THE FIRST CRUSH IS THE DEEPEST

"Are you offering me an exclusive?" Sam asked. "What's the catch?"

"Oh, how suspicious you are. Well. As it happens, I might be willing to give you that interview." Amber cleared her throat and tilted her head, well aware that she had his full attention. "But there are a few conditions we need to agree on before I talk on the record."

"Conditions. This sounds like the catch part."

"I prefer to think of them as more of a trade. You do something for me, I do something for you."

"Ah. Now we have it. You know you have the upper hand so you decided to come down here to gloat?"

"Gloat?" she repeated. "Do you really think I would do that?" Her words caught at the back of her throat. Was that how he thought of her? "I haven't changed that much, Sam. You need an interview and I have a few things I need doing, which you might be able to help me with. It's as simple as that."

"Simple? Nothing about you was ever simple, Amber."

DEAR READER,

For me, one of the delights in reading—and writing—fiction is seeing familiar places in a completely new way through the eyes of the characters on the page.

Several years ago I was fortunate enough to visit India and was stunned by the vibrant colors, amazing history and heady spices of this wonderful country.

Sam Richards had been working as a celebrity gossip columnist in major American cities. But nothing is going to prepare him for the coast of Kerala and the concert pianist he left behind ten years earlier.

Amber DuBois has her own reasons for escaping to India. And the last person she wants to share them with is the boy who was her first kiss, her first love and who broke her heart. Unless of course he can show her why she has never been able to forget him and fall in love all over again.

This is my twelfth romance novel for Harlequin, and a very special one since it introduces three very special friends. Amber, Kate and Saskia became close in high school and have drifted apart—but no longer. Now they're all back in London, all single and all working hard to make new lives for themselves.

I am particularly excited that Amber and Sam's journey to love has been included as one of the summer releases for the Harlequin KISS series.

It is wonderful to be part of this new line of fun, flirty and sensual romances that deliver all the emotional satisfaction that readers expect from the best in contemporary romantic fiction with a thoroughly modern twist.

Look out for Kate's and Saskia's stories, which will be coming soon.

I am always delighted to hear from my readers—you can get in touch via my website at www.NinaHarrington.com.

Every best wish,

Nina

THE FIRST CRUSH IS THE DEEPEST

NINA HARRINGTON

Recycling programs
for this product may
not exist in your area.

ISBN-13: 978-0-373-20719-0

THE FIRST CRUSH IS THE DEEPEST

THE WEDDING DRESS DIARIES

(Prequel to The Wedding Season continuity)

This edition published by arrangement with Harlequin Books S.A.

For questions and comments about the quality of this book, please contact us at CustomerService@Harlequin.com.

Printed in U.S.A.

www.Harlequin.com

ABOUT NINA HARRINGTON

Nina grew up in rural Northumberland, England, and decided at the age of eleven that she was going to be a librarian—because then she could read *all* the books in the public library whenever she wanted! Since then she has been a shop assistant, community pharmacist, technical writer, university lecturer, volcano walker and industrial scientist, before taking a career break to realize her dream of being a fiction writer. When she is not creating stories that make her readers smile, her hobbies are cooking, eating, enjoying good wine—and talking, for which she has had specialist training.

This and other titles by Nina Harrington are available in ebook format—check out **Harlequin.com**.

GIRLS JUST WANT TO HAVE FUN

Girls, gossip and gorgeous guys

Fabulous Harlequin KISS author Nina Harrington brings you a brand-new trilogy, exploring the lives and loves of best friends Amber, Kate and Saskia.

Don't miss Kate's story, *Last-Minute Bridesmaid*, and Saskia's story in the coming months!

CONTENTS

THE FIRST CRUSH IS THE DEEPEST   9

THE WEDDING DRESS DIARIES   215

THE FIRST CRUSH
IS THE DEEPEST

ONE

    Amber DuBois closed her eyes and tried to stay calm. 'Yes, Heath,' she replied. 'Of course I am taking care of myself. No, I am not staying out too long this evening. That's right, a couple of hours at most.'

    The limo slowed and she squinted out at the impressive stone pillars of the swish London private members club. 'Ah. I think we have arrived. Time for you to get back to your office. Don't you have a company to sort out? Bye, Heath. Love you. Bye.'

    She sighed out loud then quickly stowed her phone in a tiny designer shoulder bag. Heath meant well but in his eyes she was still the teenage unwanted stepsister who he had been told to look after and had never quite learnt to let go. But he cared and she knew that she could rely on him for anything. And that meant a lot when you were at a low point in your life.

    Like now.

    Amber looked up through the drizzle and was just about to tell the limo driver that she had changed her mind when a plump blonde in a purple bandage dress two sizes too small for her burst out of the club and almost dragged Amber out of the rain and into the foyer.

She looked a little like the mousey-haired girl who had lorded over everyone from the posh girls' table at high school.

Right now Amber watched Miss Snooty 'my dad's a banker' rear back in horror when she realised that the star of the ten-year school reunion alumni had a plaster cast over her right wrist, but recovered enough to bend forward and air kiss her on both cheeks with a loud *mmwwahh.*

'Amber. Darling. How lovely to see you again. We are so pleased that you could make our little get-together—especially when you lead such an exciting life these days. Do come inside. We want to know everything!'

Amber was practically propelled across the lovely marble floor, which was tricky to do in platform designer slingbacks. She had barely caught her breath when a hand at her back pushed her forwards into a huge room. The walls were covered with cream brocade, broken up by floor to ceiling mirrors, and huge gilded chandeliers hung from the ceiling.

It was a ballroom designed to cope with hundreds of people.

Only at that moment several clusters of extremely bored-looking women in their late twenties were standing with their hands clasped around buffet plates and wine glasses.

Every single one of them stopped talking and turned around.

And stared at her.

In total silence.

Amber had faced concert audiences of all shapes and sizes—but the frosty atmosphere in this cold elegant room was frigid enough to send a shiver down her spine.

'Look everyone. Amber DuBois made it in the end. Isn't that marvellous! Now carry on enjoying yourself. Fabulous!'

Two minutes later Amber was standing at the buffet and drinks table with a glass of fizzy water in her hand. She smiled down at her guide, who had started to chew the corner of her lower lip. 'Is everything all right?' Amber asked.

The other woman gulped and whimpered slightly. 'Yes—yes, of course. Everything is just divine. I just need to check something—but feel free to mingle, darling... mingle.'

And then she practically jogged over to a girl who might have been one of the prefects, grabbed her arm and in no uncertain terms jabbed her head towards Amber and glared towards the other side of the room.

Amber peered over the elaborate hairstyles of a cluster of chattering women who were giving her sideways glances as though scared to come and talk to her.

This was so ridiculous. So what if she had made a name for herself as a concert pianist over the years? She was still the quiet, lanky, awkward girl they used to pick on.

And then she saw it. A stunning glossy black grand piano had been brought out in front of the tall picture windows. *Just waiting for someone to play it.*

So that was the reason her old high school had gone to such lengths to track her down with an email invitation to the ten-year school reunion.

Amber sighed out loud and her shoulders slumped down.

It seemed that some things never changed.

They had never shown the slightest interest in her when she was their schoolmate—far from it in fact. Amber DuBois might have had the connections but she was not one of the posh clique of girls or the seriously academic group. She was usually on the last table and the back of the bus with the rest of the eccentrics.

Well. If there was a time to channel her inner diva, then this was it. One final performance—and the only one they would be getting from her that evening.

Cameras flashed as Amber strode, head high, canapés wobbling, across the polished wooden floor towards the ladies room.

Behind her back, Amber heard someone tap twice on the microphone but the squeaky posh voice was cut off as she stepped inside the powder room, pushed the door firmly closed with her bottom and collapsed back against it for a moment, eyes closed.

Sanctuary! If the speeches had just started she might have the place to hide out for a few precious minutes—it could even be a chance to escape.

She was just about to peek outside to check for options when the sound of something falling onto the tiled floor echoed from the adjoining powder room, quickly followed by a colourful expletive.

Amber's heels clattered on the tiles as she strolled over and peered around the corner to see where the noise was coming from.

A short brunette was standing on tiptoe, straddling two washbasins, with her arms outstretched, trying to reach the handle of the double-glazed window which was high on the wall above her. A red plastic mop bucket was lying on its side next to the washbasin.

'What's this? Kate Lovat running out on a party? I must be seeing things.' A short chuckle escaped from Amber's lips before she could stop it, and instantly the brunette whirled around to see who it was—and screamed and waved her arms about the instant she saw who had asked the question.

Which made her wobble so much that Amber rushed forwards, slid her buffet plate onto the marble counter, flipped up the bucket to create a step and then wrapped her left arm around the waist of a compact bundle of fun in a stunning cerise vintage cocktail dress.

Kate Lovat was one of the few real pals that she had made at high school.

Irrepressible, petite and fierce, Kate used to have a self-confidence which was as large as the heels she wore to push her height up to medium and a spirit to match. Today her short tousled dark hair was slicked into an asymmetric style which managed to make her look both elegant and quirky at the same time.

'Kate!' Amber laughed. 'I was praying that you were going to turn up at the reunion. You look fabulous!'

'Why thank you, pretty lady. Right back at you. You are even more gorgeous than ever.' Then Kate's mouth fell open, her eyes locked onto the floor and she gave a high pitched squeak as she grabbed Amber's arm. 'Oh my...those shoes. I want those shoes. In fact if you were not several sizes bigger than me, I would knock you down and run off with them.'

Then Kate took one step back and peered into Amber's face, her eyes narrow and her brow creased. 'Wait a minute. You look peaky. And a lot skinnier than the last time I saw you... Did I tell you that I have suddenly become clairvoyant? Because I foresee chocolate and plenty of it in your very near future.'

Then she pointed at the plaster cast on Amber's wrist. 'I have to know. Wait.' She held up one hand and pressed the fingertips of the other hand to her forehead as though she was doing her own mind-reading act. 'Let me guess. You slipped on an ice cube at some fashionista party, or was it a yacht cruising the Caribbean? It must make playing the piano a tad tricky.'

'Kate. Slow down. If you must know, I tripped over my own suitcase a couple of weeks ago. And yes, I have cancelled everything for the next six months so my wrist has a chance to heal.' Then she paused. 'And why do you need to sneak out of the window at our school reunion when you could be catching up on the gossip with the rest of our class?'

Kate took a breath, her lower lip quivered and she seemed about to say something, then changed her mind, broke into a smile and waved one hand towards the door. 'Been there. Done that. This has been one hell of a rotten day and the kidnappers have blockaded the doors to stop us from getting out.'

Then Kate lifted her chin. 'But here is an idea,' she said, her dark green eyes twinkling with delight. She gestured with her head towards the red velvet chaise at the other end of the powder room. Two buffet plates piled high with pastries and cocktail skewers were stashed on the floor.

'Who cares about them? We have a sofa. We have snacks. And the really good news is that I crashed into

Saskia five minutes ago and she is now on a mission to find liquid refreshment and cake. The three of us could have our own party right here. What do you say?'

Amber's shoulders dropped several inches and she hugged her old friend one-handed. 'That. Is the best idea I have heard in a long time. Oh, I had forgotten how much I missed you both. But I thought Saskia was still in France.'

Kate winked. 'Oh, things have certainly changed around here. Just wait until you hear what we have been up to.' Then she waved both hands towards Amber and grabbed her around the waist. 'It is so good to see you. But come on, sit. What drove you out from the chosen few? Or should that be who drove you out?'

Suddenly Kate froze and her fingers flew to her mouth. 'Don't tell me that snake in the grass Petra dared to show her face.'

Petra. Amber took a sharp intake of breath. 'Well, if Petra was in there, I didn't notice, and somehow I think I would have recognised her.'

'Damn right.' Kate scowled. 'Ten years is not nearly long enough to forget that face. A friend does not jump on her best pal's boyfriend. Especially at that pal's eighteenth birthday party.' Her flat right hand sliced through the air. 'For some things there is no forgiveness. None. Zero. Don't even ask. Oh—is that a mushroom tartlet?'

'Help yourself,' Amber replied and passed Kate her plate. Strange how she had suddenly lost her appetite the moment Petra's name was mentioned. The memory of the last time she had seen the girl she used to call her friend flittered across her brain, bringing a bitter taste of regret into her mouth. 'It takes two to tango, Kate,' she murmured. 'And, from what I recall, Sam Richards wasn't exactly complaining that Petra had made a move on him. Far from it, in fact.'

'Of course not,' Kate replied between bites. 'He was a boy and she bedazzled him. He didn't have a chance.'

'Bedazzled?'

'Bedazzled. Once that girl decided that Sam was the target he was toast.' Then Kate coughed and flicked a glance at Amber before brushing pastry crumbs from her fingers. 'He's back in London now, you know. Sam. Working as a journalist for that swanky newspaper he was always talking about.'

Amber brought her head up very slowly. 'How fascinating. Perhaps I should ring the editor and warn him that his new reporter is susceptible to bedazzlement?'

'Careful.' Kate chuckled. 'They'll be saying that I am having a bad influence on you.'

'Well, that would never do! Hi Amber,' a sweet clipped voice came from the bathroom.

'Saskia!' Kate instantly leaped up from the sofa and grabbed the plate of mini chocolate cakes that was threatening to topple over at any second. 'Look who's here.' Then she caught her breath. 'What happened to your dress?'

Saskia slid onto the sofa and lowered a screw cap bottle of Chardonnay and two glasses onto the floor in front of them so that she could give Amber a hug.

It was only then Amber noticed the red wine stain which was still dripping down the sleeve of Saskia's cream lace dress. It was almost as if someone had thrown a glass of wine at her.

Maybe things had changed? Because if Kate was the petite quirky one of their little band and Amber the lanky

American, then Saskia was the classic English beauty. Medium brown hair, medium height and size. And the one girl who would never cause a scene or make a fuss.

'Excuse me for a moment.' Saskia nodded. And, without waiting for an answer, she clenched her teeth and picked up one of the paper hand towels and tore it violently into strips lengthways. Then into smaller strips, then more slowly into squares. Only when the whole towel was completely shredded into postage stamps did Saskia exhale slowly, gather up all of the pieces and toss them into the waste basket.

'Well, I feel a lot better now.' She smiled and brushed her hands off.

Kate was still choking so Amber was the one who had to ask, 'Do you want to talk about it?'

Saskia sat bolt upright on the sofa, too proud to slouch back against the cushion, and casually mopped the stain with a paper napkin. 'Apparently I am all that is bad in the world because I refused to let the school alumni committee use Elwood House for free for the weekly soiree— you know, the one I have never been invited to? You should have seen their faces the moment I mentioned the going hourly rate. That's when the abuse started.'

She sniffed once. 'It was most unladylike. Frankly, I am appalled.'

Kate pushed back her shoulders and her chin forward. 'Right. Where are they? No one disses my pal and gets away with it. There are three of us against the whole room—no contest.'

'I have just finished ten years of training as a full-on concert diva,' Amber added. 'Want to see me in action? It can be scary.'

Saskia shook her head. 'That would be playing right into their hands. They would just love it if we made a scene. It gives them something to talk about in their shallow little lives. Let it go. Seriously. I have decided to rise above it.' Then her face broke into a smile. 'I am already having far too good a time right here. Kate. Would you be so kind as to twist open that bottle? I want to hear everything. Let's start with the obvious. My love life is on hold until Elwood House is up and running, but what about you, Kate?'

Kate looked up from pouring the wine. 'Don't look at me,' she replied in disgust. 'I seem to have an inbuilt boy repellent at the moment. One taste and they run. Unlike some people we know. Come on, Amber. What's the latest on that hunky mountain man we saw you with in the celeb mags?'

'History. Gone. Finished,' Amber replied and took a sip of wine before passing it to Saskia. 'But I live in hope. If I ever get out of this powder room I am going to start fund-raising for my friend Parvita's charity in India and, you never know, I might meet someone over the next few months. I visited the orphanage with her a few months ago and I promised the girls that I would go back if I could.' Her eyes stared over their heads at the large white tiles. 'It is the most fabulous place and right on the beach,' she added in a dreamy faraway voice.

Then her shoulders slumped. 'Who am I kidding? Heath would be furious with me for even thinking about going back to India.'

'Heath? You mean, as in your stepbrother Heath?' Kate whispered. 'Why should he object to you going to India?'

Amber took a breath and looked over at Saskia and

then back to Kate. 'Because he worries about me. You see, I didn't just fall over my suitcase and break my wrist. I had just got back from India and I sort of collapsed. There was an outbreak of...'

The sound of raucous laughter cut Amber off mid-sentence as a horde of noisy chattering women burst into the ladies room. Their voices echoed around the tiled space in an explosion of sound.

Amber pressed both hands to her ears. 'Sounds like the speeches are over and I have just heard the word karaoke.' She gestured towards the entrance. 'We might be able to sneak out the side entrance if we are quick. My apartment is the nearest. Then I'll tell you what really happened in India and why Heath is as worried as I am.'

TWO

———

'*Tell me what* you know about *Bambi DuBois*.'

The question hit Sam Richards right between the eyes, just as he was swallowing down the last of his coffee, and he almost choked on the coarse grounds in the bottom of the cup.

Frank Evans strode into the corner office as though he had a hurricane behind his back and waved a colour magazine in front of Sam's nose.

Sam sniffed and gave his new boss a one-handed hat tip salute. Frank had made his name in the media company by being one of the sharpest editors in the business who only worked with the best, but Sam had already been warned that Frank had not earned the editor's desk through his personnel skills.

'And good morning to you too, Frank,' Sam replied. 'And thank you for your warm welcome to the London office.'

'Yeah, yeah.' Frank shooed a hand in Sam's direction and pointed to the desk. 'Take a seat. Monday madness. Worse than ever. You know what it's like. The chief is on my back and it's not nine o'clock yet. Time to rock and roll. You talk. I listen. Let's hear it. Show me that you're not completely out of touch with the London scene after all those years out in the wilderness.'

Sam stifled a laugh. *So much for an easy first day in the new job.*

Frank settled the seat of his over tight suit onto the wide leather chair on the other side of the modern polymer table and ran his short stubby fingers through his receding grey hair before drinking down what must now be cold milky coffee.

His cheap tie was already tugged down a couple of inches and his shirt sleeves had missed the iron, but in contrast his eyes sparkled with intelligence as he leant his arms on one of the cleanest and most organised desks Sam had ever seen.

Bambi DuBois? The shock of hearing her name kept Sam frozen to the spot, cup in hand, before his brain kicked in and he frowned as though thinking about an answer. A few manly coughs gave him just enough time to pull together a casual reply to the editor who he had previously only spoken to twice on the telephone.

The editor who had the power to decide whether he had a future career in this newspaper—or not.

This was definitely not the perfect start to his dream job that he had imagined!

Lowering his cup onto a coaster, Sam assumed his very best bored and casual disinterested journalist's face. His career depended on this man's decision.

'Do you mean Amber DuBois? English concert pianist. Blonde. Leggy. Popular with the top fashion designers, who like her to wear their gowns at performances.'

He shrugged at the newspaper editor and new boss who was staring at him so intently. 'I think she was the face of some cosmetic company a few years ago. And I would hardly call Los Angeles the wilderness.'

Frank slid a magazine across the desk. 'Make that the biggest cosmetic company in Asia and you are getting close. But you seem to have missed something out. Have a look at this.'

Sam took his time before picking it up and instantly recognised it as the latest colour supplement from their main competitor's weekly entertainment section. And any confusion he might have had about Frank's question vanished into the stiflingly hot air of the prized corner office.

The cover ran a full colour half page photograph of Amber 'Bambi' DuBois in a flowing azure dress with a jewel-encrusted tiny strapless bodice.

The shy, gangly teenage girl he had once known was gone—and in her place was a beautiful, elegant woman who was not just in control but revelling in her talent.

Amber was sitting at a black grand piano with one long, slender, silky leg stretched out to display a jewelled high heeled sandal and Sam was so transfixed by how stunning she looked that it took him a microsecond to realise that his new boss was tapping the headline with the chewed end of his ballpoint pen.

International Concert Pianist Amber DuBois Shocks the Classical Music World by Announcing her Retirement at 28. But the Question on Everyone's Lips is: Why? What Next for 'Bambi' DuBois?

Sam looked up at his editor and raised his eyebrows just as Frank leant across the desk and slapped one heavy hand down firmly onto the cover so that his fingers were splayed out over Amber's chest.

'I smell a story. There has to be some very good reason why a professional musician like Amber DuBois suddenly announces her retirement out of the blue when she is at the top of her game.'

Frank aimed a finger at Sam's chest and fired. 'The rumour is that our Amber is jumping on the celebrity bandwagon of adopting a vanity charity project in India to spend her money on, but her agent is refusing to comment. As far as I am concerned, this is a ruse to get the orchestras begging her to come back with a solid platinum hello. And I want this paper to get in there first with the real story.'

Frank sat back in his wide leather chair and folded his arms.

'More to the point—I want *you* to go out there and bring back an exclusive interview with the lovely Miss DuBois. You can consider this your first assignment.'

Then Frank shrugged. 'You can thank me for the opportunity later.'

The words stayed frozen in the air as though trapped inside an iceberg large enough to sink his new job in one deadly head-on collision.

Thank him?

For a fraction of a second Sam wondered if this was some sort of joke. A bizarre initiation ceremony into the world of the London office of GlobalStar Media, and there was a secret camera hidden in the framed magazine covers behind Frank's head which were recording just how he was reacting to the offer of this amazing *opportunity*.

Sam flexed out the fingers of both hands so that he wouldn't scrunch up the magazine and toss it back to Frank with a few choice words about what he thought of his little joke, while his normally sharp brain worked through a few options to create a decent enough excuse as to why Frank should find another journalist for this particular gig.

Sam inhaled slowly as each syllable sank in. It had taken him three months to arrange a transfer from the Los Angeles office of the media giant he had given his life to for the past ten years. He had worked himself up from being the post room boy and sacrificed relationships and anything close to a social life to reach this point in his career.

This was more than just a jump on the promotion ladder; this was the job he had been dreaming about since he was a teenager. The only job that he had ever wanted. *Ever.* No way was he going to be diverted from that editor's chair. Not now, not when he had come so far.

Sam blinked twice. 'Sorry, Frank, but can you say that again? Because I think I must have misheard. I've just spent the last ten years working my way from New York to Los Angeles on the back of celebrity interviews. I applied to be an investigative journalist not a gossip columnist.'

Frank replied with a dismissive snort and he bit off a laugh. 'Do you know what pays for this shiny office we are sitting in, Sam? Magazine sales. And the public love celebrity stories, especially when it concerns a girl with the looks of Amber DuBois. It's all over the Internet this morning that orchestras have been lining up and offering her huge bonuses to come and work for them for one last season before she retires. And then there is her publicity machine. The girl is a genius.'

He raised one hand into the air and gave Sam a Vee sign. 'She has only ever been seen with two dates in the last ten years. *Two.* And not your boring classical musician—oh, no, our girl Amber likes top action men. First there was the Italian racing car driver who she cheered on to be World Champion, then that Scottish mountaineer. Climbing Everest for charity. With the lovely Amber at Base Camp waving him farewell with a tear in her eye. She is the modelling musical sweetheart and her fans love her—and now this.'

The pen went back to some serious tapping. 'Think of it as your first celebrity interview for the London office. Who knows? This could be the last fluff piece you ever write. Use some of that famous charm I've been hearing about—the lovely Miss DuBois will be putty in your hands.'

His hands? Sam's fingers stretched out over his knees. Instantly his mind starting wheeling through the possibility that someone had tipped off this shark of an editor that ten years ago those same hands had known every intimate detail about Amber 'Bambi' DuBois. Her hopes, her dreams, the fact that she always asked for extra anchovies on her pizza and had a sensitive spot at one side of her neck that could melt her in seconds. The way her long slender legs felt under his fingertips. Oh, yes, Sam Richards knew a lot more about Amber DuBois than he was prepared to tell anyone.

This job was going to make or break his career, but he

had promised himself on the night they'd parted that, no matter how desperate he was for money or fame, he would never tell Amber's story. It was too personal and private. And he had kept that promise, despite the temptation—but the world he worked in did not see it that way.

Sam had seen more than one popular musician or actor pull celebrity stunts to get the attention of the media, and he had learnt his craft by writing about their petty dramas and desperate need for attention, but Amber had never been one of them. She didn't need to. She had the talent to succeed on her own, as well as a body and a face the camera loved.

Frank shuffled in his chair. *Impatient for his reply.*

Sam took one look into those clever, scheming eyes and the sinking feeling that had been in the bottom of his stomach since he had walked into the impressive office building that morning turned into a gaping cavern.

He was just about to be stitched up.

What could he do? He did not have the authority to walk into a new office and demand the best jobs as though they owed him a future. Just the opposite. But Frank might have waited until his second day as the new boy.

'I'm sure you're right, Frank. But I was looking forward to getting started on that investigation into Eurozone political funding we talked about. Has it fallen through?'

Frank reached into his desk drawer and handed Sam a folder of documents.

'Far from it. Everything we have seen so far screams corruption at every level from the bottom up. Take a look. The research team have already lined up a series of interviews with insiders across Europe. And it's all there, waiting for someone to turn over the stones and see what is crawling underneath.'

Sam scan read the first few pages of notes and background information for the interviews and kept reading, his mind racing with options on how he could craft a series of articles from the one investigation. And the more he read, the faster his heart raced.

This was it. This was the perfect piece of financial journalism that would set him up as a serious journalist on the paper and win him the editor's job he had sacrificed a lot to achieve. And it had to be the London office. Not Los Angeles or New York. London.

'Does your dad still have that limo service in Knightsbridge? We've used them a couple of times. Great cars. Your dad might get a kick out of seeing your name on the front page.'

Might? His dad would love it.

His father had sacrificed everything for him after his mother left them. He had been a single parent to a sullen and fiercely angry teenager who was struggling to find his way against the odds. Driven by the burning ambition to show the world that he was capable of being more than a limo driver like his dad.

Sam Richards had made his father's life hell for so many years. And yet his dad had stuck by him every step of the way without expecting a word of thanks.

And now it was payback time.

This promotion to the GlobalStar London office was a first step to make up for years of missed telephone calls and flying Christmas visits.

Shame that his shiny new career was just about to hit an iceberg called Amber DuBois.

Aware that Frank was watching him with his arms crossed and knew exactly how tempting this piece was, Sam closed the folder and slid it back across the desk. This was no time to be coy.

'Actually, he sold the limo business a few years back to go into property. But you're right. He would be pleased. So how do I make that happen, Frank? What do I have to do to get this assignment?'

'Simple. You have built up quite a reputation for yourself as a hard worker in the Los Angeles office. And now you want an editor's desk. I understand that. Ten years on the front line is a long time, but I cannot just give you a golden story like this when I have a team of hungry reporters sitting outside this office who would love to make their mark on it. All I am asking you to do is show me that you are as good as they say you are.'

Frank slid the dossier back into his desk drawer. 'If you want the editor's desk, you are going to have to come back with an exclusive interview from the lovely Amber. Feature length. Oh—and you have two weeks to do it. We can't risk someone else breaking Amber's story before we do. Do we understand each other? Excellent, I look forward to reading your exposé.'

Sam rose to shake hands and Frank's fingers squeezed hard and stayed clamped shut. 'And Sam. One more thing. The truth about "Bambi's Bollywood Babies" had better be amazing or you will be back to the bottom of the ladder all over again, interviewing TV soap stars about their leg-waxing regime.'

He released Sam with a nod. 'You can take the magazine. Have fun.'

Sam closed the door to Frank's office behind him and stood in silence on the ocean of grey plastic industrial carpet in the open-plan office, looking out over rows of cubicles. He had become used to the cacophony of noise and voices and telephones that was part of working in newspaper offices just like this, no matter what city he happened to be in that day. If anything, it helped to block out the alarm sirens that were sounding inside his head.

This was the very office block that he used to walk and cycle past every day on his way to school. He remembered looking up at the glass-fronted building and dreaming about what it must be like to be a top reporter working in a place like this. Writing important articles in the newspapers that men like his dad's clients read religiously in the back seat of the limo.

The weird thing was—from the very first moment that he had told his dad that he wanted to be a journalist on this paper, his dad had worked all of the extra hours and midnight airport runs, week after week, month after month, to make that possible. He had never once doubted that he would do it. Not once.

And now he was here. He had done it.

The one thing he had never imagined was that his first assignment in his dream job would mean working with Amber.

Sam glanced at the magazine cover in his hand. And reflected back at him was the lovely face of the one woman in the world who was guaranteed to set the dogs on him the minute he even tried to get within shouting distance.

And in his case he deserved it. The nineteen-year-old Sam Richards had given Amber DuBois very good reason to never want to talk to him again.

He might have given Amber her first kiss—but he had broken her heart just as fast.

Now all he had to do was persuade her to overlook the past, forgive and forget and reveal her deep innermost secrets for the benefit of the magazine-reading public.

Fun might not be the ideal word to describe how he was feeling.

But it had to be done. There was no going back to Los Angeles. For better or worse, he had burnt those bridges. He needed this job. But more than that—he wanted it. He had worked hard to be standing on this piece of carpet, looking out, instead of standing outside on the pavement, looking in.

He owed it to his dad, who had believed in him when nobody else had, even after years of making his dad's life a misery. And he owed it to himself. He wasn't the second class chauffeur's son any longer.

He had to get that interview with Amber.

No matter how much grovelling was involved.

THREE

———

'And you are quite sure about that? No interviews at all? And you did tell Miss DuBois who was calling? Yes. Yes I understand. Thank you. I'll be sure to check her website for future news.'

Sam flicked down the cover on his cellphone and tapped the offending instrument against his forehead before popping it into his pocket.

Her website? When did a professional talent agency direct a journalist to a website? No, it was more than that. His name was probably on some blacklist Amber had passed to her agent with instructions that she would not speak to him under any circumstances.

He needed to think this through and come up with a plan—and fast.

Sam wrapped the special polishing cloth around his fist and started rubbing the fine polish onto the already glossy paintwork on the back wheel arch of his dad's pride and joy. The convertible vintage English sports car had been one of the few cars that his dad had saved when he had to sell the classic car showroom as part of the divorce from Sam's mother.

It had taken Sam and his dad three years to restore the sports car back to the original pristine condition that it was still today. Three years of working evenings after school and the occasional Sunday when his dad was not driving limos for other people to enjoy.

Three years of pouring their pain and bitterness about Sam's mother into hard physical work and sweat, as though creating something solid and physical would somehow make up for the fact that she had left Sam with his dad and gone off to make a new life for herself with her rich boyfriend. A life funded by the sale of his dad's business and most of their savings.

But they had done it. *Together.* Even though Sam had resented every single second of the work they did on this car. Resented it so much that he could cheerfully have pushed it outside onto the street, set it on fire and delighted in watching it burn. Like his dreams had burnt the day his mother left.

In another place, with another father and another home, Sam might have taken his burning fury out in a sports field or with his fists in a boxing ring or even on the streets in this part of London.

Instead, he had directed all of his teenage frustration and anger and bitterness at his father.

He had been so furious with his dad for not changing jobs like his mother had wanted him to.

Furious for not running after her and begging her to come back and be with them—like he had done that morning when he came down for breakfast early and saw her going out of the front door with her suitcases.

He had followed that taxi cab for three streets before his legs gave way.

She had never even looked back at him. Not once.

And it was all his dad's fault. The arguments. The fights. They were all his fault. He must have done something terrible to make her leave.

Sam's gaze flicked up at the thin partition wall that separated the cab office from the workshop. Just next to the door was a jagged hole in the plaster sheet the size of a teenage fist.

Sam's fist.

It was the closest he had ever come to lashing out at his dad physically.

The screaming and the shouting and the silent stomping about the house had no effect on this broken man, who carried on working as though nothing had happened. As though their lives had not been destroyed. And to the boy he was then, it was more than just frustrating—it was a spark under a keg of gunpowder.

They'd survived three long, hard years before Sam had taken off to America.

And along the way Sam had learnt the life lessons that he still carried in his heart. He had learnt that love everlasting, marriage and family were outdated ideas which only wrecked people's lives and caused lifelong damage to any children who got caught up in the mess.

He had seen it first-hand with his own parents, and with the parents of his friends like Amber and the girls she knew. Not one of them came from happy homes.

The countless broken marriages and relationships of journalists and the celebrities he had met over the years had only made his belief stronger, not less.

He would be a fool to get trapped in the cage that was marriage. And in the meantime he would take his time enjoying the company of the lovely ladies who were attracted to luxury motors like free chocolate and champagne, and that suited him just fine.

No permanent relationships.

No children to become casualties when the battle started.

Other men had wives and children, and he wished them well.

Not for him. The last thing he wanted was children.

Pity that his last girlfriend in Los Angeles had refused to believe that he had no intention of inviting her to move into his apartment and was already booking wedding planners before she realised that he meant what he said—he cared about Alice but he had absolutely no intention of walking down an aisle to the tune of wedding bells any time soon. If ever.

No. Sam had no problem with using his charm and good looks to persuade reluctant celebrities to talk to him—and he was good at it. Good enough to have made his living out of those little chats and cosy drinks.

But when it came to trust? Ah. Different matter altogether.

He placed his trust in metal and motor engineering and electronics. Smooth bodywork over a solid, beautiful engine designed by some of the finest engineers in the world. People could and would let you down for no reason, but not motors. Motors were something he could control and rely on.

He trusted his father and his deep-seated sense of integrity and silent resolve never to bad-mouth Sam's mother, even when times had been tough for both of them. And they had been tough, there was no doubt about that.

But there had always been one constant in his life. His dad had never doubted that he would pass the exams and go to university and make his dream of becoming a journalist come true.

Unlike his mother. The last conversation that they ever had was burned into his memory like a deep brand that time and experience would never be able to erase.

What had she called him? *Oh, yes.* His own mother had called him a useless dreamer who would never amount to anything and would end up driving other people around for a living, just like his father.

Well, he had proven her wrong on every count, and this editor's job was the final step on a long and arduous journey that began the day she left them.

It was time to show his dad that he had been right to keep faith in him and put up with the anger. Time to show him that he was grateful for everything he had done for him.

All of which screamed out one single message.

He needed that interview with Amber. He knew that she was in London—and he knew where her friends lived. He *had* to persuade her to talk to him, no matter what it took, even if it meant tracking her down and stalking her. He had come too far to let anything stand in his way now.

Amber DuBois. *The girl he left behind.*

His hands stilled and he stepped back from the car and grabbed a chilled bottle of water from the mini-fridge in the corner of the workshop and then pressed the chilled bottle against the back of his neck to try and cool down. Time to get creative. Time to...

The bell over the back door rang. Odd. His dad didn't like customers coming to the garage. This was his private space and always had been. No clients allowed.

Sam turned down the radio to a normal level and was just wiping his hands on a paper towel when the workshop's wooden door swung open.

And Amber 'legs up to her armpits' Bambi DuBois drifted into his garage as though she was floating on air.

He looked up and tried to speak, but the air in his lungs was too frozen in shock. So he squared his shoulders and took a moment to enjoy the view instead.

Amber was wearing a knee length floral summer dress in shades of pastel pink and soft green which moved as she walked, sliding over her slim hips as though the slippery fabric was alive or liquid.

Sam felt as though a mobile oasis of light and summer and positive energy had just floated in on the breeze into the dim and dingy old garage his dad refused to paint. The dark shadows and recesses where the old tins of oil and catalogues were stored only seemed to make the brightness of this woman even more pronounced.

She took a few steps closer, her left hand still inside the heart-shaped pocket of her dress and he felt like stepping backwards so that they could keep that distance.

This was totally ludicrous. After all, this was his space and she was his visitor.

His beautiful, talented, ridiculously lovely visitor who looked as though she had just stepped out from a cover shoot for a fashion magazine.

She was sunlight in his darkness—just the same as she had always been, and seeing her again like this reinforced just how much he had missed her and never had the courage to admit it.

Amber looked at him with the faintest of polite smiles and slipped her sunglasses higher onto her nose with one fingertip.

'This place has not changed one bit,' she whispered in a voice what was as soft and musical and gentle and lovely as he had remembered. A voice which still had the power to make his blood sing.

Then she glanced across at the car. 'You even have the same sports car. That's amazing.'

Sam had often wondered how Amber would turn out. Not that he could avoid seeing her name. Her face was plastered on billboards and the sides of buses from California to London. But that was not the real Amber. He knew that only too well from working in the media business.

No. This was the real Amber. This beautiful girl who was running the manicured fingertips of her left hand along the leather seat of the sports car he had just polished.

Maybe she had decided to forgive him for the way they had parted.

'My dad kept it.' He shrugged. 'One of a kind.'

Amber paused and she sighed. 'The last time I saw this car was the night of my eighteenth birthday party and you were sitting in the front seat with your tongue down the throat of my so called friend Petra. About twenty minutes after you had declared your undying love for me.'

She gave a strangled chuckle. 'Oh, yes, I remember

this car very well indeed. Shame that the driver was not quite as classy.'

Or maybe she hadn't.

Sam pushed his hand down firmly on the workbench behind him.

So. *Here we go.* In her eyes he was *still* the chauffeur's son who had dared to date the rich client's daughter. And then kissed her best friend.

Goodbye editor's desk.

Time to start work and turn on the charm before she chopped him into small pieces and barbecued him on the car's exhaust pipe.

'Hello, Amber. How very nice to see you again.' He smiled and stepped forward to kiss her on the cheek but, before he got there, Amber flipped up her sunglasses onto the top of her head and looked at him with those famous violet-blue eyes which cut straight through any delusion that this was a social call.

Her eyes might have sold millions of tubes of eye make-up, but close up, with the light behind her, the iridescent violet-blue he remembered was mixed with every shade from cobalt to navy. And, just for him today... blue ice.

The contrast between the violet of her eyes and her straight blonde hair which fell perfectly onto her shoulders only seemed to highlight the intensity of her gaze. The cosmetic company might have chosen her for her peaches and cream ultra-clear complexion, but it had always been those magical blue eyes that Sam found totally irresistible. Throw in a pair of perfect sweet soft pink lips and he had been done for from the first time he had seen her stepping out of his dad's limo with her diva mother screaming out orders from behind her back.

She didn't seem to know what to do with her long legs, her head was down and she peered at him through a curtain of long blonde hair before brushing it away and blasting his world with one look.

Now she was standing almost as tall as he was and looking him straight in the eyes. The smile on her lips had not reached her eyes and Sam had to fight past the awkwardness of the intensity of her gaze.

'My agent mentioned that you were back in town. I thought I might pop in to say hello. Hope you don't mind.'

Her gaze shifted from the casual trainers he had found stuffed in the bottom of the wardrobe in the spare bedroom, faded blue jeans and the scraggy, oil-stained T-shirt he kept for garage work. 'I can see that your fashion sense hasn't changed very much. Shame, really. I was hoping for some improvement.'

Sam glanced down at his jeans and flicked the polishing cloth against his thigh. 'Oh, this little old outfit? Don't you just hate it when all of your chiffon is at the dry cleaner's and you can't find a thing to wear?' He crossed his arms. 'And no, Amber, I don't mind you popping in at all, especially since my editor has been harassing your agent for weeks to arrange an interview. He will be delighted to hear that you turned up out of the blue, expecting me to be here.'

Amber floated forward so that Sam inhaled a rich, sweet floral scent which was almost as intoxicating as the woman who was wearing it.

A whirlwind of memories slammed home. Long summer days walking through the streets of London as he memorised routes and names and places for the limo business. Hand in hand, chatting, laughing and enjoying each other's company as they shared secrets about themselves that nobody else knew. Amber had been his best friend for so long, he hadn't even realised how much she had come to mean to him until they were ripped apart.

'Don't flatter yourself. May I sit?'

Sam gestured to the hard wooden chair his dad used at the makeshift desk in the corner. 'It may not be quite what you're used to, but please.'

She nodded him a thanks and lowered herself gracefully onto the chair and turned it around so that she was facing him.

Sam shook his head. 'You are full of surprises, Amber DuBois. I thought that it would take a very exclusive restaurant in the city to tempt you to come out of your lair long enough to give me an interview.'

Her reply was to lift her flawless chin and cross her legs. Sam took in a flash of long tanned legs ending in peep toe low wedge sandals made out of plaited strips of straw and transparent plastic. Her toenails were painted in the same pale pink as her nails, which perfectly matched her lipstick and the colour motif in her dress.

She was class, elegance and designer luxury and for a fraction of a second he wanted nothing better than to pick her tiny slim body up and lay it along the bonnet of the car and find out for himself whether her skin felt the same under his fingertips.

'What makes you think that I am here to give you an interview?' she replied with a certain hardness in her voice which plunged him back into the cold waters of the real world. 'Perhaps I am here to congratulate you on your engagement? Has your fiancée come with you from Los Angeles and my wedding invitation is in the post? I can see that you would want to give me heads-up on that.'

He reeled back. 'My what?'

'Oh—didn't you announce your engagement in the Los Angeles press? Or is there another Samuel Patrick Richards, investigative reporter and photojournalist of London, walking the streets of that lovely town?'

Sam sucked in a breath then shrugged. 'That was a misunderstanding. My girlfriend at the time was getting a little impatient and decided to organise a wedding without asking me first. Apparently she forgot that anything to do with weddings brings me out in a nasty rash. It's a long-standing allergy but I have learnt to live with it. So you can save your congratulations for another time.'

Amber inhaled very slowly before speaking again. 'Well, it seems that this garage is not the only thing that hasn't changed, is it, Sam? You do seem to make a habit out of running out on girls. Maybe we should all get together and form a support group.'

She raised both of her arms and wrote in the air. '"Girls Sam Richards has dumped and ran out on." We could have our own blog. What? What is it?'

Sam crossed the few steps which separated them and gently tugged at her cardigan. 'Your arm is in plaster. Hell, Bambi, what happened? I mean, you have to play the piano...'

She pulled her cardigan over the plaster, but lifted her left arm across her chest.

'I broke my wrist a few weeks ago and I'm officially on medical leave. And that is strictly off the record. My career is fine, thank you. In fact, I am enjoying the holiday. It is very restorative.'

Sam shook his head. 'Must make your daily practice interesting...but are you okay? I mean there won't be any lasting damage?'

She parted her lips and took a breath before answering, and for some reason Sam got the idea that she was about to tell him something then changed her mind at the very last minute. 'Clean break, no problem. The exercises are working well and I should be as good as new in a few months.'

'Glad to hear it. This brings us right back to my original question. What are you doing here?'

He stepped forward and stood in front of her, with one hand on each arm of his dad's old wooden chair, her legs now stretched out in front of her and trapped between his. He was so close that he could feel her fast breath on his cheek and see the pulse of her heart in her throat.

Her mouth narrowed and this time it did connect with the hard look in her eyes.

But, instead of backing away, Amber bent forward from the waist, challenging him, those blue eyes flashing with something he had never seen before. And when she spoke her voice was as gentle and soft as a feather duvet. And just as tempting.

'Okay. It goes like this. I understand that you want to interview me in the light of my recent press release concerning my retirement. I'm curious about what it is that you think you can offer me which is so special that I would want to talk to you instead of all the other journalists who are knocking at my door. You have never been the shy or modest type, so it must be something rather remarkable.'

'Absolutely. Remember that dream I used to talk about? The one where I am a big, important investigative journalist working at that broadsheet newspaper my dad still reads every day? Well, it turns out that to win the editor's desk I have to deliver one final celebrity interview.' Sam pointed at Amber with two fingers pressed tight together and fired his thumb like a pistol trigger.

Amber nodded. 'I thought it might be something like that.' Her eyebrows went skywards. 'I take it your editor doesn't know about our teenage fling?'

'Fling? Is that what you call it? No. He certainly doesn't, or he would have sent me to your last known address with a bunch of supermarket flowers and a box of chocolates as soon as I walked into his office. No. That part of my life is filed under "private". Okay?'

She gave him a closed mouth smile. 'Why? I know you must have been tempted. I can see the headline now. "The real truth about how I broke Amber Du Bois' heart"? Yes, there are plenty of television reality shows who would love to have you on their list. I could hardly sue, could I?'

'I suppose not, but let's just say that I was saving that for a financial emergency. Okay?'

'An emergency? You were saving me to get you out of some money crisis? I don't know whether to be flattered or insulted. Or both. I'm not sure I like being compared to a stash of used notes which you keep under the mattress.'

'Oh—is that where you keep yours? I prefer banks myself. Much more secure.'

Her eyes narrowed and she licked her lower lip as

though she was trying to decide about something important.

He could remember the first time he'd kissed those lips. They had just come out of a pizza restaurant and got caught in a heavy rain shower. He had pulled her under the shelter of his coat, his arm around her waist and, just as they got to the car, laughing and yelling as the rain bounced off the pavement around them, she had turned towards him to thank him and her stunning face was only inches away from his. And he couldn't resist any longer. And he had kissed her. Warm lips, scented skin, alive and pungent in the rain, and the feeling of her breath on his neck as she rested her head on his shoulder for a fleeting second before diving into the warm, dry car.

Not one word, but as he'd raced back to the driver's door, there was only one thing on his mind.

She was the passenger and he was the driver. Her chauffeur. The hired help. And that was the way it was always going to be. Unless he did something to change it.

Which was precisely what he had done.

Except to Amber he would always be the rough diamond she broke her teeth on. Girls like this did not date the help.

Sam stepped back and chuckled as he tidied away the polishing kit.

'Relax, Amber. It takes a lot of hard work to become a journalist in today's newspaper business. I earned this new job in the London office. Besides, I don't need to trawl through my past history to score points with my editor. Frank Evans is far more interested in what you are doing in your life right now. Not many people retire at twenty-eight. That's bound to cause some interest.'

'And what about you, Sam? Are you interested in what I am doing in my life right now?'

He looked up into her face, which was suddenly calm, her gaze locked on him.

Was he interested? A wave of confusion and a hot, sweaty mixture of bittersweet memories surged through Sam. His breathing was hot and fast and for a fraction of a second he was very tempted to lean back and give her the full-on charm offensive and find out just what kind of woman Amber had become by being up close and personal—and nothing to do with his job.

Fool. Eyes on the prize.

'The only thing I am interested in is the promotion to the job I have been working towards for ten long years in the trenches. Sorry if that disappoints you, but there it is.'

'Ah—so your editor needs a story and you thought you could use our teenage connection to wangle the real truth from my lips. Tut, tut. What shameful tactics. And if I even hear the words "for old times' sake", I promise that I will pretend to cry my eyes out and sob all the way home to my good friend Saskia's house and my girl gang will be round with my legal team in an hour. And I will do it. Believe me.'

'Oh—cruel and unnecessary. I think I just cut myself on your need for revenge. Well, think again, because I have no intention on wandering down memory lane if I can avoid it.'

Just for a second her lips trembled and the vulnerability and tender emotion of the girl he used to know was there in front of him but, before he could explain, her lips flushed pink and she chuckled softly before answering.

'I'm pleased to hear it, because I have something of

a business proposition to put to you. And it will make things a lot simpler if we can keep our relationship on a purely professional basis.'

'A business proposition? Well, there's a change. The last time we met your stepbrother and your mother were doing a fine job running your life. As I remember, you didn't have much of a business sense of your own back then.'

And the moment the words were out of his mouth Sam regretted them.

How did she do that?

He made his living out of talking to celebrities and teasing out their stories with charm and professionalism, but one look at Amber and he slotted right back into being an angsty teen showing off and saying ridiculous things. Trying to impress the girl he wanted.

Yes, Amber's mother had been furious when she found out that her musical prodigy of a daughter was sneaking out to see the chauffeur's son, but he didn't have to listen when she told him how a boy like him was going to hold her daughter back and ruin her career.

He was the one who'd taken the cheque Amber's mother had waved in front of him.

He was the one who'd marched out of Amber's eighteenth birthday party alone, only to find a warm and receptive Petra waiting for him in the car park.

Maybe that was why it still smarted after all of these years? Because the young Sam had fallen for her mother's lies, just as she had planned he should. Because she'd been right. What hope did Amber have if she was trapped with a no-hoper like Sam Richards?

It did not excuse what he'd done. But at least her

mother cared about what happened to her child. Unlike his mother.

Amber's head tilted to one side and she peered around his side to focus on the sports car that he had just been polishing before answering in the sweetest voice, 'Well, some of us have moved on in the last ten years.'

The silence between them was as rigid as steel and just as icy.

Then Amber shuffled forwards in his dad's chair and raised her eyebrows. 'Do you know what? I have changed my mind. Perhaps it was a mistake coming here after all. Best of luck with the new job and please say hello to your dad for me. Now, if you will excuse me, I have an appointment with the features editor at another newspaper in about an hour and I would hate to be late.'

She pushed herself to her feet and waved a couple of fingers in the air. 'See you around, Sam.'

And, without hesitating or looking back, Amber strolled towards the garage door on her wedge sandals, the skirt of her floaty dress waving back and forth over her perfect derrière as she headed out of his life, taking any chance of a career in London with her.

FOUR

————

'Aren't you going to ask me what it feels like to finally work in that shiny glass office I used to drag you down to ogle every week?' Sam called after her. 'I would hate for you to stay awake at night wondering how I'm coping with being a real life reporter in the big city. Come on, Amber. Have you forgotten all those afternoons you spent listening to my grand plans to be a renowned journalist one day? I know that you're curious. Give me another five minutes to convince you to choose me instead of some other journalist to write your story.'

Amber slowed and looked back at Sam over one shoulder.

And her treacherous teenage heart skipped a beat and started disco dancing just at the sight of him.

Just for an instant the sound of her name on his lips took her right back to being seventeen again, when the highlight of her whole day, the moment she had dreamt about all night and thought about every second of the day, was hearing his voice and seeing Sam's face again. Even if it did mean sitting in the back of the limo and in dressing rooms around the country as her mother's unpaid assistant and general concert slave for hours on end.

It was worth it when Sam took her out for a pizza or a cola for the duration of the concert she had heard so many times she could play it herself note perfect.

She had adored him.

He had not changed that much. A little heavier around the shoulders and the waistline, perhaps, but not much. His smile had more laughter lines now and his boyish good looks had mellowed through handsome into something close to gorgeous. She was sorry to have missed the merely handsome stage. But, if she closed her eyes, his voice was the same boy she used to know.

And the charm? Oh, Lord, he had ramped up the charm to a level where she had no doubt that any female celebrity would be powerless to resist any question he put to them.

Sam had always had a physical presence that could reach out and grab her—no change there, but she had not expected to feel such a connection. Memories of the last time she came to this very garage flooded back. His ready laughter and constant good-natured teasing about watching that she didn't knock her head on the light fittings. The nudges, the touches, the kisses.

Until he betrayed her with one of her best friends on her eighteenth birthday. And the memories of the train wreck of the weeks that followed blotted out any happiness she might have had.

Amber turned back to face Sam and planted her left hand on her hip.

'Perhaps I am worried about all of those hidden tape

recorders and video feeds which are capturing my every syllable at this very moment?'

He smiled one of those wide mouth, white teeth smiles and, in her weakened pre-dinner state, Amber had to stifle a groan. What was wrong with the man? Didn't Sam know that the only respectable thing for him to do was to have grown fat and ruined his teeth with sugary food? He had always been sexy and attractive in a rough-edged casual way, as relaxed in his body as she had been uncomfortable in her tall gangly skin. But the years had added the character lines to his face, which glowed with vitality and rugged health. Confidence and self-assurance were the best assets any man could have and Sam had them to spare.

'In this garage? No. You can say what you like. It's just between us. Same as it ever was.'

The breath caught in Amber's throat. Oh, Sam. Trust you to say exactly the wrong thing.

She flicked her hair back one-handed and covered up the bitter taste of so much disappointment with a dismissive choke. He must be desperate to go to such lengths for this interview. She had no idea how much journalists earned, but surely he didn't need the job that much?

Drat her curiosity.

Of course she remembered the way he used to talk about how he was going to work his way through journalism school at all of the top London newspapers and be the star investigative journalist. His name would be on the front page of the big broadsheet newspapers that his dad read in the car as he waited for his clients to finish their meetings or fancy events.

Maybe that was it?

Maybe he was still hungry for the success that had eluded him. And this interview would take him up another rung in that long and rickety ladder to the front page.

She was a celebrity that he wanted to interview for his paper to win the extra points he needed for the big prize. And the bigger the story the more gold stars went onto his score sheet.

And that was all. Nothing personal. He had walked—no, he had *run* away from her at the first opportunity to make his precious dream of becoming a professional journalist a reality.

She did not owe him a thing.

'Same as it ever was? In your dreams,' she muttered under her breath, just loud enough for him to hear. 'That editor of yours must really be putting the pressure on if you're resorting to that line.'

Sam shrugged off her jibe but looked away and pretended to tidy up the toolbox on the bench for a second before his gaze snapped back onto her face.

'What can I say? Unlike some people, I need the job.' Then he laughed out loud. 'You always had style, Amber, but retiring at twenty-eight? That takes a different kind of chutzpah. I admire that.'

He stepped forward towards her and nodded towards her arm, his eyes narrowed and his jaw loose. 'Is it your wrist? I know you said that it was a clean break, but...'

'No,' she whispered. 'It's nothing to do with my wrist.'

'I am glad to hear it. Then how about the other rumours? A lot of people think that you are using this announcement to start a kind of bidding war between rival orchestras around the world. Publicity stunts like this have been done before.'

'Not by me. I won't be making a comeback as a concert pianist. Or at least I don't plan to.'

Amber swallowed down her unease, reluctant to let Sam see that she was still uncertain about where her life would take her.

She had made her decision to retire while recovering in hospital and she'd imagined that a simple press statement would be the easiest way to close out that part of her life. Her agent was not happy, of course—but he had other talent on his books and a steady income from her records and other contracts—she was still valuable to him.

But the hard implications were still there on the horizon, niggling at her.

Music had been her life for so long that just the thought of never performing in public again was so new that it still ruffled her. Playing the piano had been the one thing that she did well. The one and only way that she knew to earn her mother's praise.

Of course Julia Swan would have loved her daughter to choose the violin and follow in her footsteps, but it soon became obvious that little Amber had no talent for any other instrument apart from the piano.

For a girl who was moving from one home to another, one school to another, one temporary stepdad to another, music had been one of the few constants in her life. Piano practice was the perfect excuse to avoid tedious evenings with her mother and whatever male friend or violin buff she was dating at the time.

The piano was her escape. Her refuge. It was where she

could plough her love and devotion and all of the passion that was missing in her life with her bitter and demanding, needy and man-hunting mother.

So she had worked and worked, then worked harder to overcome her technical problems and excel. It was her outlet for the pain, the suppressed anger. All of it. And nobody knew just how much pain she was in.

Because there was one thing that her mother never understood—and still did not understand, even when she had tried to explain at the hospital. And then in the endless texts and emails and pleading late night phone calls begging her to reconsider and sometimes challenging her decision to retire.

Amber had always played for the joy in the music.

She was not an artist like her mother, who demanded validation and adoration. She just loved the music and wanted to immerse herself in the emotional power of it.

And Sam Richards was the only other person on this planet who had ever understood that without her having to explain it.

Until this moment she had thought that connection between them would fade with the years they had spent apart.

Wrong.

Sam was looking at her with that intense gaze that used to make her shiver with delight and anticipation of the time that they would spend together and, just for a second, her will faltered.

Maybe this was not such a good idea?

Getting her own back on Sam had seemed a perfectly logical thing to do back in the penthouse, but here in the garage which was as familiar as her own apartment, suddenly the whole idea seemed pathetic and insulting to both of them. She had made plenty of poor decisions over the past few years—surely she could forgive Sam the mistakes he had made as a teenager desperate to improve his life?

Amber opened her mouth and was just about to make an excuse when Sam tilted his head and rubbed his chin before asking, 'I suppose this is about the money?'

And there it was. Like a slap across the face.

Her lower lip froze but she managed a thin smile. 'Are you talking about the blood money you took from my mother to leave me alone and get out of London? To start your new career, of course.'

His mouth twisted and faltered. 'Actually, I was thinking more about the generous donation the paper will be contributing to your favourite charity. Although I should imagine that we are not the only ones to offer you something for your time. Not that you need the money, of course. Or the publicity.'

'You don't think that I need publicity?'

'Come on, Amber, your face was on billboards and the sides of buses, your last CD went into the top ten classical music charts and you have set new records for the number of followers you have on the social media sites. Publicity is not your problem.'

'It goes with the job—I am in showbiz. Correction. Was in showbiz. That doesn't interest me any longer.'

'Okay then. So why are you even talking to me about doing an interview? Seeing as you don't need the publicity.'

'Logistics. I thought that the press would get bored after a couple of weeks and move onto the next musician.

Wrong! I was almost mobbed outside the record company this morning. So it makes sense to do one comprehensive interview and get it over with.'

She waved one hand in the air. 'One interview. One journalist.'

Sam shoved his hands deep into the pockets of his jeans, his casual smile replaced by unease.

'Wait a minute. Are you offering me an exclusive?' he asked. 'What's the catch?'

'Oh, how suspicious you are. Well. As it happens, I might be willing to give you that interview.' She cleared her throat and tilted her head, well aware that she had his full attention. 'But there are a few conditions we need to agree on before I talk on the record.'

'Conditions. This sounds like the catch part.'

'I prefer to think of them as more of a trade. You do something for me, I do something for you. And, from what I have seen so far, you might find some of them rather challenging. Still interested?'

'Ah. Now we have it. You know you have the upper hand so you decided to come down here to gloat?'

'Gloat? Do you really think I would do that?' she repeated, her words catching at the back of her throat. Was that how he thought of her? As some spoiled girl who had come to impress him with her list of achievements?

'I haven't changed that much, Sam. We've both done what we set out to do. You need an interview and I have a few things I need doing which you might be able to help me with. It's as simple as that.'

'Simple? Nothing about you was ever simple, Amber.'

Sam leaned back against the workbench and stretched out his long arms either side of him so that his biceps strained against the fabric of his T-shirt across his chest and arms. The sinewy boy she had known had been replaced by a man who knew his power and had no problem using it to get his way.

And the tingle of that intense gaze sent the old shivers down the back of her legs and there was absolutely nothing she could do to stop them. Her heart started thumping and she knew that her neck was already turning a lovely shade of bright red as his gaze scanned her face.

She could blame it on the hot May sunshine outside the garage door, but who was she trying to kid?

What had Kate said about Petra? That she had bedazzled Sam that night? Well, the Sam who was scanning her body was quite capable of doing his own bedazzling these days.

Sam had been the first boy who had ever given her the tingles and there had only been two other men in her life. All god-handsome, all rugged and driven and all as far removed from the world of music and orchestral performance venues as it was possible to imagine.

And every single one of them had swept her off her feet and into their world without giving her time to even think about what she was doing or whether the relationship had a chance. Little wonder that she had ended up alone and in tears, bewildered and bereft, wondering what had just happened and why.

But one thing was perfectly clear. Sam had been the first, and there was no way that she was going to go through that pain again, just to score a few points on the payback scoreboard.

Decision time.

If she was going to do this, she needed to do it now,

and put the tingles down to past stupidity. Or she could turn around and run as fast as she could back to the penthouse and lock the door tight behind her. Just as her kind friends thought that she should. Just as she would have done only a few months earlier, before her life had changed.

'I hadn't planned to give any more interviews after the press release. That part of my life is over,' she said, her chin tilted up. 'But I have a few things you could help me with and you need this interview to impress your editor and make your mark in the London office. Am I getting warm?'

He shrugged and tried to look casual. But there was just that small twitch at the side of his mouth which he used to have when things were difficult at home and he didn't want to talk about it. 'Warm enough.'

'Warm? If I was any hotter I would be on fire. If I go to another paper, you will be waiting on the pavement for movie stars to stagger out from showbiz parties wearing their underpants as hats.'

Sam's hands gripped onto the bench so tightly that his knuckles started to turn white. 'Ah. Now I am beginning to understand. You want to see me suffer.'

Amber winced and gave a small shoulder shrug. 'You walked out on me and broke my heart. So yes, it would be a shame to miss the opportunity for some retribution. And I am not in the least bit ashamed.' She took a breath. 'But that was a long time ago, Sam. And I am keen to put that away in a box labelled "done and dusted". I think this will help me do that.'

Sam closed his eyes and shook his head from side to side before blinking awake and laughing out loud. 'Done and dusted, eh? I am almost frightened to ask what form my punishment is going to take. But please, do continue, let's get it over with.'

He stood to maximum height, pushed his shoulders back and lifted his chin. 'Hit me.'

Amber strolled into the garage and focused her attention on the sports car, her fingertips lingering on the old leather seats, her face burning with awareness that Sam's gaze was still locked onto her. 'I want to get this done as soon as I can, but time is tight. I'm redecorating my apartment and the girls want to celebrate my birthday this week.'

She almost turned around at the sound of Sam's sharp intake of breath. 'May eighteenth. Hard to forget.'

Amber flung her head up and twisted around at the waist, ready with a cutting remark, but bit it back when she saw the look on Sam's face was one of sadness and regret.

His lips twitched for a second before he replied. 'Busy week. No problem. Just give me your email address and I can send over some questions so you can work on them when you have time.'

'Email questions? Oh, no. This interview has to be in person.'

Sam coughed twice. 'Are you always so awkward?'

She tilted her head slightly to one side before replying. 'No. Just with you.'

He laughed out loud and planted a fist on each hip. 'Don't try and kid me, girl. You have been planning this for ages and are having way too much fun teasing this out.' He flicked his chin in her direction. 'You could have asked your agent to make the call and organised the interview over the phone. But that wouldn't have been nearly so satisfying, would it?'

He waved her spluttering away. 'And I understand that perfectly. Really. I do. I made a horrible mistake and treated you badly, and now you're going to make me pay.'

Then his stance softened and his gaze darted from side to side. 'I'm not proud of what happened the last time we met. Far from it. But that was ten years ago and we're different people now. At least I am. I'm not sure about you.'

'What do you mean?'

'You never had a vindictive thought in your life, Amber DuBois. So why don't you just take me through that list of little things you want me to help you with and we can get this over and done with, and we can put the past behind us?'

Amber inhaled slowly and turned to face Sam, her head tilted slightly to one side, and she carefully pushed the slip of paper deeper into the heart-shaped pocket of her dress.

'What makes you think I have a list?' she asked in the best innocent and surprised voice she could muster at short notice.

'Amber. You always had a list. For everything. A list of things to do that day, a list of how long you practised that week. You are a listy type of person and people don't change that much. So it makes sense for you to have a list of all the things I am going to have to do in exchange for one interview.'

He shot her a glance which made her eyes narrow. Why did he have to remember that small detail, of all things? There was no way she could talk him through her list now.

'I prefer to think of them as challenges. But you are right about one thing—I have thought about what you could possibly give me in exchange for an exclusive, and you can take that smirk off your face right now. You would not be so lucky. So I came up with a new approach.'

She crossed the space between them until her face was only inches away from his and licked her lips before speaking.

'Look, Sam,' she said in low, calm voice as her gaze locked onto his. 'I know people are interested in why I decided to retire when I did, but my reasons are very personal and very close to my heart.' She took a breath and swallowed before rolling her shoulders back a little. 'It would be very easy for a reporter to do a hatchet job with some crazy headline just to sell more papers. So...I need to know that I can trust the journalist I go for to give me a fair hearing.'

'That's not going to be easy,' he replied in a voice which sang with resignation and disappointment.

'I know. This is why you are going to have to prove to me that you are the right man for the job before I say a word on the record.'

His eyebrows went skywards. 'Any ideas on how I do that?'

'Oh, yes,' she sniffed. 'You are going to have to pass an audition before I give you the job. You see, this week is crazily busy and my wrist is a problem. So I need someone to be my Man Friday for the next few days. Unpaid, of course, and you provide your own uniform. But all refreshments are provided by the management. And I just know how much Saskia and Kate are looking forward to having you around the place.'

'A Man Friday,' Sam repeated, very, very slowly. 'So, basically, I have to be your man slave for the next week before you'll even think about giving me the interview?'

Amber picked her business card out of her dress pocket with two fingers, gave Sam her sweetest camera-ready smile and looked deep into his startled eyes as she held the card high in the air. 'Well, it's good to know that your powers of deductive reasoning are as sharp as ever. The audition starts at my apartment at ten tomorrow morning. Oh—and just to make it a little more interesting, I'll have a new challenge for you every day. See you there, Sam. If you are man enough to accept the challenge.'

The air bristled with tension for all of ten seconds. Then Sam took two powerful steps forward, his brows low and dark-eyed, his legs moving from the hips in one smooth movement. Driven. Powerful.

And, before Amber had a chance to complain or slip away, Sam splayed one hand onto her hip and drew her closer to him. Hip to hip.

Amber's breath caught in her throat as his long clever fingers pressed against the thin silk of her dress as though it was not there. She could feel his hot breath on her face as she inhaled a scent that more than anything else she had seen or experienced today whipped her right back to being held in Sam's arms. It was car oil, polish, man sweat, dust and ambition and all Sam. And it was totally, totally intoxicating.

His gaze locked onto her eyes. Holding her transfixed.

'Bambi, I am man enough for anything that you have to offer me,' Sam whispered in a voice which was almost trembling with intensity, one corner of his mouth turned up into a cheeky grin as though he knew precisely what effect he was having on her blood pressure. And there was not one thing she could do about it.

Then, just like that, he stepped back and released her, and it took a lot to stay upright.

And then he winked at her.

'See ya tomorrow—' he smiled with a casual lilt in his voice '—looking forward to it.'

FIVE

_____

'No Mother. Seriously. I don't need another expert medical opinion. Every specialist I have seen recommends six months' recovery time. Yes, I am sure your friend in Miami is excellent but I am not pushing my wrist by trying to practice before it is ready.'

Amber closed her eyes and gave her virtuoso violinist mother two more minutes of ranting about how foolish she was to throw away her career before interrupting. 'Mum, I love you but I have to go. Have a great cruise. Bye.'

Amber closed the call, strolled over to the railing of her penthouse apartment and looked out over London. The silvery River Thames cut a wide ribbon of glistening water through the towering office blocks of glass and exposed metal that clung to the riverbanks. Peeking out between the modern architectural wonders were the spires and domes of ancient churches and imposing carved stone buildings that had once been the highlights of the London landscape.

Even five storeys up, the hustle and bustle of traffic

noise and building work drifted up to the penthouse, creating the background soundtrack to her view of modern city life.

Everywhere she looked she saw life and energy and the relentless drive for prosperity and wealth. Investment bankers, city traders and financial analysts jostled on the streets below her on the way to their computer trading desks. Time was money.

The contrast to the tiny beachside orphanage in Kerala where Parvita was celebrating her wedding could not be greater.

The seaside village where the girls' orphanage was based had running water and electricity—most of the time.

She would love to go back and see them again. *One day.* When she was not so terrified of catching another life-threatening infection.

A cold shiver ran across Amber's shoulders and she pulled her cashmere tighter across the front of her chest.

Heath and her mother were right about one thing. *As always.* Even if she wasn't scared, she *could* raise more income for the orphanage by staying in London or Boston or Miami and fund-raising than risk returning to Kerala, where she had caught meningitis only a few months earlier.

Now all she had to do was come up with a way of doing precisely that.

Not by playing the piano. That was for sure.

No matter how much her mother nagged her to reconsider and plan a comeback concert tour. A year ago she might have gone along with it and started rigorous training but that part of her life was over now.

Wiped away by meningitis and a few months of enforced bed rest when she had to ask some hard questions about the life she was living and how she intended to spend it in the future.

Amber closed her eyes and inhaled and exhaled slowly a couple of times. *No going back, girl. No going back. Only forward. This was her new start. Her new beginning.*

The sun was warm on her face and when she opened her eyes the first thing she saw was the braided cord bracelet that Parvita had made and woven onto her right wrist that last day she was at the orphanage.

She was so lucky.

Heath and her mother loved her and that was what she had to focus on. Not their nagging. She would go back to Boston and start work with the fund-raising committee for Parvita. Benefit concerts were always popular and between her mother and their network of professional musicians they could pull together some top name soloists who could raise thousands for the charity.

This was her chance to do something remarkable. And she was going to grab hold of it with both hands and cling on tight, no matter how bumpy the road ahead was.

First hurdle? Talking to Sam.

Amber glanced at her wristwatch and a fluttering sensation of apprehension blended with excitement bubbled up from deep inside. In another place and time she might have said that the thought of seeing him again face to face was making her nervous. That was totally ridiculous. This was her space and he was here to help her out, as he had promised.

This was not the time to get stage fright.

She was an idiot.

They had agreed to make a trade. His time in exchange for one interview. Nothing more. *What else could there be?*

Her thoughts were interrupted by a petite bundle of energy.

'One good thing came out of that whole school reunion fiasco.' Kate laughed and threw her arms around Amber's waist. 'The three of us haven't been in the same city at the same time for far too many years. And that is a disgrace. So all hail school reunions.'

Amber laughed out loud and stepped back to clink her mug of coffee against Kate's. 'With you on that. I still cannot believe that it's the middle of May already. April was just a blur.'

Kate groaned and slumped into the patio chair facing Amber. 'Tell me about it. London might be suffering from the economic recession but bespoke tailoring is booming and I have never been so busy. It's great. Really great. But wow, is it exhausting.'

'Well, here is something to keep you going.' Saskia El-wood came out from Amber's penthouse apartment with a tray of the most delicious-looking bite-sized snacks, which she wafted in front of Amber. 'Test samples for your birthday party. I need you to taste them all and tell me which ones you like best.'

Kate half rose out of her chair. 'Hey, don't I get to try them too? I could scoff the lot. And breakfast was hours ago.'

'You're next but the birthday girl has first pick. Besides, she needs fattening up a bit. What did they feed you in that hospital, anyway? I can't have you coming to my dining room looking all pale and scrawny.'

Amber munched away on a mini disc of bacon and herb

pizza and made humming sounds of appreciation before speaking between bites. 'No appetite. It was so hot and I was asleep most of the time. And the food certainly wasn't as good as this. These are fantastic.'

'Thought you would like it and there are lots more to come. So tuck in.'

Kate snatched a tiny prawn mayo sandwich and chewed it down in one huge bite before sighing in pleasure. 'Oh, that is so good. Amber DuBois, it was a genius idea to have your birthday party at Saskia's house.'

'It was the very least I could do. Ten years is a long time and all three of us have come a long way,' Amber replied and raised her coffee as a toast. 'I missed you both so much. To the goddesses.'

'The goddesses,' Kate and Saskia echoed and all three of them settled back in their chairs in the sunshine with the tray of snacks between them, hot Italian blend coffee and the sound of the city way below to break up the contented sighs.

'So what have you been up to, Amber?' Saskia asked, her eyes shielded with a hand as she nibbled on a fresh cream profiterole drizzled with chocolate sauce. 'It must get you down when you're unable to practise for hours like you usually do.'

Amber waved her right arm in the air and turned the plaster cast covering her wrist from side to side. 'Frustrating more than anything, but the exercises are keeping my fingers working and I have to get used to being one handed for a few more weeks. Only that isn't the problem. There is something missing and somehow...' Then she gave a chuckle and shook her head. 'Oh, ignore me. I'm just being silly.'

'Oh, no, you don't,' Saskia said in a low voice. 'We can tell that there is something bothering you. And you know that we're not going to let it drop until you tell us what the problem is. So come on. Spill. Out with it.'

Amber focused her gaze on the terrace. Bright flowering plants and conifers spilled out of colourful planters in front of a panoramic view across the London city skyline.

'Yesterday I was feeling down in the dumps so I pulled out my favourite music scores. If I have a spare hour or two on tour I can usually visualise the performance in my head and it is the one thing that is always guaranteed to cheer me up and have me bouncing with excitement.'

She paused and sighed low and slow. 'But not this time. I didn't feel a thing. There was nothing that made me want to tear off this plaster cast and play. *Seriously.* It's as though all of my passion for the music has gone out of the window.'

She paused and looked from Saskia to Kate and then back to Saskia again. 'And that's scary, girls. I don't know how to do anything else.'

The silence echoed between the three of them before Kate put her mug down on the metal mesh table with a dramatic thud.

'Amber? Sweetie? It might have something to do with the fact that you have just spent months in hospital recovering from the infection you caught in India. And yes, I know that it is still our secret. We won't tell anyone. But you have to give yourself time to recover and get your mojo back. Maybe even be kind to yourself and let your body heal, instead of running from place to place at top speed. How about that for a crazy idea?'

Amber blew out long and slow. 'You're right. This is

the first time in years that I have been in London long enough to take stock. I just feel that I am lost and drifting on my own. Again.'

Saskia slid over to the end of Amber's lounger and wrapped her fingers around her arm. 'No, you're not. You will always have a home at Elwood House. And don't you dare forget that.'

Amber smiled into the faces of her two best friends in the world. Friends who had somehow got pushed lower and lower on her priority list over the past few years, and yet they were the very people who had come running the first time she asked.

'I don't know what I did to deserve you two. Thanks. It means a lot. But I won't put you out too much.'

'Decision made, young lady,' Saskia said in a jokey serious voice. 'You are coming to stay with me at Elwood House as my birthday present, and you are going to be cosseted, whether you like it or not.'

'Oh, that sounds good,' Kate said, and snuggled back further onto the soft cushion of the patio lounger. 'Can I come over and be cosseted in exchange for making curtains and cushions? I could use a good cosset.'

'You and your needlework skills are welcome any time.' Saskia laughed and gestured towards Amber with her head. 'I'm going to need some help keeping this one from wearing herself out getting ready for her birthday party.'

Amber dropped her head back and closed her eyes as bright warm sunshine broke through the light cloud cover. Then she turned back to face Saskia and Kate, who were looking at her. 'It's going to be like old times. The three of us, camped out at Elwood House. But at least this time I'm not running away from home to spite my mother by eloping with Sam Richards.'

Saskia peered at her through narrowed eyes. 'Ah, yes. Sam.' She nodded. 'Were you okay? With seeing him again? Because I still cannot believe that you went there on your own.'

'Ah. So you think I would be safe from the evil clutches of the teenage boy who broke my heart and betrayed me with one of my best friends if I stayed here in my ivory tower penthouse like a fairy tale princess waiting to be rescued.'

She laughed and said with a snort, 'Not a chance, gorgeous. I refuse to be turned into some kind of recluse just because the press want to know why I decided to retire. Besides, I've been working with reporters like Sam Richards for years. He doesn't bother me.'

Kate shuffled to the edge of her seat, her bottom jiggling with excitement while Saskia just chuckled softly to herself. 'Really?'

Amber pushed out her famous moisture lipstick slicked lips. 'Oh, yes. My musician friend Parvita runs a wonderful charity in India who could certainly use the fee, only...' she sighed with a slight quiver in her voice and Saskia and Kate instantly leant closer towards her '...I've had enough of that circus who think that they can make up any kind of story and get away with it. I have helped the media sell newspapers and magazines for the last ten years. And now I'm done with it. I am not playing that game any more. And they are going to have to get used to the idea. This time I call the shots.'

Kate's eyebrows lifted. 'I knew it! You're going to charge them megabucks for a full page nude shot with you sitting at a white grand piano with only discreet pieces of sheet music and fabulous jewels to cover your modesty? That could be fun.'

Amber and Saskia both turned and stared at Kate in silence.

'What? So I have a vivid imagination?' Kate shrugged.

Amber frowned at Kate for a moment and then blinked. 'Not exactly what I had in mind and no, it wouldn't be fun, not even for the megabucks. But do you know what? The more I thought about it, the more I got to thinking that maybe Sam does have something we can trade with after all.'

Kate drew back and squinted at her suspiciously. 'Go on.'

'I need to get the past off my back. Parvita's charity and my birthday party are going to take all of my time and energy, and the last thing I need is a troop of paparazzi making my life even more of a nightmare.'

'You really are serious about retiring?'

'Totally,' Amber replied and smiled at Saskia. 'But talking to you two has reminded me where my real priorities lie.' And then she reached out and squeezed Saskia's hand for a second. 'Your aunt Margot gave me a sanctuary at Elwood House, and I haven't forgotten it. I owe you. This is why I'm thinking of doing something rather rash.'

'What do you mean by rash?' Saskia asked in her low, calm, gentle voice.

Amber took a long drink of coffee, well aware that both of her friends were waiting for her to speak.

'When you told me all about your plans to convert Elwood House into a private meeting and dining venue I was amazed that we hadn't thought about it before. Your dining room is stunning.'

Her voice drifted away dreamily. 'I gave my first piano recital in that house. I'll never forget it. The crystal chandeliers. The flickering firelight. It was magical. This is why I want to do as much as I can to help make Elwood House a success.'

Saskia shook her head. 'You have already invited half the fashion models in London, their agents, their posh friends and the music industry to your birthday party this week. I couldn't ask for better publicity.'

'And yet you still don't have a decent website or booking system or photo gallery to showcase the house. And that. Is where I come in. And you can stop shaking your head; I know that you won't take my money. So I am going to ask a professional photographer to come over and put together your full marketing package and organise the website. Free. Gratis. Won't cost you a penny.'

'Really?' Saskia replied and lifted her mug towards Amber in a toast. 'That's fantastic. Is he one of your fashion pals?'

Amber licked her lips and took a sip of water before answering.

'Not exactly. I think Sam Richards is calling himself a photojournalist these days. More tarts, anyone?'

Amber paused and looked at Kate, who was groaning with her head in her hands. 'Don't worry about Sam. He knows that he has to be on his very best behaviour if he has any chance of that interview. Saskia needs those photos and Sam seems to know which end of a camera to point. And no, I haven't forgiven him yet. Think of this as part of the payback. So please don't kill him. At least not in front of the party guests. Saskia does not want bloodstains on her nice carpet.'

The words had barely left Amber's mouth and the shouts were still ringing in her ears when the oven timer bell rang and Kate shook her head slowly from side to side before diving back into the kitchen to get fresh supplies of snacks.

'Don't burn your mouth by eating them straight out of the oven,' Saskia called out to Kate, but then her mouth relaxed into a half smile. 'Payback. I suppose that is one way of looking at it and I have no doubt that he would do a good job. But sheesh, Amber. I am worried for you.'

Amber was just about to rattle off a casual throwaway remark, but instead she paused before answering one of her few real friends in the world. The old Amber would have laughed off her friend's concern with a flippant gesture as some sort of silly joke, but the new Amber was slowly getting used to opening up to people she loved and trusted. 'You always did like Sam, didn't you?'

Saskia gave a brisk nod. 'I suppose so. Not in any sort of romantic way, of course, nothing like that, but yes, I did. His dad had driven my aunt Margot around for years and sometimes he brought Sam along with him. I suppose that's why I suggested that your mum use his limo service to take her to venues.'

Saskia lifted one hand. 'I think I might even have introduced you. So blame me for what happened. But yes, I thought he was okay.' Her brow squeezed together. 'Why do you ask me that now?'

'Because it was so weird. Over the years I sometimes imagined what I would say if I met up with Sam unexpectedly at some airport or hotel, or if he came to one of my performances. But when I saw him yesterday? All those clever, witty put-downs just fled. He was still the same Sam, working in his dad's garage. And I was right back to feeling like a gawky, awkward, six feet tall seventeen-year-old with big feet who was trying to sound all grown-up and clever around this handsome, streetwise city boy.'

Amber looked up at Saskia and shrugged. 'I trusted him then and he let me down just when I needed him the most. How do I know that I can trust him now? The orphanage in India is too important to me to see the real message buried under some big celebrity exposé which is around the world in seconds. Can you imagine the headlines? "Brave Bambi DuBois cheats death from meningitis. Career in tatters." Oh, they would love that.'

'Which is why you are taking control. Maybe there is too much history between the two of you for him to be objective. But we agreed that we would give him an audition for the job, and that is what we are going to do. Okay?'

'Absolutely okay. If he can stand it, then so can I.'

'Right. And on the way you can make sure that Sam gets the message that you have moved on to even more handsome and successful boyfriends. But fear not. Kate and I will make sure that we rub it in at regular intervals that he made a horrible mistake when he let you go and you are so totally over him.'

'Saskia! I didn't say anything about being cruel. And as for being over him? Sam only had to smile at me yesterday and I got the tingles from head to toe. Which is so ridiculous I can hardly admit it. The last time that happened I ended up on a plane to Kathmandu with a suitcase full of evening wear and piano music and no clue about what I was going to do when I got there.'

'Mark the mountaineer?'

Amber nodded. 'And three years before that it was Rico. Racing car driver. One kiss on the cheek and a cuddle in the pits and I smelt of diesel fumes for months.'

Amber sighed dramatically and slumped back. 'I am a hopeless case and I know it. I mean. *A mountaineer*? What was I thinking? I got the tingles and that was that.' She blinked a couple of times. 'The only scientific explanation is that I was cursed at birth. You know how it goes. The good fairy godmother blesses me with some musical talent, and the evil one says, "Oh, that's sweet, but in exchange you are going to fall for men who will only ever be interested in their obsession. So you had better get used to the idea."'

'You weren't thinking. You were taking a chance on love with remarkable men,' Saskia replied wistfully. 'You know. Not all of us have had a chance to be cuddled by racing car drivers or kissed at Everest base camp. I envy you for having the courage to take that risk.'

Amber instantly sat up and wrapped her arm around Saskia's shoulder. 'You'll meet someone—I'm sure of it. Especially now you're opening up Elwood House. Think of all the handsome executives who will be queuing up to sample your tasty treats.'

'From your lips... But in the meantime, where does that leave our Sam Richards? Because, to me, this little plan of ours could go in one of two ways. Either you keep your cool and freeze out his tingle power so that you can finally get Sam out of your system and your life. Or...'

Saskia smiled and pushed out her lips. 'You might be

tempted to try out the new and improved version to see if the quality of those tingles has improved over the years. And don't look at me like that. It's a distinct possibility. Dangerous, scary and not very clever, but a possibility...and that worries me, Amber. I know how much you cared about Sam. I was there, remember? I don't want to see you running back to Elwood House in tears over Sam Richards.'

'Sam?' came a squeaky voice from the bedroom and a second later its owner appeared on the patio and she was not carrying more snacks.

Kate was wearing a huge fascinator in the shape of a red tropical flower on her head and several strings of huge beads cascaded below bundles of silk scarves. 'You don't have time to think about boys, woman!'

Kate gestured with her head towards the dressing room, which had long since given up any hope of being used as a second bedroom. 'Amber DuBois, you are officially one of the worst hoarders I have ever seen. And I make clothes for women who are still wearing their mother's hats. You have been crushing stuff into those cupboards for years. I am frightened to open those wardrobes in fear of avalanche.'

Amber waved one slender hand in the air. 'I know. I spent most of yesterday trying to root out casual day clothes to wear and ended up going to the shops. I have got so used to just dumping my stuff here that when I want something I cannot find it.'

Amber frowned and pushed her lower lip out. 'Is it normal to have more performance dresses than pants? I love dressing up for my audiences, but I find it so hard to refuse when designers start giving me free gorgeous things to wear. Most of those dresses have only had to survive one recital. It does seem a shame to just stash them until they gather dust. Unless, of course...'

She grinned and looked from side to side. 'Ladies. I have been looking for some way of raising funds. What do you say to a spot of dressing up in the name of decluttering? I am talking Internet auctions and second-hand designer shops.' A wide grin creased her face as she was practically deafened by shrieks from Saskia and Kate. 'I'll take those screams as a yes. Right. Then let's get started on those ball gowns. But girls—there is one condition. You do not touch the sacred shoes. Okay? Okay. Let's do it. I'll race you.'

SIX

———

Sam Richards leant against the back wall of the elevator, propped his camera bag against his foot and crossed his arms as he enjoyed the view.

Two tall, very slender brunettes dressed from head to toe in black had rushed in at the last minute from the cream and caramel marble reception area to Amber's apartment building, gushing thanks and flooding the space with giggling, floral perfume and an empty garment rail which took up the whole width of the elevator. Judging by their sideways glances, indiscreet nudging and body language, they were not too unhappy with being crushed into the space with him, and any other time and place he might have started chatting and enjoying their company.

But not today.

His morning had already got off to a poor start when his dad had phoned from France saying that he was going to stay on a few more days because for once the weather in the Alps was perfect for a spot of touring.

Perhaps it was just as well. His dad had not exactly

been sympathetic when Sam had told him about Amber's little scheme. In fact he had laughed his head off and told him to behave himself.

As if he had a choice.

Sam pressed his hands flat against the cool surface of the elevator wall.

Amber had the upper hand and he was going to have to go with it, but it didn't mean to say that he liked it. One. Little. Bit. He had stopped being at other people's beck and call the day he'd left London and there was no way he was going to step into the role of Amber's fool and like it.

But he would get through it and move on. He could survive being pulled back into Amber's high class life as a diva for a few days.

If she could stand it—then so could he.

Sam inhaled the perfumed air, which was suddenly overheated and cloying. He had no interest in this world of fashion and celebrity—he never had. The A-list party and clubbing circuit had long lost their appeal for him. It was his job and he worked hard to create something interesting and new out of the same old shallow gossip and the relentless need for fame and riches fuelled by the public obsession for celebrity—an obsession he helped to foster, whether he liked that fact or not.

Past tense. He had paid his dues and earned the right to sit behind that editor's desk, doing the job he had been trained for. And he wasn't going to let that slip away from him without a fight.

He had come a long way from the raw teenager with a fire in his belly that Amber had known.

Man enough for the job? Oh, yes, he was man enough for the job all right.

Even if he had no clue what the actual job was. Her text message had asked him to bring his camera bag and a screwdriver over and they were all the clues she had given him.

Sam rolled his shoulders back as the elevator slowed and the girls starting fidgeting with the clothes rail.

The elevator doors slid open on the floor number Amber had given him but, before he could stride forward with his bag, the girls swept out into the wide corridor of pale wood and pastel colours.

Interesting.

Unless, of course…

With a tiny shoulder shrug Sam slowly followed the girls towards the penthouse apartment. Lively disco dance music drifted out through an open door towards him, the beat in perfect tune with the rattle of their high heels on the fine wooden floor.

Disco music? If this was Amber's place, she must be out shopping for the morning. The only music Amber DuBois liked was written by men with quill pens and dipping ink hundreds of years ago.

The girls rolled the garment rail into the apartment, waved at someone inside, then swept back past Sam out into the hallway, arm in arm in a flutter of perfume and girly giggles.

He paused for a second to admire them, then turned to face the door.

This was it. Show time. He took a deep breath, pushed the door open another few inches, stepped inside the apartment and instantly went into sensory overload.

What looked like the entire contents of a large fashion boutique was scattered over every surface in the living room. Handbags, shoes, hats and assorted female fripperies were draped across sofas, chairs and tables in a wild riot of colours and patterns, illuminated by the daylight streaming in from the floor to ceiling patio doors at the other end of the room.

His first reaction was to step back into the corridor and call the whole thing off. Right then and there. Apparently there were some men who enjoyed going clothes shopping with their wives and girlfriends. He had never understood how they could do that. There was probably medication for that kind of mental self-affliction.

He had never done that kind of crazy and he had no intention of starting now.

But he couldn't leave. And she knew it. Which meant that Amber had to be here to witness the payback in person.

Time to get this over with.

Sam sniffed, pushed his shoulders back, stashed his bag behind the sofa so that it was out of the mayhem and by stepping over the entire contents of a luggage department, he wound his way through the obstacle course that was the corridor towards the source of the disco music.

He had been on racing circuits which had fewer chicanes than this room.

Sam paused at the open bedroom door and leant casually on the door frame, his arms crossed.

It was a long, wide room but surprisingly simply furnished with a large bed with an ivory satin quilt, a small sofa covered in a shiny cream fabric with flights of butterflies painted on it and a wide dressing table next to more patio doors.

One complete wall was covered with a floor to ceiling mirror.

And standing in front of the mirror were three girls he had last seen together at Amber's eighteenth birthday party, what felt like a lifetime ago.

Amber, Saskia and Kate were wearing lemon-yellow oversized T-shirts with the words 'ALL SIZES' printed on them in large black letters. Kate was in the middle, moving her hips from side to side and jiggling along to the disco music and holding a hairbrush to her mouth as a microphone. Saskia and Amber were her backup singers. Kate could not be more than five feet four inches tall in heels, Saskia was a few inches taller in flat shoes and Amber—Amber had been six feet tall aged sixteen.

It stunned him to realise that he could recognise Amber's voice so easily. She could sing like an angel and often had at Christmas concerts and birthday parties. Kate was the best singer in their little schoolgirl clique so Amber had left her to it and stayed on the keyboard, but she had such a sweet, clear voice. He had missed that voice. And whether he liked it or not, he had missed the sound of Amber whispering his name as she clung on to him with her arms looped around his neck.

Sam pressed back against the door frame.

A memory of those same three girls wearing those same yellow T-shirts at Margot Elwood's house came drifting back. It was someone's birthday party and the girls had put together a little musical routine for Saskia's aunt and Amber had asked Sam to join in the fun. Strange. He had not thought about Elwood House in years.

These three girls looked the same—but he knew that

they had all changed more than he could have imagined. But these three girls? In those T-shirts? It was a blast from a happier time when they all had such wonderful dreams and aspirations about what they were going to do with their lives.

This was a bad time to decide to become sentimental. Time to get this started.

He banged hard on the door with the back of his knuckles and called out in a loud voice, 'Is the lady of the house at home? The help has arrived.'

They were so intent on singing along to the words of some pop tune from the nineteen nineties that it was a few seconds before Saskia even glanced in his direction.

She instantly stopped dancing, put down her can of hairspray microphone and nudged Amber in the ribs before replying, 'Hi, Sam. Good to see you.'

'Hey. We were just getting to the chorus,' Kate complained, then turned towards him and planted a fist on each hip and tutted loudly, but Sam hardly looked at the support band.

His whole attention was focused on the girl who was peeking out at him over the top of Kate's head.

In contrast to the fresh, floral Amber who had waltzed into his dad's garage, this version of Amber had donned the uniform of the full-on casually elegant fashion world.

The T-shirt was V-necked and modest enough to cover her cleavage but fashionably off centre so that a matching azure bra strap was exposed over one shoulder as she moved. Her collarbone formed a crisp outline.

Amber had never been overweight, but it seemed that she was paying the price of working with fashion designers.

She was too skinny. *Way too skinny.*

She had tied her broken wrist into a long blue scarf with pink and gold threads which ran through it to form a kind of halter neck.

The shade of blue matched the colour of her violet eyes. Perfectly. And, without intending to, Sam's gaze was locked onto those eyes as though he was seeing them for the first time.

Her hair was clipped back behind her head in a simple waterfall. She wasn't wearing any make-up from what he could see and did not need any.

He wondered if she realised how rare that truly was. Yes, he had met stunning girls in Los Angeles—the city was full of them.

But Amber DuBois was the real deal.

No doubt about it.

The lanky, awkward girl who had never known what to do with her long legs and arms and oversized feet was gone.

For good.

Replaced by a woman who looked totally comfortable and confident in her own skin.

This was the Amber he had always known that she would become one day, and he was suddenly pleased that she had realised just how lovely she truly was. And always had been.

Now the world had the chance to see Amber the way he had once seen her. As a beautiful, confident woman with the power to take his breath away. Just by looking at her.

'Hi, trouble,' she replied casually with a bright smile as though she were greeting an old friend, which was about right. 'You are right on time.'

He gave her a mock salute. 'Reporting for duty as ordered.'

Her small laugh turned into a bit of a cough, then she turned back to Kate and Saskia and pressed her cheek lightly to each of them in turn. 'Thanks, girls. I'll see you the same time tomorrow. Oh—and don't forget to check online about the shoes. Bye. Bye for now.'

Amber stepped past Sam and waved to Kate and Saskia as they carefully wove their precious cargo of bags and suit carriers down the hall towards the front door, laughing and chatting as they went, with only the occasional backwards scowl from Kate over one shoulder to indicate how *pleased* they were to see him again. *Not*.

Only then did Amber turn back to face Sam, her hand resting lightly on one hip.

'I cannot believe that you actually came.'

'So you weren't serious about the audition? Great!' Sam replied, pushing himself off the door post and dusting his hands off and patting his pocket. 'Shall we get started now? I have my trusty tape recorder right here.'

Amber exhaled explosively and held up both hands. 'Not so fast. I was perfectly serious—you have to audition for this gig.'

Sam lifted both hands as he grinned at her.

'Well, here I am. This is me proving that you can trust me to keep my word and do whatever it is you need me to do. Your personal slave is ready for action. So let's get started.'

'Oh, now don't tempt me,' Amber murmured under her breath, then she lifted her chin and peered at him through creased eyebrows. 'You had better come into my bedroom.'

Sam blinked several times. 'I am liking the sound of this already.'

She closed her eyes and shook her head. 'And I am regretting it already. Do not even try and flirt with me because it won't work. Okay?'

'Methinks the lady doth protest too much,' Sam replied, then winced at the searing look she gave him. 'Okay, I get the message. I am a snake who cannot be trusted. So. Let's get this game of charades started. What is the first thing on that long list of yours?'

Amber pressed her forefinger to her full, soft pink lips and pretended to ponder.

'You may have noticed that I am having a bit of a declutter at the moment.'

'Declutter? Is that what you call it? I have to tell you that, despite reports to the contrary, my knowledge of female clothing is not as great as you might imagine. So if you are looking for fashion advice...'

Amber jabbed her finger towards the bedroom wall right in front of them, which was covered with a framed collection of artwork, portraits of Amber and old sheets of music manuscripts.

'I need someone to take my pictures down so I can decorate. It is a bit tricky one-handed and some of them are quite valuable. I vaguely recall that you can handle a screwdriver. Think you can manage that?'

Sam stepped forward so that they were only inches apart.

'Bambi, I can handle anything you throw at me.'

She took a step closer, startling him, but there was no way that he was going to let her know that.

'Oh, this is only the start. I have a very, very long list.'

'I expected nothing less.'

He turned to go back into the living room, and then looked back at Amber over one shoulder. 'And don't worry. I won't tell anyone that you couldn't wait to drag me into your bedroom the first chance you could get.' He tapped one side of his nose with his forefinger. 'It will be our little secret.' And with that he strode away from Amber, leaving her wide-mouthed with annoyance, delighted that he had managed to squeeze in the last word.

SEVEN

————

Two hours later Sam had taken down the framed pictures from the walls of two bedrooms, a kitchen and a hallway, covered them in bubble wrap and packed them into plastic crates already stacked two high along the length of Amber's hall, before starting on the living room.

The barrage of noise, telephone calls and visitors had slowly faded away as the morning went on so that by the time he had unscrewed the last of the huge oil paintings and modern art installations in the living room, he didn't have to worry about stepping on Amber's peep toe sandals as she worked around him, or accidentally brushing plaster dust onto some fabulous gown which had been casually thrown over a chair or garment rail.

It took superhuman effort but for most of that time he kept his eyes on the rawl plugs and loose plaster behind the pictures instead of the long, lean limbs of the lovely woman who brushed past him at regular intervals in the hallway, leaving a trail of scented air and a cunning giggle in her wake.

Decluttering? When he'd cleared out his furnished Los Angeles apartment, he had walked out with two suitcases and a laptop bag. The same way he had found it. All of his car magazines and photos were safely scanned and digitised. The rest had been recycled or passed on to his pals. He never had to go through this palaver.

Sam stood back and tilted his head to look at a pair of large oil paintings made up of small shapes inside larger shapes inside larger shapes which was starting to give him a headache.

And some of the picture frames had sticky notes on the front with the letter S written in purple marker pen. Purple, he snorted. What did that mean?

Right. Finish this little collection. Then it was time to go and find the lady and find out.

No need. Here she was, ambling towards him. Head down, a large garment bag over one shoulder and a cellphone pressed against her ear, oblivious to his presence.

From the corner of one eye he watched her flip the phone back into her pocket and pick up several scarves from the top of the piano. Then Amber paused and ran two fingertips along the surface of the keys without pressing them firmly enough to make music.

Only as he watched, her lovely face twisted into a picture of sadness and regret and pain that was almost unbearable for him to see.

He turned around to face her, but it was too late—the moment was lost as Amber suddenly realised that she was being observed. A bright smile wiped away the trauma that had been all there to see only a few seconds earlier, startling him with how quickly she could turn on her performance face, and she lowered the lid on the piano. 'Plaster dust,' she whispered. 'Not a good idea.'

'Don't let me put you off playing,' Sam quipped and gestured towards the piano with his screwdriver. 'I brought my own earplugs in case you were holding a rehearsal session.'

'Very funny, but your ears are safe. I am not playing today.' She took a breath and raised her plaster cast towards him. 'My wrist is hurting.'

Her chin lifted and she angled her head a little. 'You can tell your lovely readers that I simply cannot tolerate second best. My standards are just as high as ever.'

'Yeah.' He nodded. 'Right. It's just weird that you haven't even tried to play. It used to be the other way around. I spent a lot of time trying to drag you away from the nearest keyboard.'

Sam looked into her face with a grin but her gaze was firmly fixed on the scarves in her bag.

'That was a long time ago, Sam. People change.' And with that she turned away and strolled back to her bedroom. In silence.

As he watched her slim hips sway away from him, every alarm bell in his journalist's mind started ringing at the same time.

Music used to be the one thing that gave Amber joy. She used to call it her private escape route away from the chaos that was her mother's life.

Well, it didn't look like that now.

Something was not right here. And it was not just her wrist that was causing Amber pain.

And, damn it, but he cared more than he should.

* * *

Amber ran her fingers over the few dresses still left in her wardrobe and stifled a self-indulgent sniff. She had loved wearing those evening gowns which were now on their way to a shop specialising in pre-loved designer wear. But she had plenty of photos of the events to remind her what each dress had looked like if she wanted a walk down memory lane.

Which she didn't.

She had never been sentimental about clothes like some of the other performers. There was no lucky bracelet or a corset dress which was guaranteed to have her grace the cover of the latest celebrity magazine. They were just clothes—beautiful clothes which had made her feel special and beautiful when she had worn them. But clothes just the same.

So why did it feel so weird to know that she would never wear them again?

Amber sniffed again, then mentally scolded herself.

This was pathetic! She was still Amber Sheridan DuBois. She was still the girl with the first class degree in music and the amazing career. The same Amber who had flown so very high in a perfect sky which seemed to go on for ever and ever.

Until she had gone to India and fate had sent her tumbling back down to earth with a bang.

The sound of an electric screwdriver broke through her wallow in self-pity and Amber shivered in her thin top. All in the past. She was over the worst and her wrist would soon be better. She was lucky to have come through the infection more or less intact, and that was worth celebrating.

So why did she feel like collapsing onto her bed and sleeping for a week?

She was overtired. That was it. *Idiot.* The doctors had warned her about overdoing it, then her mother and Heath and now so had Kate and Saskia—and Parvita, who had offered to delay the wedding because she felt so guilty about inviting her friends to perform a concert at the orphanage. She had had no clue that there was a meningitis outbreak sweeping across Kerala.

Of course she had told Parvita not to be so silly— the astrologers had chosen a perfect wedding day and that was precisely what Parvita was going to have. A perfect wedding back in her home village without having to worry about an exhausted concert pianist who should be in Boston resting in glorious solitude at her stepbrother's town house.

Pity that she had not factored in the mess in her apartment, and surviving a birthday party at Elwood House. And then there was the ex-boyfriend who had suddenly popped into her life again.

Yes. Sam might have something to do with her added stress levels.

Good thing he had no idea how her body was on fire when he was in sight or she would never live it down.

He had no idea that she had tossed and turned most of the night with an aching wrist, wondering would have happened if she had fallen into Sam's arms that night of her eighteenth birthday. Would they still be together now? Or would their relationship have fizzled out with recriminations and acrimonious insults?

She would never know, but there was one thing she was sure about.

Ever cell in her body was aware that Sam Richards was only a few feet away from her in the next room. His boyish grin was locked into her memory and, whether she liked it or not, her treacherous body refused to behave itself when he was so close. Her hands were shaking, her legs felt as though they belonged to someone else and it had nothing to do with the fact that she was supposed to be resting. Nothing at all.

All she had to do was survive a few more days and Sam would be out of her life.

Amber rolled her stiff and sore shoulders and rearranged her sling.

Shaking her head in dismay, she stretched up to tug at the boxes on the top shelf of her dressing room but they slid right back into the corner and out of her reach.

Grabbing the spare dining room chair Kate had used earlier to find the hat boxes, Amber popped the headphones of her personal stereo in her trouser pocket over her ears, and hummed along to the lively Italian baroque music as she jumped up onto the chair and stretched out on tiptoe to reach the far back corner of the shelf.

She had just caught hold of the handle of her old vanity case and was tugging it closer when something touched the bare skin below her trouser leg.

As she whipped around in shock, her left hand tried to grab the chair, which had started to wobble alarmingly at the sudden movement, throwing her completely off balance. The problem was that her fingers were already tightly latched onto the vanity case and as it swung off the shelf it made contact with the side of Sam's head as he stepped forwards to grab hold of her around the middle and take the weight of her body against his.

She dropped the case, and it bounced high before settling down intact.

Not that she noticed. Her fingers were too busy clutching onto Sam Richards as she stared into his startled face.

Time seemed to stand still as she started to slide down the front of his hard body, her silky top riding up as she did.

Sam reacted by holding her tighter, hitching her up as though she was weightless, his arms linked together under her bottom, locking her body against his.

'Sorry about that,' she said, trying to sound casual, as though it was perfectly normal to have a conversation while you were being held up against the dusty T-shirt of the man who had once rocked your world. 'Good thing I didn't hit anything important.'

He bit his lower lip, as though he was ready to hit back with some comment and then thought better of it, then one corner of his mouth turned up and he slowly, slowly, started to bend his knees until her feet were on the floor. But all the time his arms were locked behind her back as though he had no intention of letting her go.

Why should he? Amber thought. Sam was having way too much fun.

Strange that his breathing seemed to be even faster than hers, if that was possible, and she could see the blood pulsing in his neck. Hot and fast.

His wide fingers slid up from her hips to her waist, holding her firm, secure, safe but being careful not to crush her plaster cast.

Amber inhaled the warm spicy aroma of some masculine scent that had a lot of Sam in the blend and instantly became aware that she could feel the length of his body pressed against hers from chest to groin.

His breathing became stronger. Louder. And his fingers stretched to span the strip of exposed skin below her top, gently at first and then moving back and forth just a little against her ribcage. Amber felt like closing her eyes but didn't dare because his gaze had never left her face.

He felt wonderful. He smelt better.

Sam tilted his head and looked at her. Really looked at her. Looked at her with an intensity that sent shivers and tingles from her toes to the ends of each strand of hair.

It had been such a long time since any man had held her like this, with that fire in his eyes.

Bad fire.

Bad tingles.

Bad, bad heart for wanting him to finish what he had started.

It would be so easy to kiss him right now and find out if his kiss was still capable of making her weak at the knees.

Bad Amber for wanting him, when that was the worst thing that could happen to either of them.

Her back stiffened and she lifted her chin slightly.

'You can put me down now if you like,' she said in a jokey voice which sounded so false and flat. Her words seem to echo around the narrow dressing room until they found their target.

'And what if I don't like?' Sam replied and leant closer to breathe into her neck while his fingers moved in slow circles at her waist.

Suddenly Amber wished that she had installed air conditioning in the apartment because the air was starting to heat up far too quickly in this small space. And so close to her bed...

Amber lifted her hand from Sam's shoulder and reached behind and gently slid her fingers around his wrist and released him.

And, just like that, the connection was broken, leaving her feeling dizzier than she wanted to admit.

Without his support, her legs felt so wobbly that she had to swivel around and sit down on the chair—anything but the bed. That would be far too dangerous with this man around and she would hate to give him ideas.

His brow creased and Sam crossed his arms in front of his chest as he stared at her, his legs wide, his shoulders back and squared, his gaze locked onto her face. As he stared his eyes narrowed as though they were concerned about something. And her foolish girly heart gave a little leap at the idea that he might still care about her.

'Hey, Bambi. I thought we had a deal. It's time you kept to your side of the bargain.'

'Will you please stop calling me Bambi? Yes, I know you came up with the name in the first place, but Amber will do fine. And what do you mean? My side?'

'Okay, then. Amber, I brought my own work uniform...' Sam waved a hand down his clothing.

'But you promised me refreshments. So far all I have seen are a small plate of girly mini cupcakes and one mug of weak Earl Grey tea.'

He winced and shook his head slowly from side to side. 'That. Is not refreshments as I understand them. What's more, I have just raided your refrigerator and there is nothing more than a couple of low fat yoghurts and some supermarket ready meals.'

He stood back and ogled her, then reached out and pinched her arm.

She wriggled away. 'Hey. Ouch. What was that for?'

'Too skinny and too pale and wobbly. By far. That decides it. We, young lady, are going out to get some food. What is your fancy? Mexican? Pub food? Take your pick.'

Amber looked around the bedroom in horror at the debris.

'I can't leave now. The flat is a mess and it will take me ages to tidy it up.'

'But the girls have gone for the day...right?'

'Well, yes. I don't have any more appointments.'

'Good. Because it is two o'clock in the afternoon and neither of us have eaten since breakfast. Right?'

Amber sighed and checked her wristwatch, and then her shoulders sagged. 'I am flagging a bit. I suppose it would make sense to eat some late lunch...and what are you doing?'

'Looking for your coat. And which one of these is your handbag? Come on, girl. The sun is still shining and there is nothing fit to eat in this apartment. What do you say? We get some lunch and I volunteer to carry your shopping home from the supermarket on the way back. You can't get a better offer than that.'

'Can't I?'

Amber leant backwards and pulled out her mobile phone from her trouser pocket and was about to sling her cashmere wrap over one shoulder when Sam stepped behind her and wrapped it around her shoulders, gently pressing the collar into her neck, his fingertips touching her, and she blinked in delight then cursed herself for being so needy.

'Actually, I might have a better idea, but I need to make a phone call. This restaurant can get extremely busy around lunchtime.'

Sam groaned. 'I might have known. How many awards does it have? Because I have to tell you—I am not in the mood for mini tasting portions served on teaspoons made out of toast.'

She sniffed dismissively. 'Several. But wait and see. You might just like it. And the table has the most amazing view over London.'

'I don't believe that you ordered home delivery,' Sam exclaimed and put down his screwdriver as Amber sauntered into the kitchen swinging a large brown paper bag. 'Don't tell me that the famous Amber DuBois has suddenly got cold feet about being seen out in public. Or were you worried that I would make you pay the bill?'

Amber sniffed dismissively in reply. 'Well, someone has a very high opinion of themselves.' Then she sighed in exasperation and gestured with her head towards the cabinets. 'Only now I am out of hands. Would you mind bringing the plates and cutlery? Have a rummage in that drawer. Yep. That's it.'

'You are avoiding my question,' Sam said as he followed Amber out onto the sunlit terrace and spread the picnic kit out onto the table, where Amber was already pulling out foil containers. 'Why not go out to some fabulous restaurant so the waiters can fawn all over you?'

She looked up at him and gave a half smile. 'Two reasons. First, I want some peace and quiet to enjoy my meal, and the restaurant this food came from is always crushed jam-tight. And secondly—' she paused and looked out towards the skyline '—I have only used this apartment on flying visits these past few years and never stayed long enough to enjoy the view.' She nodded towards the railing. 'Feel free. This is your city, after all. And I know how much you love London.'

Sam took the hint and walked the few steps over to the railing. And exhaled slowly at the awe-inspiring scene spread out in all directions in front of him. The stress of the past few days melted away as he took in the stunning view over the Thames and along both sides of the river for miles in each direction. His eyes picked out the locations which were so familiar they were like old friends. Friends like Amber had once been.

'You always were the clever one. This is a pretty good view, I'll give you that. And yes, London is my city, and it always has been. And what is that amazing smell?'

He turned back towards Amber and instantly his senses were filled with the most amazing aromas which instantly made his mouth water.

'Are those Indian dishes? You used to hate spicy food.'

'That was before I tasted real southern Indian food like this. Home-cooked traditional recipes from Kerala. The restaurant doesn't usually do take out but I know the owner's cousin. Willing to risk it?'

'Are you kidding me?' Sam replied and flung himself into the seat. 'I loved living in Los Angeles, but you cannot get real Indian food unless you cook it yourself. Pass it over and tell me what you ordered.'

'Vegetable curry, chickpea masala, coconut rice and a thick lamb curry for you. And just this once we are allowed to eat it using a fork and plates instead of fingers and a banana leaf. Go ahead and tuck in. I ordered plenty. What do you think?'

Sam held up a fork and dived into the nearest dish, speared some lamb and wrapped his lips around it.

Flavour and texture exploded on his tongue and he moaned in pleasure and delight before smiling and grabbing each dish in turn and loading up his plate with something of everything.

'This is seriously good. But now I'm curious. How do you know the owner of a Keralan restaurant in London? That doesn't seem to fit with a career musician.'

Amber swallowed down a mouthful of vegetables and rice and gave a tiny shrug before taking a sip of water.

'The orchestra I tour with has an amazing cellist who has become one of my best friends in the business. Parvita is one of those totally natural talents who has been winning awards all over the place—but it was only when I got to know her that I found out just how remarkable she really is.'

Amber topped up her plate as she spoke, but there was just enough of a slight quiver in her voice to make Sam look at her as he chewed. 'Parvita was left at an orphanage for girls when she was only a toddler. Her widowed mother was too poor to feed another daughter. She needed her boys to work their farm in Kerala and knew that the orphanage could give a little girl an education and a chance to improve her life.'

Amber chuckled. 'I don't think that Parvita's family were expecting her to win scholarships to international music schools and then build a career as a concert cellist. But she did it, against all of the odds.'

Amber raised her water glass. 'And along the way my

friend introduced me to real home-cooked food from Kerala. The chef who runs this restaurant is one of her cousins and is totally passionate about fresh ingredients and cooking with love. I think it shows.'

Sam lifted his fork in tribute. 'This is probably the best Indian food that I have ever eaten. Although it does make me wonder. Aren't you going to miss your friend Parvita? Now that you have decided to retire?'

Amber closed her lips around the fork and twirled it back and forth for a second before replying. 'Not at all. She is still my friend so I will make the effort to keep in touch. She even invited me to her wedding next week and sent me a fabulous hot pink sari to wear.'

'Now that is something I would like to see. Just tell me which fabulous and exclusive London venue is having the privilege of hosting this happy event and I'll be right there with my camera.'

'Oh, she isn't coming to London. The wedding party is in Kerala. I've already sent my apologies—' Amber shrugged '—but the newlyweds will be passing through London in a few weeks, and we can catch up then.'

'So you are not going to the wedding after all?'

She shook her head as she chewed and pointed to her plaster.

'That's interesting.' Sam nodded. 'If one of my friends was getting married I wouldn't let a simple thing like that stop me from going. Unless, of course, there is more to it than that. Hmm?'

Then he leant back and crossed his cutlery on his plate and shook his head from side to side.

'Well, well. Why do I get the feeling that some things have not changed that much after all? Let me guess. Your mother ordered you not to go, didn't she? Or was Heath Sheridan worried that his little stepsister is going to get sunburnt if she goes to India? How is your stepbrother doing these days? Still trying to interfere in your life? Um. I take that glaring scowl as a yes.'

He sniggered off her rebuke, and dived back into his food. 'You surprise me, Amber. You're twenty-eight years old, with a brilliant career, an international reputation and the kudos to match, and you still cannot get out from under their thumb, can you? Well, shame on you, Amber DuBois. I thought you were better than that.'

EIGHT

———

'Shame on me? Shame. *On me*?'

Amber felt the heat burn at the back of her neck which had nothing to do with the Indian food and she crashed her hand down onto the table hard enough to make both Sam and the plates jump, and leant forwards towards him.

'*How dare you?* How dare you tell me that I should be ashamed of the fact that my family love me and care what happens to me? No, I don't always agree with what they tell me, but at least they make an effort to be part of my life. But you know all about that, don't you? How are you getting on with your dad these days? And remind me of the last time you saw *your* mum?'

The words emerged in harsh outbursts which seemed to echo around her patio and reflect back from the stone-faced man sitting opposite. And she instantly regretted them.

It shocked her that Sam was capable of making her so spiteful and hard. She was one of the few people who knew how hard it had been for him when his mother abandoned her husband and son. But that didn't mean that she had to throw his pain back in his face.

She was better than that. Or at least she was trying to be.

'In fact I don't know why I am even listening to you in the first place.' She blinked and tossed her head back and calmly sipped her water. 'You are hardly qualified to take the moral high ground. I certainly don't need a lecture on making decisions from you, Sam. Understood?'

'Perfectly.' Sam nodded, then leant forward and rested his elbows on the table while his gaze locked onto her face. 'Is your little tantrum over now, Miss DuBois? Because I would really like to get this so called interview over and done with as soon as possible. I have a real assignment waiting for me back at the paper, so can we move on, please?'

'Absolutely,' Amber replied, trying to calm her heart rate and appear to be more or less in control again. 'But it does make me wonder. What are you *really* doing back here in London? Because whatever it is must be very important to persuade you to go through with this little game of charades.'

Sam tried to savour more of the delicious food as slowly as he could while his brain worked at lightning speed, trying to form an answer, but his appetite was gone and he pushed his meal away.

Amber had fired her arrow and hit her target right in the centre.

Strange how this girl was one of the few people alive who knew just what his emotional hot buttons were and was not afraid to press them down hard when she needed to.

Just as he had pressed hers.

That was the problem with working with people who understood you.

Touché Amber.

If this was a game, then it was one point to each of them.

Sam sat back in his chair and watched Amber as she turned away from him and looked out over the city, all joy in her food and apartment forgotten.

The warm sunlight played on her pale skin and delicate features. Up close and personal, she was even lovelier than the girl on the magazine cover. Her chest rose and fell and he could sense the emotional strain these last few minutes had cost her.

Strain he was responsible for.

Shame on him.

Amber DuBois was gunpowder and those few minutes they had just shared in the dressing room had proved just how explosive getting within touching distance could be.

Any ideas he might have had about staying distant and professional had just gone out of the window the instant his fingers touched her skin.

He might be over his teenage crush but this woman he was looking at now had the power to get under his skin and bother him.

Bother him so badly that suddenly it felt easier to keep his change of heart towards his father to himself. If she had a whiff that he was some sort of self-sacrificing martyr who desperately wanted to make it up to his dad for all those angry years, she would never let him forget it.

A few days. He could stay cool and professional for a few days for his dad's sake.

His eyebrow lifted. 'I told you. I need the promotion and the boss made it clear that I will only get that if I come back with an exclusive from, and I quote, "the lovely Miss DuBois". That's it, job done,' and Sam went back to the food.

No way was he going to fall into Amber's trap and start spouting on about how guilty he felt about leaving his dad all alone for years on end while he lived the high life in California. This was Amber he was talking to. She would be only too ready to believe that he was a heartless son who had only come back to London for the job and the status.

After what had just happened in the dressing room he intended to keep as far away from her as physically possible.

He had to keep up the pretence that he was still the self-absorbed young man who would let nothing come between him and his career. Which was not so far from the truth. Happy families were for other men. Not men like Sam Richards.

'Job done. Right,' Amber replied and picked up her water glass. 'Come on, Sam. Out with it. From what I hear, you can get a job anywhere you like. Why here? Why now? And why do I suspect that there is a lovely lady involved in the answer?'

'You think I came back to London for a woman? Oh, no. Sorry to burst your romantic bubble, but this was strictly business all the way.'

'Um,' Amber replied. 'Pity. I could have given her a few tips. Such as run for the hills now, before he breaks your heart. That sort of thing. But not to worry, it will keep for another time.'

And she smiled sweetly at him over her water glass. 'But do tuck into your lunch. You are going to need it for this afternoon's opportunity to shine.'

'More pictures?'

'Yes, but that is for later when you deliver the paintings to Saskia and hang them up for her,' Amber replied. 'But in the meantime I have something which is much more suited to your...talents.'

She narrowed her eyes and rested her elbows on the table so that she could support her chin with one hand. 'Did you bring your camera and tripod? I'll take that nod as a yes. Super. My shoes really do need the right angle to look their best.'

Sam spluttered into his water glass. 'Shoes? You want me to photograph your shoes?' he asked in complete disbelief.

'Eighteen pairs of designer loveliness.' Amber sighed. 'Worn once or not at all. Gorgeous but unloved. Kate wanted them but she has tiny feet so I am selling them on the Internet.'

'You are selling your shoes.' Sam snorted and tossed his head with a sigh. 'Things must be desperate. Cash flow problems?'

Her tongue flicked out and she licked her lips once. And right there and then he knew that she was keeping something from him.

'Don't try and hide your enthusiasm. I knew that you would be excited by the opportunity. This is just part of the modern girl's annual clearing out of last season's couture so that she can buy new ones to take their place—

and all the money goes to charity. Oh—and tomorrow gets even better. The lovely Saskia is trying to launch Elwood House as a private dining venue and her online presence is just not cutting it. She needs a professional writer to redesign the website and create a whole new photo gallery—and it has to be complete in time for my birthday party on Thursday.'

'Is there any good news in all of this?' he spluttered, while shovelling down more chickpeas and rice.

'Of course. You have a front row seat at my birthday party, hobnobbing with the great and good of the London scene. Even if you are taking the photographs for Saskia's website at the same time.'

Sam blew out slowly. 'I am so grateful for your kind consideration. So that's Saskia covered. Are you sure that Kate Lovat wouldn't like me to stand in her shop window modelling a tartan dinner suit in my copious spare time?'

'Hey, that's not a bad idea. You might be able to fit it in after you have cleaned the spiders and mouse droppings out of her attic tomorrow. Oh. Didn't I mention that? Silly me. And after you have sorted the ladies out, then you can pop back here. By then I should have sorted out my unwanted lingerie. I am sure you can come up with some suitable slogan like "as worn by Amber" when you put together the adverts for the Internet auction.'

Amber tilted her head to one side as he glared at her through slitted eyes.

And this was the girl he was thinking of asking to be his friend.

'Not lingerie. Shoes I can understand. But I draw the line at photographing lingerie unless you intend to model it in person.'

'But this is your audition, sweetie. Have you forgotten so quickly? Of course, if you are refusing to carry out my perfectly reasonable requests, well, I shall have to phone the journalist on the other paper and see if she is still interested... And no, my modelling days are over.'

She leant her chin on the back of one hand and fluttered her eyelashes at him.

'You're looking a little hot under the collar there, Mr Richards.' Amber smiled. 'How about some ice cream to cool you down? It's delicious with humble pie.'

'Well. What do you think? The emerald and diamond drop necklace or the sapphire white gold collar?'

Amber held one necklace then the other to her throat, slowly at first, then faster and then faster, using two fingers of her plastered wrist to prop them up against her skin.

'Hey. Slow down, I'm still thinking about it.'

Kate sat back against Amber's bed pillows in Saskia's best spare bedroom and stretched both arms out above her head.

'Decisions, decisions.' Then she sniffed. 'The sapphires. They are absolutely perfect with that dress. Although, if it was me, I would wear both and go totally overboard on the bling. Especially since you won't be wearing either of them again.'

Amber smiled and dropped the emerald necklace, which had been a present from a fashion designer who had been trying to woo her into being their cover girl, back into the velvet tray. 'True. But the way I look at it, some other girl has the chance to enjoy them and the charity gets the loot. The last thing I need is a load of expensive jewellery in a safety deposit box which has to be insured every year at huge expense. It makes sense to sell it back to the jewellers while it is still in pristine condition.'

Kate shuffled to the edge of the bed. 'Don't let the spy hear you say that. Can you imagine the headlines? "Injured pianist forced to sell her jewellery to make ends meet".' Then Kate pushed herself off the bed. 'Here. Let me help with the earrings. I'm thinking some serious dangle and maximum sparkle and that is a tricky thing to pull off one-handed.'

She peered into the tray and pulled out a pair of chandelier diamond and sapphire drops. 'Ah. Now we are talking...' Then she took another look at the maker on the box and blew out hard. 'Wow. Are these for real? My fingers are shaking. I never thought I would be holding anything from that jeweller. Oh, Amber.'

Amber reached up and wrapped one arm around Kate's shoulders but, as her friend laughed and reached up to fit her earrings, she shook her head. 'Not until you have tried them on first. Go on. I want to see you wear those earrings—and that necklace.'

'What? My neck is too short and my ears are tiny. Nope. These are serious jewels for serious people. I'll stick to my pearls, thanks all the same.'

'Kate Lovat, I won't take no for an answer. I know that my clothes and shoes are huge on you, so please, just this once, be nice and do what I ask. It is my birthday.'

Amber pushed her lips out and pretended to sulk.

'Oh, stop it,' Kate replied with a dramatic sigh. 'You are ruining your make-up and it has taken me the best part of an hour to make it look natural. Okay, okay, I'll try the jewellery on. But only because it's your birthday, Look, I'm doing it. And… Oh, Amber.'

Kate stepped behind Amber and rested her head on her shoulder as Amber smiled back at her. 'Absolutely gorgeous. Told ya. Right, that's sorted. You're wearing the jewels that Heath gave me. Done. Or do you want them to sit in the box up here in the bedroom unused and unloved because you have rejected them?'

Kate replied by reaching for a tissue. 'Oh. Now look what you have made me do. Pest.'

Then Kate peered at herself in the mirror. 'Do you think that Heath would like me in these?'

'Pest right back. And he would definitely like you in those earrings,' Amber replied and wrapped her arm around Kate's waist. 'Does Heath still hold the prize for the best emergency school party date a girl could hope for?'

Kate rested her head on Amber's shoulder before answering with a small shrug. 'Absolutely. Which must make me the stupidest girl in London. Here I am, surrounded by loads of handsome boys, and the only one who comes close to being my personal hero is living in Boston and doesn't remember that I even exist unless you are around. Mad just about describes it.'

'Oh, Kate. Don't worry. You'll find someone special, I know you will.'

Kate grinned and ran a tissue across the corner of both eyes. 'Damn right. Who knows? My soulmate could be on his way to this very party this evening. How about that?'

'Absolutely. Now shoo. I have to finish getting ready and you need to show your loveliness to all and sundry. Go. Have fun at the party. And Kate…make sure that Sam the spy takes your picture. You can't miss him—he'll be the one with the camera around his neck.'

'You've got five minutes, young lady—then the posse will be up here to drag you downstairs.'

'I would expect nothing less,' Amber replied and waved to Kate as she waltzed across the carpet on her tiny dainty heels and the bedroom door swung closed behind her.

Only when she heard Kate's sandals on the marble floor of the entrance did Amber feel it was safe to flop back down on her bed.

So her best friend Kate was still in crush with her stepbrother Heath. Oh, Kate. Maybe it was a good thing that Heath had already spoken to her from his lecture tour in South America and was not turning up for this party after all. He might have brought his lovely girlfriend Olivia with him. Not good. *Not good at all.*

Her wrist was aching, her head was thumping and she could quite easily pull the quilt over her legs right then and there and sleep for days. But she couldn't. She might have organised her birthday party at the last minute, but she was still the star of the show—and she had to make her appearance.

Time to turn up and give the greatest performance of her life.

All smiles and confidence and clear about what she was doing and why. Exploring. Taking a break. Enjoying herself. Fund-raising for charity. What fun!

That was the official line and she was sticking to it. She could count the number of people who knew the truth on one hand—and that was how she wanted it to stay. Until she was ready. And then she would have to add Sam Richards to the list.

Sam.

What was she going to do about Sam?

Was he Sam the spy as Kate called him? Could she trust him again?

He had kept his side of the bargain and worked hard at every ridiculous task that the three of them had thrown at him over the past few days without much in the way of complaint.

He could never know that she had spent two nights tossing and turning in her bed as his words roiled in the pit of her stomach. She did listen to Heath—she always had and probably always would. He was her sensible older stepbrother. But these past two days, every time he had told her to do something rather than ask or suggest, she kept thinking about what Sam had said. Maybe she was still under his thumb more than she liked? Maybe he had a point.

Of course going back to Kerala would be scary. She would be a fool not to be worried. But she had made a vow in hospital that her life would be different from now. She *wanted* to see Parvita married and share her happiness.

She *wanted to* go back and yet it was so risky. Doubt rolled over Amber in waves, hard and choppy, buffeting and threatening to weaken her resolve.

Turning her life around was harder than she had expected.

The jewel tray was still open on the dressing table and Amber slithered off her bed and lifted out the top tray. Hidden inside a tiny suede pouch at the very bottom was a small gold heart suspended from a thin gold chain.

Sam had given it to her at her eighteenth birthday

party, just before they had escaped out of the kitchen door and taken a ride in his dad's vintage open top sports car.

Amber smiled as she let the chain slip between her fingers. Sam had let her stand up tall on the passenger seat with her arms outstretched to the sky as they rode through the London streets—the wind in her hair and the sound of their laughter and the hoots from passing motorists reverberating through every bone in her body.

She had been so very, very happy, and she should be grateful to Sam for showing her what true happiness felt like. It was a joyous memory.

The sound of party music drifted up the stairs and Amber grinned. She had survived meningitis more or less intact, she had friends waiting for her downstairs and more on their way.

She looked at herself in the mirror and, without another moment of hesitation, she winked at her reflection and dropped the gold chain back into the pouch and closed the lid down on the box with the rest of her past.

She was a lucky girl.

Time to rock and roll and *enjoy herself.*

Taking a deep calming breath, Sam Richards strolled across the luxurious marble-floored hallway of the Victorian splendour that was Elwood House.

He paused to check his reflection in the Venetian hall mirror above a long narrow console table, and lifted up his chin a little to adjust his black bow tie.

Not bad. Not bad at all.

For a chauffeur's son from the wrong part of London.

At least this time he had been welcomed at the front door!

Which had certainly not been the case ten years ago when he had stood in the hallway of another house and another birthday celebration.

Amber might have invited him to her eighteenth birthday party but her mother had taken one look at him standing on her front doorstep, snorted and closed the door in his face. Just to make sure that he got the message loud and clear.

Sam Richards was not good enough for her daughter. Oh, no. Nowhere near.

Of course he wasn't going to put up with that—he had plans for Amber's birthday and there was no way that her mother was going to thwart his little scheme.

So he'd climbed over the garden fence and sneaked in through the conservatory where the young people were having fun.

Suddenly there was the tinkle of laughter from the kitchen and Sam grinned as he strolled into the warm, light, open space of the huge kitchen sun room that Saskia's aunt Margot had built. Every worktop was covered with plates and bowls and platters of foodstuffs— but his attention was focused on the two women who were walking towards him.

Here come the girls.

Saskia's arm was around Kate's shoulder, which was not difficult, considering that Kate could just about make five feet four inches if she stretched. Although tonight she looked stunning in a dark green taffeta cocktail dress with real jewels. Saskia was in midnight-blue crushed velvet with a real pearl choker and gorgeous lilac kitten heels.

They were like dazzling stars transported from a catwalk fashion show into this London kitchen. English style and elegance. Not too much flesh on show, and all class.

Kate hissed at him, but Saskia nudged her with a glare and moved forward to shake his hand.

'Hello, Sam. Nice to see you again. I appreciate your help with my website—it's ten times better than I could have thought of on my own. We're having a few drinks on the patio before the hordes of locusts arrive. Why don't you come and join us?'

'Perfect. Thanks. And I'm pleased I could help.'

'You go ahead. One more thing to bring out of the oven,' Saskia replied, and waved Kate and Sam onto the terrace.

The second they were out of sight of the kitchen, Kate grabbed Sam's sleeve, whirled around and planted a hand on each hip as she stared up at him with squeezed narrow eyes.

'I'm watching you, Sam Richards. If you step out of place tonight or do anything to spoil Amber's evening I'll be on to you like a shot.'

He raised both hands in surrender.

'I came here to work. And help Amber have a good time along the way. Okay?'

Kate replied by jabbing her second and third fingers towards her eyes then stabbed them towards his face, then back to her eyes.

'Watching you,' she hissed, then broke into a wide-mouthed grin and popped one of Saskia's mini tomato tarts into her mouth and groaned in pleasure as Saskia strolled up with the most delicious-smelling tray.

Kate raised her glass of white wine in a toast. 'Fab. You always know exactly how to pull off the perfect party, Saskia. Always have.'

'Hold that thought, gorgeous. Special order for the star of the show. Mini pizza. Extra anchovies. Okay?'

'Did someone say mini pizza?'

Amber sidled up to Saskia and kissed her on the cheek before biting into the crisp pastry and nodding. 'Delicious.' Only then did she look across at Sam and smile. 'Hello, Sam. What perfect timing.'

And she took his breath away.

Her long sensitive fingers were wrapped around the stem of a wine glass which Kate was topping up with sparkling tonic water rather than wine. A diamond bracelet sparkled at her wrist and flashed bright and dazzling as she moved in the sunlight.

But that was nothing compared to the crystal covered dress and jewelled collar she was wearing.

Sam dragged his eyes away from Amber's cleavage before Kate noticed and stabbed him with the corkscrew.

Her earrings moved, sparkling and bright, and helped him to focus on her face. Stunning make-up showed her clear, smooth complexion to perfection, and her eyes glowed against the dark smudge of colour. Her lips were full, smooth. Her whole face was radiant.

Amber had never looked so beautiful or more magical.

This was the Amber he had always imagined that she would look when she was happy in her own skin—and she had exceeded his wildest imagination.

He had often wondered over the years if Amber had

stayed the sweet, loving girl that he had fallen for, under the surface gloss and razzmatazz, and it only took a few seconds of seeing her now with her friends to realise that she had somehow managed to keep her integrity and old friendships alive.

Now that was something he could admire.

He would give a lot to be here as her date this evening. To know that those lovely violet-blue eyes were looking at him with love instead of tolerance.

He had walked away from a great love.

Maybe his only love. And certainly the only girl that he had ever truly wanted in his life.

Which made him more than a fool. It made him a stupid fool.

The best that he could do was try and capture this moment for ever. So that when they were back in their ordinary worlds on other continents he had something to remind him of just how much he had lost.

She was the star. And he was a reporter who was working for her.

Because that was what he was here for, wasn't it? To work?

Not as one of the guests.

Oh, no.

The likes of Sam Richards did not come to these events as a guest. He was the one parking cars and taking the coats.

Strange to think that he had some standing on the A-list circuit in Los Angeles. But it took London to put him right back in his place.

As one of the help.

Pity that he had no intention whatsoever of fitting

in with someone else's idea of who and what he was. He was here because they needed him as much as he needed Amber.

An equal trade. Yes. That was better. He could work with that.

He was done with being second best. To anyone.

Instantly Sam smiled. 'You look lovely, Amber—and not a day over twenty-eight. In fact, you ladies look so stunning as a group that I think this would make a charming example of a perfect summer drinks party. Early evening cocktails for a private party? So if you could just hold that pose? Lovely. And a little more to the right, Kate? Gorgeous—and don't forget to smile, Kate. Much better than sticking your tongue out at me. That's it.'

Sam stepped back and by the time the girls had straightened their dresses and rearranged the canapés his digital camera had already captured the trio from several angles, taking in the conservatory, the lovely sun-lit garden and the happy women enjoying themselves.

Of course Amber had no idea that he had taken several shots for his personal album. And every one of them was of Amber.

'Fantastic. And a few more with you choosing something from the tray and pouring more wine. Excellent. Now. Saskia. How do you want to showcase the patio? With or without the food?'

NINE

———

Five hours later, every canapé, savoury and dessert that Saskia had served had been eaten, empty bottles of champagne stood upside down in silver wine buckets and the eighty or so guests had been entertained by some of London's finest musical talent.

One Spanish musician had even brought along a classical guitar and Amber had kicked off the flamenco dancing with great gusto and much cheering. It was amazing that the glass wear had survived the evening.

He had taken hundreds of photographs in every public room, with and without guests, from every possible angle. But there was no doubt who was the star of the show.

Sam could only watch in awe as Amber laughed and chatted in several languages to men and women of all ages and dress styles. Some young and unkempt, some older and the height of elegance, but it did not seem to matter to her in the least. The fashion models and media people were introduced to classical artists and quite a few popular musicians with names that even he had heard of.

Everyone from the costume designers to hairdressers and international conductors were putty in Amber's fingers. He had never expected to hear a sing-song around the grand piano where four of the world's leading sopranos improvised a rap song with an up-and-coming hip hop star.

It took skill to make a person feel that they were the most important person in the room—and Amber had that skill in buckets.

He was in awe of her.

It was only now, as Saskia and Kate chatted away to old friends and lingering guests, that he realised that Amber had already slipped away into the kitchen before he had a chance to thank her and say goodnight.

He quickly scanned the kitchen for Amber and waved to the waiting staff that Saskia had set to work on the washing-up. He had just turned away when he saw a splash of blue on the patio and slowly strolled out of the hot kitchen into the cool of the late May evening.

Amber was sitting on the wooden bench on the patio, humming along to the lively Austrian waltzes being played on the music system in the conservatory only a few feet away.

Her eyes were closed tight shut and her left hand was twisting and moving as though it was dancing in the air, her right arm waving stiffly along in time, the plaster cast forgotten.

Her face was in shadow but there was no mistaking the expression of joy which seemed to shine from inside outwards, illuminating her skin and making it glow.

She was happy. Beautiful. And content. And he yearned to be part of that happiness and share that little window of joy with this amazing woman.

This was the Amber he had fallen in love with ten years ago and then fallen in love all over again in the first ten seconds when she'd walked into his dad's garage and knocked his world off its axis.

And the fact that he had been in denial until this moment was so mind-boggling that all he could do was stand there and watch as she sang along to the music, all alone in the light of the full moon and the soft glow streaming out from the conservatory where the last guests were mingling in the hallway.

He stood in the shadows, watching her for minutes until the music changed to a new track and she dropped her hands onto her lap and clasped hold of her knees and blinked open her eyes.

And saw him.

'Hi, Sam,' she said, and her eyes met his without hesitation or reluctance. Almost as if she was pleased to see him there. 'Are we on our own?'

Sam swallowed down the lump in his throat and strolled over to the bench in the soft light and lifted up her feet and sat down, her legs on his knees, well aware that he probably had a huge man crush grin all over his face.

'More or less. The girls are seeing the last of the guests out. It was a great party. Did you have a good time?'

Amber sighed and snuggled sideways on the arm rest. 'The best. Even though I am now completely exhausted. How about you?'

Sam half turned to face her and as she shuffled higher, her legs resting on his thighs and her arm on her lap, he inhaled a wonderful spicy, sweet perfume that competed with the full musk roses and lavender which Saskia had planted behind the bench. It was a heady, exotic aroma that seemed to fill his senses and make him want to stay there for as long as Amber was close by.

He wanted to tell her that she looked beautiful.

But that would be too close to the truth. So he covered up his answer and turned it into something she would be expecting him to say.

'I had an interesting evening. Your guest list was inspired. I suspect the birthday present swag will be excellent.'

'Birthday presents? Oh. No, I only had a few. I asked people to make a donation to Parvita's charity instead.'

She looked at him. Really looked at him. Her gaze moved so slowly from his feet upwards that by the time it reached his face Sam knew that his ears were flaming red.

'Nice suit. You look positively dangerous. Was it safe to let you out on your own? I'm sorry I didn't have much time to talk. Did you get all of the shots Saskia needs?'

'I can usually be trusted to behave myself if the occasion demands. And yes, I think I can do something creative for a website and make the most of the venue.'

'Really? That almost sounds professional. Then things truly have changed. And not just the suit.'

'Oh, no compliments, please; you'll have me blushing.'

'I noticed you working the room with your camera. Hasn't Saskia done a lovely job?'

'I have been to this house so many times with my dad but I'd forgotten how stunning it is. Judging from some of the comments from your guests, I think she might be on to a winner.'

Amber hunched up her shoulders. 'I hope so. She's had a rough time since her aunt Margot died. This is why it's important to me that you do a good job and help Saskia out. Elwood House is her home but it's also her business. She needs a decent marketing and promotional campaign to get it off the ground.'

'There are expert companies out there who could make it happen.'

'Yes, there are. And they cost serious amounts of money. And Saskia won't accept my help. I have plenty of colleagues and casual friends in my life. You met some of them this evening. But nobody comes close to real friends like Kate, Saskia and her aunt Margot. They made me believe that, despite everything that happened with my mother, I could make a real home in London and create something close to a normal school life for myself. And that was new.'

'I know, I was there. Remember?'

Then she laughed out loud. 'Oh, yes, I remember very well indeed. But I refuse to be angry with you on my birthday. Life really is too short. I have had enough of all of that. And yes, you can record that little snippet on your handy pocket tape recorder and do what you like with it.'

He patted his pockets. 'Oh, shame. I seem to have left it at the office. Fancy that. The last time I came to your birthday party I had to climb over the garden fence. It makes a nice change to come in through the front door.'

She chuckled before answering. 'How could I forget?' She laughed out loud. 'You strode into my eighteenth birthday party as though you were the guest of honour and hadn't just climbed over the fence to avoid the security on the front entrance. And then you kidnapped me when my mother was in the salon with all of the stuffy, important guests she had invited who I had never met, and you whisked me away in your dad's sports car. It was magical and you were the magician who made it possible. It was like some happy dream.'

She shook her head, making her chandelier earrings sparkle, and brought her knees up to her chest. 'My mother still hasn't forgiven you for the fact that I missed my own birthday cake, eighteen candles and all. Heath had to blow them out for me.'

'Your mother is a remarkable lady. As far as she is concerned, I will always be the chauffeur's son, but do you know what? I am proud of the fact that my dad used to drive limos for a living before he moved into property. I always have been. No matter what you and your family think.'

Amber inhaled sharply and tugged her hand away from his.

'Wait a minute. Don't you dare accuse me of treating you differently because your dad was our driver. Because I didn't. I never did, and you know that. You were the one who was always defending yourself. Not me.'

'Your mother...'

'I'm not talking about my mother. I'm talking about you and me. I would never, ever have looked down on you because of the job you did. And maybe it's about time to get over that stupid inferiority complex of yours so that you can see all of the amazing things you have achieved in your life.'

'You mean like being an international concert pianist who is able to perform in front of thousands of people? Or my wonderful career as a fashion model and cosmetics guru? Is that what you mean?'

'I was in the right place at the right time and I got lucky. And you are insufferable.'

'And you are deluded.'

Amber glared at him for several seconds before she took a slow breath and shook her head slowly from side to side, before flicking her long hair back over her left shoulder.

'Parents. They have a lot to answer for. And that includes mine as well as yours. It's a good thing that we have both been able to rise above them to become so independent and calm and even-tempered.'

'Isn't it just.'

Amber slowly lowered her legs to the floor and shuffled closer to him on the bench so that there were inches and ten years of lost time between them. So close that he could hear her breathing increase in speed with his.

'Which reminds me...' Sam smiled and released her to dive inside his jacket pocket and pull out a long slim envelope which he passed to her. 'Happy birthday, Amber.'

And, without waiting for her to reply, he leant forwards and kissed her tenderly but swiftly on the cheek. Lingering just long enough to inhale her scent and feel her waist under his fingertips before he drew back.

She looked at him with wide, startled eyes. 'Thank you. I mean, I wasn't expecting anything. Can I... Can I open it now?'

'Please. Go ahead.'

Sam looked around the garden for the few seconds it took for her to slide a manicured fingernail under the flap of the envelope and draw out a slim piece of faded paper.

'Sam? What is this? It looks like...' And then she understood what she was holding and her breath caught at the back of her throat.

'Is this what I think it is?'

Then she shook her head and sat back away from him, head down, reading the letters in the dim light before speaking again. And this time her voice came out in one long breath.

'This is the cheque my mother gave you to leave me alone.'

She looked up at him and her gaze darted from the cheque to his face and then back to the cheque again. 'I don't understand. She told me that she had offered you enough cash to take you through journalism school.'

Amber dropped the cheque into her lap and took hold of his hand, her eyes brimming with tears. 'Why? Why didn't you use this money, Sam? The damage had already been done.'

Sam raised his hand and stroked her cheek with his fingertips, until they were on her temple, forcing her to look into his eyes.

'Your mother knew the real thing when she saw it. I was dazzled by you, Amber. Dazzled and scared about how deep I was getting into a relationship I never saw coming. She took one look at me and saw a terrified young man who had barely survived his parents' divorce and was determined not to make the same mistake myself. She knew that we cared about each other very much. Too much. You were so beautiful and talented and for some crazy reason you wanted to be my friend and were even willing to sacrifice your music scholarship to stay in London with me. She couldn't let that happen.'

Sam made a slicing motion with the flat of his hand through the air.

'So she did the only thing she knew. She used my feelings for you to break us up.'

The air was broken by the sound of Amber's ragged breathing but Sam kept going. If ever there was a time and a place for the truth to come out, this was as good as any.

'All she had to do was put the idea in my head that you were looking for a ring on your finger and a house and two kids and that was it. She didn't need to spell it out. Staying with me would mean the end of your career as a concert pianist and my grandiose fantasy scheme to be an intrepid international reporter.'

Sam turned to face the garden so that he could rest his elbows on his knees, only too well aware that Amber's gaze would still be fixed on his face.

'That was the weird thing. I didn't believe her at first. I kept telling myself that she simply wanted me to leave you alone because she didn't think that I was good enough or ambitious enough for you.

'The problem was, when I went back into the party, you were talking to your rich friends from the private school who were all in designer gear and real jewels, chatting away about yacht holidays, and the more I thought about it, the more I realised that maybe she had a point. What future did we have together? If you stayed with me, I would be holding you back. You would be better taking the scholarship and spending the next three years in Paris with people who could further your career. People who sat in the back of limos. Not in the driver's seat.'

'Sam—no!' Amber exploded. 'How could you even think that? Why didn't you come and talk to me about what she had said? I would have put that idea out of your head right then and there.'

He shook his head. 'Clever woman, your mother. She knew that my dad was on his own because my mum had walked out on us. All she had to do was plant the idea in my head that if I wasn't good enough for my own mother—then how could I possibly be good enough for her beautiful and talented daughter who deserved the very best in life? The big chip on my shoulder did the rest.'

Amber took his hand in hers and squeezed but he dared not look at her. Not yet. 'It was all too much; my head was thumping with the champagne and I couldn't deal with everything with the sound of the party going on around me. So I slipped out of the kitchen door and into the car park to get some air.'

Sam looked up into the sky, where the stars were already bright. 'And you know who was there, waiting for me in the convertible?'

'Petra,' she replied in a shaky voice.

He nodded. 'She had a bottle of champagne and two glasses and my mind was so racing with all the possibilities and problems and options that it never even occurred to me to wonder why she was outside in the first place. It was only later that I found out—Petra knew that I was going to be coming outside.'

'My mother sent Petra out to wait for you? Is that what you're saying?'

Sam nodded. 'Petra called a few days later to tell me that her folks were taking her to their villa in Tuscany for the whole of the summer before finishing school in Switzerland. I think she was genuinely sorry that she had been used the way she was, but by then it was too late. You had already left for Paris. It was too late. She had done it. She had broken us up.'

Amber pushed off the bench and walked across the

patio to the flower beds and stood with her back to Sam, her shoulders heaving up and down with emotion.

Every word that Sam had said echoed around inside her head, making it impossible for her to reply to him.

Her good arm wrapped tight around her waist, trying to hold in the explosion of confusion and regret that was threatening to burst out of her at any moment.

And not just about what had happened on her eighteenth birthday.

She had been so totally trusting and gullible! But the more she thought about it, the more she recognised that Sam was right. She was still dancing to her family's tune eleven years later—and the worst thing was, she was the one who was allowing them to do it.

So much for her great plans to make a new life for herself!

She was still too afraid to make her own decisions and follow her heart.

No longer.

That ended tonight.

From now on, she chose what to do and where. And who with.

Starting with Parvita. She wanted to see her friend get married so very much and that was precisely what she was going to do. Risk be damned.

Before Amber could calm her beating heart, she sensed his presence and seconds later a strong hand slid onto each side of her waist, holding her firm. Secure. She breathed in his aftershave, but did not resist as he moved closer behind her until she could feel the length of his body from chest to groin pressed against her back.

She had not even realised that she was shivering until

she felt the delicious warmth and weight of Sam's dinner jacket as he dropped it over her shoulders.

Sam's arms wrapped tighter around her waist, the fingers pressing oh so gently into her ribcage and Amber closed her eyes, her pulse racing. It had been a long time. And he smelt fabulous. Felt. Fabulous.

Sam pressed his head into the side of her neck, his light stubble grazing against her skin, and her head dropped back slightly so that it was resting on his.

Bad head.

Bad need for contact with this man.

Bad full stop.

One of his hands slid up the side of her neck and smoothed her hair away from her face so that he could press his lips against the back of her neck.

'It was all my fault,' he said, and his low, soft voice sounded different. Strained. Hesitant. 'I was trying to do the right thing and in the end I caused you pain. I'm so sorry.'

Amber sighed and looked up at the twinkling stars in the night sky, but sensed her shoulders lift with tension.

'There's nothing for you to be sorry about. It was eleven years ago and we were both so young and trying to find our way. It's just...it never crossed my mind that you were trying to do the noble thing by walking out on me. I wasted a lot of angry tears. And that is just sad, Sam.'

Sam continued to breathe into her neck, and one of his hands slid up from her waist to move in small circles on her shoulders under his jacket, and Amber suddenly began to heat up at a remarkably rapid rate.

'I know you're tired. No wonder. I've watched you dance the night away and I'm glad that I was here to see that. So thank you again for inviting me. Although Kate was watching me like a hawk to make sure that I wasn't making any moves on you.'

And that did make Amber grin. 'Kate the virtue keeper. I like that.'

Sam said nothing, but the hand tracing circles slid down her arm from shoulder to wrist, and he moved impossibly closer, his hand moving slowly up and down her arm.

'And necessary. You look very beautiful tonight.'

Amber smiled wide enough for Sam to sense her movement. 'Thank you. And thank you for finally telling me the truth about what happened.'

She slowly lifted one of Sam's hands from her waist and pushed gently away from him, instantly sorry that she had broken the touch, but turned back to face him.

'It's gone midnight. And I have had a very bad year, Sam. In so many ways. I don't want to start the next year of my life with regrets and bitterness.'

The smile on his lips faded and his upper lip twitched a couple of times. Amber knew that move. He couldn't be nervous. *Could he*?

She looked into his face and smiled a closed mouth smile. 'We both made mistakes. And I'm the last person who should be judging anyone. So how about starting the next year of my life as we mean to go on? As old friends who have just met up again after a long break. Can you do that?'

'Old friends,' he replied and lifted her fingers to his lips, his eyes never leaving hers. 'I'll drink to that. How about...'

But, before Sam could finish speaking, a fat lounger

cushion whacked him on the side of the head. And then a second time.

'You can stop that right now, Sam Richards. I mean it. Stop or I'll go and find the rolling pin and wrap it around your ears.'

'It's okay, Kate.' Amber sighed and rolled her eyes. 'Sam has just passed the audition. He'll be coming to India to interview me next week. You can put the pillow down.'

Sam stopped ducking his head and whipped around. 'What did you just say?'

'I have changed my mind about going to Parvita's wedding.' Amber smiled, her eyebrows high. 'Isn't that exciting?'

TEN

———

Hey Goddesses

Greetings from another gorgeous day in Kerala. The girls are still trying to settle down after all of the excitement of Parvita's wedding so lots to do, but my wrist is feeling a lot better today—despite all of the sitar playing!

Sam's flight was an hour late leaving London so he won't arrive until very late in the evening, which is probably a good thing considering this pre monsoon heatwave. No doubt he is bursting to get this interview over and done with so he can get back to his nice cool London office. Especially since I asked the janitor to pick Sam up at the airport in his rusty old motor, which is definitely on its last legs. Just for Kate.

Will report back tomorrow. Have fun. Amber

Sam Richards slid his rucksack off his shoulder and mopped the sweat from his brow and neck with one of his dad's pocket handkerchiefs as he strolled up the few steps to the single storey white building. If it was this hot at dusk he was dreading the midday temperature. But he would find out soon enough.

Great! *Not*.

The school janitor, who had picked him up at the airport, had pointed him towards the main entrance to the girls' home but Sam had barely been able to hear what he said since he kept the wreck of a car engine going just in case it broke down before he made it home.

The last hour had been spent in a bone-shaking car from the nineteen-sixties driven by a friendly janitor who seemed oblivious to the fact that he was hitting every pothole on the dirt road between the local airport and the girls' home in a car with bald tyres and no suspension.

Sam was amazed that the patched up, barely intact motor had lasted the journey without breaking down in a coconut grove or rice paddy. But it had got him here and for that he was grateful.

Slipping his sunglasses into his shirt breast pocket, Sam stretched his arms tall and tried to take in the sensory overload that was the Kerala coastline at sunset.

And failed.

The sea breeze from the shockingly beautiful crescent shaped bay was blocked by the low brick wall which formed the boundary of the property, creating a breathless oasis of fruit trees, a vegetable garden and exotic flowering plants which spilled out in an explosion of startlingly bright colours from wooden tubs and planters.

The immaculately kept gardens stretched down to the ocean and a wide strip of stunning white sand which glowed in the reflected shades of deep rich apricot, scarlet and gold from the setting sun. His view of the lapping waves was broken only by the thin trunks of tall coconut palms, banana plants and fruit trees.

It was like a poster of a dream beach from the cover of a holiday brochure. Complete with a long wooden fishing boat on the shore and umbrellas made from coconut palm fronds to protect the fishermen and occasional tourists who were out on the beach this late in the evening.

Coconuts. He was looking at real coconut palm trees. Compared to the grey, drizzly London Sam had left the previous afternoon the warm breeze was luxuriously dry and scented with the salty tang from the sea blended with spice and a tropical sweet floral scent.

A great garland of bougainvillea with stunning bright purple and hot pink flowers wound its way up the side of the school entrance and onto the coconut fibre roof, intertwined with a wonderful frangipani which spilled out from a blue ceramic pot, attracting bees and other nectar-seeking insects to the intensely fragrant blossoms. The perfume almost balanced out the heavy red dust from the dirt road and the bio odours from the cows and chickens who roamed freely on the other side of a low coconut matting fence.

He loved writing and his life as a journalist. He always had, but it was only when he came to villages like this one that it really struck home how much of his life was spent in open plan offices under fluorescent light tubes.

Even the air tasted different on his tongue. Traffic from the coast road roared past. Trucks in all colours, painted auto rickshaws and bright yellow buses competed with birdsong and the chatter of people and motor scooters. Everywhere he looked his eyes and ears were assaulted by a cacophony of life.

But as he relaxed into the scene, hands on his hips, the sound of piano music drifted out through the partly open door of what looked like a school building to his left and Sam smiled and wandered over, his shirt sticking to his back in the oppressive heat and humidity.

Amber was sitting on a very frail looking low wooden bench in front of an upright piano which had definitely seen better days. The polish was flaking off, the lid was warped and, from where he was standing, it looked as if some of the black keys were missing at the bottom of the scale.

But it didn't matter. Because Amber DuBois was running the fingers of her left hand across the keyboard and suddenly the old neglected instrument was singing like a nightingale.

She was dressed in a blue and pink long-sleeved cotton tunic and what looked like pyjama bottoms, her hair was held back by a covered elastic band and, as her feet moved across the pedals, he caught a glimpse of a plastic flip-flop.

And, for the first time in his professional life, Sam Richards did not know what to say.

Amber DuBois had never looked more beautiful in her life.

Exotic. Enchanting. But at that moment there was something else—she was totally and completely relaxed and content. Her eyes were closed and, as she played, she was humming along gently to the music as it soared into flights of soft and then dramatic sections of what sounded to Sam's uneducated ears as some great romantic composer's finest work.

Her shoulders lifted and fell, her left arm flowing from

side to side in brilliant technique while her plastered hand moved stiffly from octave to octave. But that did not matter—the music was so magical and captivating that it reverberated around this tiny school room and into every bone of his body.

The tropical garden and birdsong outside the window disappeared as he was swept up in the music.

This was her joy and her delight. The thing she loved most in the world.

He was looking at a completely different woman from the one who had flounced into his dad's garage, or the fashion model who had haughtily gossiped with the designer goddesses as she decluttered her apartment.

This was the real Amber. This was the girl he used to know. The girl whose greatest joy was playing the piano for her own entertainment and pleasure.

She was back!

And Lord, the longer he looked at her and listened to her music, the more he liked what he saw and the more he lusted. The fire that had sparked the second his fingers had touched her skin in that ridiculous penthouse dressing room suddenly flared right back into a blazing bonfire.

The heat and humidity of Kerala in May was nothing compared to the incendiary fire in his blood which pounded in his neck and ears.

Did she know? Did Amber have any clue that when she played liked this she was revealing to the world how much inner passion was hidden inside the cool blonde slender frame?

He had thought that he had been attracted to her

before, but that was nothing compared to the way he felt now.

He wanted her. And not just in his bed. He wanted Amber in his life, even if it was only for a few days, weeks or months. He wanted to be her friend and the man she wanted to share her life with. The music seemed to soak into his heart and soul and fill every cell with a fierce determination.

Somehow he was going to have to find a way of winning her back and persuading her to give him a second chance, or risk losing her for ever.

His bag slumped onto the floor.

Sam walked slowly into the room and slid next to Amber on the very end of the child-sized wooden bench. She did not open her eyes but smiled and slowly inhaled before giving an appreciative sigh.

'They say you can tell a lot about a man from the aftershave he has chosen. Very nice. Did you buy it at the airport?'

Her hands never missed a note as he gave a short dismissive grunt in reply. 'Then you won't mind if I move a little closer.'

Sam was blatantly aware that the fine wool cloth of his trousers brushed against the loose cotton trousers Amber was wearing as he slid along the shiny wooden surface until the whole side of his body seemed to be aligned against her.

'Hello. How was the flight?'

He started to say something, changed his mind, and left her staring at his mouth for just a few seconds too long. Much too long. His eyes scanned her face as though he was trying to record the images like a digital camera in his memory.

He had been worried about how awkward this moment was going to be. But, instead of watching every word, it was as though he was meeting one of his best friends in the world—and his heart lifted.

'You're playing nursery rhymes. From memory.'

She shook her head slowly from side to side. 'It sounds terrible and I am totally out of practice.'

'But you are trying. In your apartment last week, I couldn't help wonder if the old piano-playing business had lost its appeal. Am I right?'

Her fingers slowed down but did not stop. 'Full marks to the man in the sweaty shirt. You're right. I didn't want to play. No. That's wrong. I didn't want to perform.' She gave a little giggle and her left hand played a trill. 'This is not performing. This is having fun. And I have missed that. Do you know what I spent this afternoon doing? Making up tunes and songs around nursery rhymes these girls have never heard before. We had a great time.'

'Wait a minute. Are you telling me that you don't enjoy performing? Is that why you decided to retire? Because you do know that you are brilliant, don't you? I even splashed out and bought your latest album!'

She stopped playing, sat back and smiled, wide-eyed.

'You did? That was very kind.'

'No, it wasn't kind. It was a delight. And you haven't answered my question.'

Her gaze scanned his face as though looking for something important and Sam suddenly remembered that he needed a wash and a shave. 'That depends on who is asking the question,' she replied in a low, soft voice with the power to entrance him. 'My old pal Sam who I used to trust once upon a time, or the newest super-journalist at GlobalStar Media who I am not sure about at all.'

He swallowed down a moment of doubt but made the tough choice. Editor be damned. 'Let's try that first option.'

'Okay. Let's.' She looked down at her left hand and stretched out the fingers on the piano keys. 'Well. *Off the record.* These past few years have been very hard going. I haven't given myself enough time to recover from one tour before launching into rehearsals for the next. Combine that with all of the travelling and media interviews and suddenly I'm waking up exhausted every morning and nothing I do seems to make any difference.'

Her gaze shifted to his eyes and locked on tight. Shades of blue and violet clashed against the faint golden tinge to her skin. 'Every night was a struggle to make myself play and dive into the music to try and find some energy. I lost my spark, Sam. I lost my joy.'

'That's not the girl I used to know talking.'

'I'm not that same girl any more.'

'Aren't you?' Sam replied and reached up and touched her cheek. 'Are you quite sure about that? Because when I came in just now you had that soppy girly look on your face like you used to have when you sat down at a piano.'

'What do you mean, soppy?'

'Soppy. It means that you are your old self again—and I am very glad of it. This place seems to be doing you a lot of good.'

He glanced down and shocked her by gently lifting up her left hand and turning it over, his forefinger tracing the outline of the beautiful scrolls and flowers drawn in henna on the back of her hand.

'Take this, for example. I've never seen anything like it. Totally amazing. How was the wedding?'

His fingers stroked her palm, then lifted the back of her hand to his lips so that he could kiss her knuckles and was rewarded with an intense flash of awareness that told him that she knew exactly what he was saying. It was not the henna he found amazing.

She tutted twice, took her hand back then turned to face him. 'It was a fabulous wedding and I wouldn't have missed it for the world.' She gestured with her head towards the window. 'Parvita's family organised a flower arch in the garden and the service was so simple. A few words spoken by a man and a woman from completely different worlds, and yet it was totally perfect. There was not a dry eye in the house.'

'You cried at your friend's wedding? Really? And there is no such thing as a perfect marriage, just a decent wedding day.'

'Yes, I cried, you cynic,' Amber replied and scowled at him and pulled her hand away. 'Because this was the real thing. They didn't need a huge hotel with hundreds of guests who they would never have a chance to meet and talk to. All they wanted was their friends and family to help them celebrate. The little girls were all dressed up and throwing flowers. It was perfect. So don't mock.'

Sam held up both hands in surrender.

'Hey. Remember my ex-girlfriend who tried to lure me into a wedding without asking me first? Not all of us believe in happy endings, you old romantic.'

Amber thumped him on the arm. 'Well, that is just sad and pathetic.'

'Maybe you're right,' Sam replied and looked around, suddenly desperate to change the subject. 'Is this one of your school rooms?'

She nodded. 'The building work is going flat out before the monsoon rains so this is a temporary teaching room. I like it but I can't wait until the new air conditioned school is ready.'

'Have you decided on a name for the school you are paying for?' Sam asked as he picked up his bag and they strolled out into the evening air. 'The DuBois centre? Or the DuBois School for Girls. What is it to be?'

'Oh, you would like that, wouldn't you? No. I suggested a few names to the board of governors and they came back with one winner: the Elwood School.'

'Elwood? You named the school after your friend Saskia? Why did you choose that name?'

Amber leant back and gestured towards the girls who were playing on the grassy lawn under the mango and cashew nut trees. 'Do you see these lovely girls? They are so talented and bursting with life and enthusiasm. And yet not one of them has a home to go to. They are not all orphans as we would define orphans—far from it. Most of them have parents who cannot look after them or there were problems at home which mean that they only see their parents for a few months every year. But one way or another they have found their way here to this girls' home, where they can feel safe and protected by people who love them.'

Amber turned back to Sam with moisture sparkling in the corners of her eyes and when she spoke there was a hoarseness in her voice which clutched at Sam's heart and squeezed it tight. 'Well, I know just what that feels like. Saskia and her aunt Margot gave me a safe refuge when I needed to get away from my mother and whatever man she was living with who struggled to recall my name.'

Then she shook her head with a chuckle. 'They even let me stay with them after the mega-row I had with my so called parents after the disaster that was my eighteenth birthday party.'

Sam coughed, twice. 'You had a fight with your mother? I haven't heard that part of the story.'

She sniffed. 'I had no idea that those particular terms of abuse were in my vocabulary until I heard them come out of my mouth. Harsh words were exchanged about the expensive education I had been subjected to. It was not my moment of shining glory. And then I stomped out of the house with only my handbag and walked around to Elwood House. And Saskia and her aunt Margot took me in and looked after me as though I was one of their own.'

Amber sat up straight and curled her right hand high into the air with a flourish. 'Ta da. Elwood School.' Then she blinked and gave a curt nod. 'It may surprise you but I do have something in common with Parvita and these girls.'

Then she shivered and chuckled. 'Well, I did tell you that this article was going to be a challenge. I cannot wait to see what you do with that little insight, if it was on the record.'

'Any more like that?'

'Plenty. Just wait and see what tomorrow brings.'

ELEVEN

———

From: Amber@AmberDuBois.net
To: Kate@LondonBespokeTailoring.com; Saskia@Elwood-House.co.uk
Subject: My fiendish plan

Well, this is turning out to be a very odd week.

I came out first thing this morning to find Sam halfway up a jackfruit tree tossing fruit down to the girls below. He claims that he couldn't sleep because of the heat but he is now their official hero in long pants and is mobbed wherever he goes. I have just peeked outside and he is showing his little gaggle of fans the slideshow of photos on his digital camera. Amazing!

He even had me playing Christmas carols and nursery songs to amuse the girls during meal times in exchange for helping to organise the juniors. They adored him. I think he may never be allowed to leave!

My fiendish plan is to steal Sam away long enough for a walk along the beach at dusk and talk him into working on Parvita's story instead of mine. It is worth a try. Otherwise I don't know how long I can keep him hanging on.

The good news is that my wrist is feeling a lot better and I am enjoying playing for the first time in ages.
Cheers from Kerala. Amber

From: Kate@LondonBespokeTailoring.com
To: Amber@AmberDuBois.net
Subject: Sam Report
Sheesh, that man has no shame when it comes to charming the ladies. Don't be fooled. Glad that your hand is feeling better. Don't forget to drink plenty of water. Love ya. K

Sam wiped the spark plug from the janitor's ancient motor car on a scrap of cotton and held it up to the fading sunlight before deciding that the plug had lived a very long life and needed to take retirement, as of right now. He had managed to find one replacement at the bottom of a tool kit which was so rusty that it had taken hours to clean the tools to the stage where he could use them to service what passed as a car.

But at least the work had kept him close to Amber.

They still had a lot of work to do to rebuild that fragile friendship but she had seemed genuinely delighted when he helped her collect the girls together and keep them in one place long enough for her to explain about the keys on the piano and what the notes meant. With a bit of help from a couple of coconut shells, three tin buckets and a wrench.

Weird. He had surprised himself by actually enjoying playing on a makeshift set of drums.

The only thing they were not doing was talking about her career.

She might have trusted him enough to take the risk and invite him here to his magical place to see what she was doing with her life but that was as far as it went.

So far there had always been some excellent excuse why this was not a good time to record an interview and after three days he had all the background photos he might need but not the exclusive extra material he needed to create a compelling story—her story.

So what was the problem?

The sound of female laughter echoed out from the school room and he peered in through the window just in time to see Amber conducting a mini orchestra of five girls playing wooden recorders in tune with some Italian baroque music which blasted out from a cheap cassette player perched on the teacher's desk.

He smiled and dropped back down before she saw him.

It might have been his idea for her to play a few simple tunes, one note at a time, but once she got started the girls and teachers had begged her for more and now there was no stopping her.

Amber had a way with the girls that was nothing short of astonishing. It was as if they knew that she understood what they were going through and wanted to help them any way she could.

And it had nothing to do with her musical talent, although she was playing more and more every day.

Amber was giving these girls the kind of unconditional love he hadn't seen in a long time.

Seeing her with the children, it was obvious that Amber would make a wonderful mother—but how did that happen? Her own parents certainly had not been good role models. No. This came from her own heart and her ability to reach out and touch a child's life and make a little girl laugh.

Perhaps it was a good thing that Amber had thrown herself into working with the girls at the orphanage. Because the longer he spent with her and listened to her sweet voice and shared her laughter, the harder it was to kid himself that he could control this burning attraction to her.

He was falling for Amber DuBois all over again.

And that had to be the craziest thing that had happened to him in a long time.

But the worst thing that he could do right now—for either of them, was tell her how he felt. He had to be patient, even if it killed him.

Somehow he had to stay objective and cool enough to write an exclusive celebrity interview which gave no hint of how badly he wanted to be with the celebrity, talk to her and tell her how much she meant to him.

No. Forget wanted. Make that *needed* to be with her while he had the chance.

In the past few weeks he had seen Amber the cold, snarky concert pianist, Amber the fashion designers' favourite model, who happened to love Indian food as much as he did, and now he was mending the janitor's car while a stripped down, enchanting Amber taught small girls with bangles on their wrists all about Italian baroque.

And guess which version of Amber was capable of rocking his world just at the sight of her?

Every day she spent here seemed to make her even more relaxed and at ease. Happy and laughing. Enjoying her music again with every note she played and loving every minute she spent with these girls. And she could teach—that was obvious, even if she did roll her eyes at him every time he applauded after a class.

He must have told her a dozen times how good it was to hear her play with such delight—even if it was with one hand and a few fingertips, and his message seemed to be getting through. She had actually admitted over breakfast that she had never enjoyed music so much in a long time.

Maybe retiring from concert performances was not such a bad idea for Amber DuBois?

Everything he had seen and heard so far told him that she was serious about turning her back on the offers streaming in from orchestras all over the world. Frank had got that wrong. She was a lot more interested in the girls here than a prestigious career—for the moment, at least.

Sam jumped into the broken driver's seat and listened as the engine reluctantly kicked into life.

The problem was that after listening to Amber's countless stories about how wonderful her friend Parvita's wedding had been, it was fairly obvious that her idea of a happy relationship meant a ring on her finger and a house and a garden with children to play in it.

What was it with women and weddings? Why couldn't two people accept that they wanted to share their lives and be happy at that?

A few months before his ex-girlfriend Alice took the initiative in Los Angeles, they had travelled to New York for her cousin's wedding and over a very long weekend at grandiose parties he had fended off at regular intervals the constant ribbing from her relatives about when they were going to make an announcement about their wedding. Alice had done the same, only with a twist. 'Oh, Sam is not the marrying type. You can take a horse to water, but you can't make him drink. Isn't that right, Sam?'

And he had smiled and replied with yet another joke, just a bit of fun to amuse the other guests. Alice had known, even then, that they would never be together long-term, and he had been too complacent to talk to her about it. Too content to accept second best and go with the flow. Until she'd decided to take the initiative and organise the wedding on her own. And he had bolted.

Coward. After he'd left, Alice had found someone she wanted to spend the rest of her life with.

Amber was bound to do the same. She was beautiful, funny and talented and she deserved some happiness in her life. With a man who could give her what she wanted.

He wanted Amber to be happy—why wouldn't he?

The problem was, he had broken the unwritten rule. He cared about Amber. If he went back to London without telling her how he felt he would be walking away from the best thing in his life. And breaking both of their hearts all over again. And that truly would make him a coward.

'Hey there. Good news. You have just won the prize for inventing a new musical instrument. Coconut shells and buckets filled with different amounts of water make different sounds when you hit them with a wrench. Who knew? The girls loved it! What made you think of that?'

'Ingenuity. And drumming on oil cans in my dad's garage. I thought it might work.' Sam chuckled up at Amber, who was waving goodbye to the girls who were streaming out from her classroom. 'Failing that, I could always play the spoons. But I am saving that for an encore. I live in hope.'

Amber gave a small shoulder shrug. 'Either one of those would work for me. It seems that you have hidden talents after all. Are your mum and dad musical?'

'Not a bit. Nobody in our house could sing a note in tune but I like the drums. Not exactly the most subtle of instruments and my mum couldn't stand me making a noise in the house so my dad let me make loose on the oil drums. I hope I didn't scare the girls.'

'Not a bit and I was impressed. But, speaking of hope, are you free to come down to the beach for a stroll before it gets dark? It's lovely and cool down there.'

'Five minutes to wash my hands and I'll be right with you. That's the best offer I have had all day,' he replied with a sexy wink.

'Keep that up and it will be the only offer you have. Meet you under the palm tree. Second from the left.'

'It's a date,' he whispered and was rewarded with a definite flush to her cheeks before she lifted her chin in denial, rolled her eyes in pretend disgust and strolled down the lawns towards the bay.

In the end it took Sam ten minutes to wash then extricate himself from the gaggle of girls who clutched onto his legs as he made his way across the gardens towards the beach.

But it was worth it.

Sam reached for his small pocket digital camera so that he could capture the lovely image of the woman who was sitting on the edge of an old wooden fishing boat on a wide stretch of the most incredible fine golden sand, on a beach fringed with coconut palms.

She looked up as he took the shot and gave him a warm smile which came from the heart.

And he knew. Just like that. This was the photo he would use on the cover of his article—and keep in his wallet for rainy days back in London when the office got too much.

She was wearing a simple tunic and trousers, the plaster cast on her wrist covered with children's names, and her hair was tied back with a scarf. And in his eyes she was the most beautiful woman that he had ever seen in his life.

And then he saw it. Nestling at her throat. It was a gold heart shaped pendant that had cost him every penny of the money that he had been saving for spare tyres for the car his dad was working on for him.

He had given her the necklace in the car the evening of her eighteenth birthday the moment before he had turned the key in the ignition. And it had been worth every penny just to see her face light up with joy and happiness at that moment.

It was the first time she had kissed him without him prompting—and it meant the world to him.

He couldn't drag his eyes away from it. Of all the jewels she must have collected she had chosen to wear his necklace tonight. Had she chosen it to provoke him, or, and his heart swelled at the thought, to show that she had not forgotten how very close they had been?

Sam shuffled closer to her, stretched out his hand and, with two fingers, lifted the gold chain clear of her remarkable cleavage and dangled the heart pendant in the air.

'Nice necklace.'

'Thank you. It was a gift from a boy I was in love with at the time. I wear it now and again.'

'To remind yourself that you were loved?'

'To remind myself that love can break your heart,' Amber replied and reached up and took hold of Sam's fingers in hers. 'And that I was loved. Yes, that too.'

And she took his breath away with the honesty.

So much so that, instead of sitting next to her, Sam knelt down on the sand in front of Amber and looked deep into her surprised eyes before asking the question which had been welling up all day.

'Why are you avoiding our interview, Amber? What is it that you are so afraid of telling me?'

Her reply was to break off eye contact and look out over his shoulder to the sea in silence.

'We were such close friends once,' he went on. 'We used to talk about everything. Our hopes and our dreams. Our great plans for the future. *Everything*. I don't think you have any idea how much it hurts me that you find it so impossible to get past the mistake I made when I listened to your mother and walked out of your birthday party that night.'

She glanced back at him, reached out and plucked a leaf from his shoulder. 'I thought that you were the one who had thrown our friendship away as though it didn't matter.'

'You were wrong. So *wrong*. I was confused about where we could go as a couple—but never about that. You were always the friend I came to when I needed someone. Always.'

His gaze scanned her face from her brow to her chin and back again. 'You were the only real friend I had. Oh, I know that you and your pals thought that I was the popular boy around town, but the truth was harder to accept. I knew everyone in my area, played football and talked big, but I was still too raw from my parents' divorce to talk about what really mattered to anyone at school. So I kept my deep feelings to myself. Even if that meant being lonely.'

'Was that why you talked to me, Sam? Because I was an outsider?'

'Maybe.' He shrugged. 'I may also have noticed that you were not hard to look at. But hey, I was a teenage pressure cooker of hormones and bad skin. Nothing special about that.'

'Yes, you were. You were always special. To me at least.'

'I know.' His brows squeezed together. 'I think that was what scared me in the end, Amber.'

'What do you mean?'

'You took me seriously. You listened to me babbling on about what a successful journalist I was going to become and actually encouraged me to stick my neck out and pass the exams I needed to go to university. You believed in me. And that was one of the reasons why I fell in love with you.'

He heard her sharp intake of breath but ignored it and carried on. 'And it terrified me. I had seen my parents fall apart from all of the fights and arguments which they tried to keep from me, but failed miserably. You were not the only one to be dragged around from new house to new house as your mother found a new partner. I refused to go to see my mum the minute I turned eighteen but she still had the power to make my life miserable.'

Sam paused. He had not thought about that in years. Strange. 'And then you stepped out of a limo with your mother one evening. Amber Sheridan DuBois.' He grinned up into her face. 'And suddenly my life was not so miserable after all. And I will always be grateful to you for being the friend that had been missing from my life and I hadn't even realised that fact. Always. I couldn't have been happier that last year.'

'Until we became more than friends. Is that what you are saying?'

Sam nodded, lips pressed tight together. 'That night of your eighteenth when we got back to your house after our mini tour of London, and I told you that I loved you—I meant it, Amber.'

He pushed himself to his feet. 'That is why you asked me to come out to Kerala instead of giving your interview in London or over the Internet. You knew that I loved you but I still walked away. And now you are the one with the power to walk away and leave me behind.' Sam shook his head and half turned to look out across the sands to the gaggle of children playing in the surf. 'Strange,' he chuckled, 'I never thought that you would turn out to be such a diva.'

Amber gasped so loudly that Sam whirled back to look at her.

'A diva?' she repeated in a horrified voice. 'You think I am behaving like a diva? Oh, Sam. You have no idea how hurtful it is for me to hear you say those words. A diva?'

She shook her arm away as he reached out to take it and stood up. 'A diva is the very last thing I ever wanted to be.'

Sam started to follow her onto the sand, but she whirled around to face him, her hand clenched into a tight fist by her side. 'I thought that you, of all people, would understand why I despise the very word. That was what they used to call her. Remember? "The loveliest diva in the music business". Julia Swan.'

Sam groaned. 'Yes. Of course I remember. Your mum

used to relish it. But I thought...I thought you wanted star billing and your own dressing room. You have worked so hard for so many years as a soloist. Doesn't that go with the territory?'

'Of course it does. And I have worked hard. So very hard. But you still don't understand, do you?'

She stepped up to him and clenched hold of his hand. 'That wasn't what I wanted. It has never been what I wanted. I loved the music. That was the important thing.'

She released him and turned sideways to stand with her arm wrapped around her waist and look out over the ocean. 'You asked me the other day why I wanted to retire. It wasn't the work. It was me.'

Her voice faded away as though the breeze was carrying it out to sea. 'I didn't like what I was becoming, Sam. And this last tour of Asia was the final straw.'

She flung back her head so that the breeze could cool her neck. 'By the time we got to India, I started demanding things like my own dressing room and quiet hotel rooms and white cushions and stupid things like that. My pals on the tour said that it was because we were all so tired but when we got to Kerala and took a break from the tour I realised that the concert organisers were wary of me—they expected me to be demanding and difficult.'

As Sam watched, Amber closed her eyes. 'And the worst thing was that the complaining and the headaches—they had nothing to do with the love of the music and everything to do with the stress of the performances and the touring. Somewhere along the way my passion for the music had been buried under the avalanche of photo shoots and the press parties and the dresses and I hadn't even noticed. And that was so wrong.'

Amber half turned to look at Sam and she felt the tears prick the corners of her eyes even before she said the words. 'I was turning into my mother and it was killing the one thing that I had loved. I was terrified of becoming that sad and bitter and lonely diva that was Julia Swan. That's when I decided to retire, Sam. I was terrified that I was turning into my mother.'

TWELVE

———

'No,' Sam replied, resting the palms of his hands on Amber's shoulders and drawing her back to the boat to sit down. 'That was never going to happen. Never.'

His gaze locked onto her lovely eyes and held them tight. 'I've spent the last three days watching you connect with these girls. Where did you learn those skills? Not from Julia Swan and certainly not by being some diva.'

She smiled back at him but her eyes were suddenly sad. 'I can say the same thing about you. Those girls love you. But you don't understand. It had already happened. And do you know the worst thing? The moment it hit me what I was doing was when I finally understood her. After all of these years I finally understood that my mother didn't hate people—she hated her job. She hated it but she didn't know anything else, so she took her frustration out on everyone around her.'

'You might be right. But what did you do? Just walk off the tour?'

She flashed him a look. 'Hardly. No. My friend Parvita had organised a series of charity concerts in small towns and school halls in Kerala and Goa. Until then I had always said that I was too busy, but at the very last minute their solo pianist had to go to New York and Parvita asked me to take his place.'

She raised her hands then dropped them to her lap. 'What can I say? India knocked me sideways. I love everything about it. The heat, the colours, everything. We travelled with a group of incredible sitar players, and we had the best tour of our lives. And the very last day was a revelation. Can you imagine—the whole musical troupe was in a rickety bus, dodging the potholes, in the middle of nowhere heading for a string of orphanages for abandoned girls?'

She looked at Sam and managed a smile.

'Nothing can prepare you for what we found here. I thought I had seen it all. Wrong again. Same with my friends. I think I cried every night. It was tough going but Parvita worked her magic and for a short while we had a real working music school right here in this village. We had planned to do two nights at the orphanage before heading back to the airport. We stayed a week! Can you imagine? By working all around the area, we raised enough money to pay for hospital treatment for the girls with enough left over to give them a decent meal every day for a month. These girls. Oh, Sam. These amazing girls.'

She broke into a wide grin. 'You wouldn't believe the fun we all had. It was crazy. They are living in the worst conditions and they found happiness. It was very precious. I'll never forget it.'

'I can see how important it is to you. Is that why you decided to come back here for Parvita's wedding?'

Amber nodded. 'Parvita wants to create the music school but she needs help to pay the teachers' wages and keep things going. So when she left on her honeymoon I offered to stay on and help in the school before the monsoon hits.'

She paused and her eyes flicked up at Sam as he held his breath for what she was about to say next. 'I have had the most amazing fun here. You were right when you told me that I seemed happier here. The problem is—until I came here I had no idea how shallow and self-indulgent my life as a concert performer was. These girls have given me a new insight into my life.'

'You worked your whole life for your success, Amber. Hey, wait a minute. Last summer you were the new face of a huge cosmetics campaign. How does that fit in?'

Amber screwed up her face and Sam could almost see hear her jaw clench. Her face creased into a grimace. 'It was a tricky decision. My agent was thrilled and suddenly I had all of these glamorous people telling me what an asset I would be for their cosmetics. But that was not why I did it. Of course my first reaction was to laugh it off as some big joke. But then they offered me a sum of money that made my head spin. A wicked amount of money. Criminal, really. And once I had that sum in my head, it wouldn't go away. I kept thinking about my friend Parvita and all of the fund-raising work she was doing for the charity. And the more I thought about it, the more I realised that what I was actually saying was that my pride was more important than these girls having an education and healthcare. All I had to do was sit there wearing a lovely dress while make-up experts, hairdressers and lighting engineers worked their magic. This was ridiculous. I couldn't walk away from that opportunity to do something remarkable for the sake of a few hours having my photograph taken. That would be so selfish I wouldn't be able to live with myself.'

She chuckled. 'I knew that I would get a terrible kicking from the media. And I did. You and your colleagues were not very kind and it upset me at the time, but do you know what?'

Amber smiled and dropped her shoulders. 'It was worth it. I had to weigh up every cruel comment from the music press and every sniping gossip columnist against seeing a real school going up in place of the slum ruin that was here before.'

'Why didn't you tell them? That the money wasn't going into your own bank account?'

Amber turned to face him. 'You know why, Sam. How long have you been interviewing television personalities and so-called celebrities? Years, right? And how many times have you ridiculed the charity work that people do with their time and money? It doesn't seem to matter if a famous basketball player wants to visit a hospice for the day to cheer up the boys. Or a bestselling novelist donates a huge amount to a literacy campaign. They are all accused of having so much money that they can splash out on some charity or other for tax reasons and to make them look good.'

She shook her head. 'That's not for me, Sam. I wanted this project to be part of my private life, away from the media and the cameras and the concert halls. It is too personal and important. The last thing I want is my photo with the girls to be splashed over the cover of some celebrity gossip magazine. I would hate that to happen.'

'Now that I simply do not understand. Yes. Those articles help to sell newspapers and magazines, and the charity gains some free publicity at the same time. Don't you want that for the girls?'

He looked back up the hill towards the school. 'They still have a long way to go. And your name could help them get there.'

Amber started chewing on the side of her lower lip. It was an action that he had seen her do a hundred times before, usually when her mother was nagging.

'I know. And I have turned it over in my mind so many times but, in the end, it all boils down to this.'

Her gaze locked onto his face. 'I need you to write a feature article about the orphanage. And if that means using me as a hook to get readers interested—' she took a breath '—then okay, I will have my photo taken in India and splashed all over the internet and wherever the article reaches—as long—' she paused again '—as long as the article makes it clear that I am supporting the charity set up by my friend, Parvita. I'm just one member of the team working on fund-raising and teaching the pupils for free—and there is a whole long list of other professional musicians who are involved. Small cog. Big charity project. Only...'

'Only?' he asked, his head whirling with what she was asking him to do.

'I have to trust you to tell the truth about why I chose to spend my time teaching here with Parvita instead of performing in some huge concert hall, without turning it into some great fluff piece about how I am lowering myself to be here. And not one word about my mother. Can I do that? Can I trust you, Sam?'

'Amber, you don't know what you're asking. My editor, Frank, is not interested in an in-depth article on a charity in India. He wants celebrity news that will sell papers in London. And if I don't deliver, that editor's desk will go to another hungry journalist and I'll be back at the bottom of the pecking order all over again.'

She closed her eyes and his heart surged that he might be the cause of her pain. She had offered him the truth—now it was his turn.

Reaching out, he took her left hand and held it tight against his chest, forcing her to look at him.

'I need this job, Amber. My dad isn't getting any younger and I've hardly seen him these past ten years. I made his life hell after my mother left us and he had to take the blame. But do you know what? He believed in me when my mother made it clear that I was a useless dreamer who would never amount to anything. And now I have proven her wrong. That's special.'

'Your dad. Of course. How stupid of me. You finally did it. You got there. And I'm not so stupid that I can't see how much of your dad has rubbed off on you. You are terrific with the kids. But...' her brow screwed up '...now it's my turn to be confused. You always said that you wanted to write the long feature articles on the front page, and wouldn't be happy until your name was right there. On the cover.'

Then she shook her head. 'But that was years ago. I probably have got it wrong.'

Sam took a breath. 'You didn't get it wrong. I simply haven't got to the front cover yet.'

'But you will, Sam,' Amber breathed, her gaze locked onto his face. 'From the moment I first met you, I knew that you had a fire in your belly to prove your talent and were determined to be the best writer that you could be. Your passion and energy drove you on against the odds. And you have done it. Your dad should be proud of you. In fact, am I allowed to be proud of you too?'

He felt his neck flare up red in embarrassment but gave her a quick nod. 'Right back at you.'

'Thanks,' she sniffed and then lifted her chin, eyebrows tight together. 'In that case, I have an idea.'

'You always have an idea. Go on.'

'Simple. Write two articles. I will give you enough quotes for a celebrity piece about my broken wrist and taking time out with my friend at the music school—and you have those shots from my birthday party to show me in full-on bling mode. But...' her voice dropped '...the real interview starts here. At the orphanage for abandoned girl children in a wonderful country bursting with potential. You were the one who saw that they needed a teacher more than they needed a fund-raiser this week. *You get them. You understand.* That could be the feature which takes you to the front page, Sam.'

'You think I am ready for those dizzy heights?'

'I know that you have the talent—you always did have. But what do you think, Sam? You have been writing fluff pieces for years, languishing in the middle ground and peeking out now and again to write about the bigger world. Are you ready to show Frank what you are truly capable of? That is what he wants, isn't it? Or are you too scared to stick your head out above your comfort zone and take a risk in case you are shot down and rejected?'

She stepped forward and pressed her hand flat against Sam's chest. 'You have an amazing talent. I still believe that you can do this. And do it brilliantly. Do it, Sam. Do it for me, but most of all, do it for yourself.'

THIRTEEN

———

From: Amber@AmberDuBois.net
To: Kate@LondonBespokeTailoring.com; Saskia@Elwood-House.co.uk
Subject: Sam Report

Sam has just let me read his article about Parvita and it is fantastic! My boy done good! In return I have posed for some cheesy photos on the beach under the palm trees and answered lots of questions about my last concert tour and the building plans for the new school I have decided to fund here at the orphanage. I am calling it the Elwood School—I think that your aunt Margot would have approved, Saskia.

There is so much to do here and the builders are pestering me with questions and paperwork, I am really flagging. Good thing that Sam has been here to help with the tradesmen and architects.

I am going to miss him when he goes back tomorrow. And so will the girls.

This is his last evening. So it is time to have that talk I have been putting off.

Wish me luck. Amber

From: Saskia@ElwoodHouse.co.uk

To Amber@AmberDuBois.net; Kate@LondonBespoke-Tailoring.com;
Subject: Elwood School
Oh, you wonderful girl—Aunt Margot would have loved it, and I have just spent five minutes blubbing into my tea.

Re Sam the friendly spy. I think it could be time to ask that young man his intentions!

Take a chance on happiness Amber. And tell Sam that he is welcome here any time.
Good luck. Saskia

From: Kate@LondonBespokeTailoring.com
To: Amber@AmberDuBois.net
Subject: Sam Report
Love, love, love the name of the school. Do they need a needlework teacher next winter? You should tell Sam what happened pronto. Who knows? He might be okay now you have worn him down a bit with tropical beaches and hot curries.

Big might. Still scared for you.
Best of luck, gorgeous. Kate

Amber dropped down onto the fallen tree

trunk that lay among the driftwood on the shore and pressed her hand flat against the weather-smoothed exposed wood before closing her eyes. The warm wind was scented with spices from exotic flowering shrubs and the tang of the ocean waves as they rolled up on the sand in front of her. White foamed and fresh and cool, their force broken by the shallow rocks and reefs under the sand.

Which was pretty much how she was feeling at that moment. Like a spent force.

She desperately needed to calm down and focus on the coming days ahead. But her mind was still reeling from the thousand and one things on her to do list. And Sam.

Maybe things could have turned out differently for them if her mother had not scared him away.

Would they have stayed together in London and stuck it out through university and her concert tours? It would have made a difference to know that she had someone who loved her back in London, waiting for her. Someone who she could give her heart to and know that it was safe and protected.

The sound of children playing made her open her eyes as a group of boys ran across the beach, wheeling a rubber car tyre with a stick, laughing and dancing in and out of the surf. Their mothers strolled along behind them, barefoot, bright in their lovely gold braid trimmed colourful saris and sparkling bangles. Chatting like mothers all around the world.

And somewhere deep inside her body her need to have her own family contracted so fast and so painfully that she wanted to whimper with loss. Being with these girls had shown her how much she loved to share her life and her joy with open minds.

She would willingly give up her slick penthouse for a small family house with a garden and a loving husband who wanted children with her.

Sam was right. Her parents—and his—were hardly the best examples that they could have, but she still wanted to give some love to children of her own one day. At least she knew what *not* to do.

As for Sam? Sam would make a wonderful father given the chance.

'A penny for your thoughts.'

Sam!

Amber whipped around on the sun-bleached tree

trunk so fast that her tunic snagged. But there he was. Sam Richards. This man who had come back into her life just when she'd least expected it, and was just as capable of making her head and body spin as he had ten years earlier.

It staggered her that one look at that tanned handsome face could send her blood racing and her senses whirled into a stomach-clenching, heart-thumping spin.

How did he do it? How did he turn back the clock and transform her back into a schoolgirl being taken out for a pizza and a cola by the chauffeur's son?

But those were on dull evenings back in London. She could never have dreamt that she would be with Sam on a sandy tropical beach with the rustle of coconut palms and tropical birdsong above her head.

Sam grinned and strolled along the sand towards her.

He was wearing loose white cotton trousers and a pale blue linen shirt which matched the colour of his eyes to perfection. He looked so confident and in control it was ridiculous. He moved from the hips, striding forward, purposefully, with his head high. Even on a remote beach in Kerala, Sam managed to look like a journalist ready to interview a big movie star or show business personality for the next big news story.

The Sam she was looking at belonged in the world she had left behind—the world he would be going back to in only a few hours, while she stayed behind.

Was that why she longed to hold him closer and relive the precious moments when he had held her in his arms in the apartment? To feel the tenderness of his lips on hers for one last time before they parted?

No—she dared not think about that! Amber smiled back and patted the log.

'I've saved you the best seat in the house but the show has already started.'

But when she looked up into Sam's face as he drew closer, his ready smile seemed to fade and he stopped and shrugged, almost as if he was wondering what to say to her.

His gaze locked onto her face and the look he gave her sent her body past the tingling stage and way over into melting.

'Sorry to keep you waiting. I have just been phoning London.'

'Parvita told me that you had emailed her with a few questions, even though she was on her honeymoon,' Amber said, trying her best to appear calm and unruffled. 'But you couldn't promise her much in the way of publicity.'

She peered into his face. 'Was that what you were trying to tell me yesterday, Sam? That Frank might not want to know about two crazy women who are trying to build a music school in Kerala? Especially when you are handing over the exclusive on how brave Bambi has survived her terrible trauma of being forced to play on out of tune pianos in the back of beyond?'

'Not exactly. I have just got off the phone with Frank and offered him a very interesting feature for the paper's new current affairs magazine on how girls are still being given up by their parents in some parts of India but are now being trained to be part of the technology boom. Giving them a great education and a future. And do you know what? He loved it. Two sides of an amazing developing country. In fact he loves it so much he wants to bring it forward to next month's magazine, complete with photographs and quotes from the lovely Parvita.'

Amber laughed out loud and gave him a quick one-handed hug. 'Wow. That's amazing! Congratulations. Your first feature in the London paper. And it couldn't be better publicity for what we are trying to do here. Thank you. Thank you, Sam. It means a lot—to all of us.'

Sam tilted his head sideways and grinned. 'My pleasure. And don't make me out to be some kind of hero—it's my job to spot a great story and run with it.'

Then her face relaxed into a smile. 'Of course. You were simply being a professional reporter. So the girls didn't have any effect on you at all. Of course they didn't. You were just doing your job.'

He nudged her with his elbow and she nudged him back.

'What does it feel like to be a feature writer at long last, oh, great journalist?'

'It feels okay. No. Better than okay. It feels grand. Just grand.'

He took a breath. 'There is one thing. Frank gave me a heads up on a couple of rumours flying around the Internet that you have just spent time in hospital in Boston recently.'

The cool breeze on Amber's shoulders suddenly felt icy and threatening.

Boston. Of course. Someone had tipped off the newspapers. Probably one of the hospital team back in Boston. Heath had warned her that she wouldn't be able to keep her hospital visit a secret for long and it looked as though he was right.

Great.

She inhaled slowly, then pushed down hard on the log.

His whole body stilled and he reached out and took her hand in his. 'You are still underweight, still pale despite this glorious sunshine and the other day I felt every one of your ribs. And yes, I know how hard you are working to make this new school possible before the rainy season, but there is more to it than that. Isn't there?'

Amber looked into Sam's face and saw genuine concern in his blue eyes. It was almost as if he was scared of hearing her answer.

Squaring her shoulders, she stared directly into his eyes and said, 'They are right, I was being treated for an infectious disease, but I am absolutely fine now.' She rushed on as Sam tensed up. 'Seriously. I had the all clear before I left London and don't need to take any more antibiotics.'

Then she paused and licked her lips.

'Amber. Just make it fast and tell me. Because my imagination is going wild here and you are killing me. Just how bad was it?'

Taking a deep breath, she met his gaze head-on. This was it. This was what the whole interview jag had been building up to. 'It was bad,' she whispered, her whole body trembling with the emotion and the relief that came with finally being able to tell him the secret that she had been keeping from him. She turned her head and rested her forehead against his, feeling his hot, moist skin against hers and soaking up the strength she needed to say the words.

'The last time I came to Kerala I caught meningitis. And I almost died, Sam. I almost died.'

FOURTEEN

———

The sound of motorised rickshaws and the relentless battle of car horns and truck engines from the village road rumbled across the beach towards Amber and Sam but she did not hear them. She was way too busy fighting to keep breathing, as she desperately scanned his face, which was pale and white with shock.

Sam turned sideways, lowered his body onto the log next to her and stretched out his long legs, his arms out in front of him, hands locked together, his chin down almost to his chest.

One side of his throat was lit rosy pink by the fading sun as he twisted his body around from the waist to face her, apparently oblivious to the damage he was causing to his trousers, which stretched to accommodate the muscled thighs below.

The look on that face was so pained, so tortured and so intense that Amber could barely look at him for fear that she would burn up in the heat.

They sat in silence for a few seconds but she could hear

each slow, heavy quivering breath that he took, his chest heaving as his lungs fought to gain control.

His fingers reached across and took hers and held them tight to his chest, forcing her to look up into his face.

'Oh, Amber,' he said, his pale blue eyes locked onto her face, his voice low and intense, anxious. 'Why didn't you tell me that you had been so ill?' Then he exhaled very, very slowly. 'You knew where I was working. All you had to do was ask Heath or one of your friends to lift the phone and I would have flown over to see you. Spent time with you. Help you through it, read you books, tell you crazy stories and the latest gossip from Hollywood. Anything. Anything at all.'

She swallowed down hard and took a long juddering breath. 'You would?'

'In a heartbeat, you foolish, stubborn woman,' Sam answered with a faint smile, and reached up and stroked a strand of her hair back over her ear, his fingertips gently caressing her forehead as he did so.

His touch was so tender and so very gentle that Amber almost surrendered to the exhaustion that keeping her secret from Sam had caused.

'You might be right about the stubborn bit. I had intended to tell you before you left,' she whispered through a throat that felt as though she had swallowed a handful of sharp gravel, 'but there never seemed to be a good time. But I had to be sure, Sam. Really sure, before I told anyone the truth.'

'Sure of what? That I would do a good job telling your story? Or that you could trust me enough to be honest with me?'

His brows screwed together and for a terrifying moment Amber thought that he was going to jump up and walk out on her. But instead, Sam closed his eyes and when he opened them she was stunned to see a faint gleam of moisture in the corners.

Moisture she was responsible for putting there by her selfish behaviour.

And the sight sucked the air from her lungs, rendering her speechless.

'That was why you decided to retire,' Sam said, his gaze scanning her face.

All she could do was nod slowly in reply. 'I was already back in Boston when I collapsed. I don't remember breaking my wrist when I fell over my suitcases. And I only have snatches from that first week in the hospital. I think I scared the hell out of Heath.'

'I'm not surprised. You are doing a pretty good job with me right now,' Sam replied with a tremble in his voice that she had never heard before.

'The doctors told him that I was in danger for the first twenty-four hours—but when I was in the ambulance I made Heath promise not to tell anyone. This was one time I did not want the media following every second of my life. I couldn't hide the fact that I had broken my wrist—but I could hide the fact that I broke it when I collapsed. I don't want the world to feel sorry for me. Pity me. Can you understand that?'

'Not a bit. Why not?' Suddenly Sam's voice switched from desperate and sad to excited and enthusiastic. 'Let me tell the world how you survived this trauma and came out of the other side with a new purpose in life. That's an amazing story. Inspiring. You could do a lot of good for the children's home if you went out and promoted it.'

'Promoted? You mean talking about the trauma of those weeks in hospital on TV chat shows and breakfast television? No. Not for me, Sam. I'm done with talking about how great I am. Because I don't feel brave or inspiring or any of those things.'

She dropped her head backwards, closed her eyes and inhaled slowly several times before going on. 'I remember the afternoon I was discharged from hospital and Heath drove me to his house and I looked out of the window in awe and astonishment. The colours were so vibrant it made me glad to be alive. The air smelled wonderful, fresh, clean, invigorating—especially compared to the hospital. Everything looked amazing, as though I was seeing the streets and the cars and even Heath's old stone house for the very first time.'

Amber raised her hand then dropped it again onto Sam's lap. 'And waiting for me was all of the clutter and admin and mess of details that comes with being a public performer.'

She shrugged. 'And do you know what? I didn't want any of it. The little things didn't matter any longer. All that mattered was being with my friends again. Living my life the way I want. In a world full of colour and hope and laughter and enthusiasm for life. That was what mattered to me now. And I knew that was not in Boston with Heath in stifling luxury, or in Paris with my dad and his new family, or in Miami with my mother on a cruise ship somewhere.'

Amber winced and pinched off a flower blossom from the tree by her side and inhaled the fragrance. 'I wanted to go where I felt at home and loved and welcome. I wanted to come here. Doing what my heart tells me is right, and not what other people and my fears tell me to do. Not any longer.'

Sam shook his head. 'I cannot believe that you came back. Hell, Amber, the same thing could happen again. Or there could be another tropical disease.'

'Or I could get knocked over by a London bus. It happens. And I'm okay with that—because this is where I want to be, Sam. This makes me happy.'

Her fingertips stroked his cheek before she tapped him on the end of his nose. 'I could have woken up with permanent brain damage or deafness, but I didn't. I don't know what I am going to do with the rest of my life but I know that I cannot go back to the life I had been living. I am so grateful for every new day that I am alive.'

She gestured towards the coconut palms. 'I have a roof over my head and food I can pick off the trees if I get hungry. And there is enough work here to last a lifetime.'

'You want to stay here? For good?' Sam asked with a look of total astonishment and disbelief.

'I've decided that I want to be happy. I choose to be happy. Whatever problems I have in my own life—sharing the magic and beauty of music with these girls and seeing the glow of excitement in my students' eyes makes everything worthwhile again. Small gestures. A hug. A smile. A kiss. A surprise when they are least expecting it. That is how I want to spend my life.'

Amber stopped talking and grinned at him as Sam sighed in exasperation.

'And I have you to thank for all of this, Sam. Now, don't look so surprised. Remember what you said over lunch at the penthouse? You challenged me to come here for Parvita's wedding and somehow I found the courage to take that first step and make it happen. Thank you. It's been a long journey, Sam.'

'Right back at you. We've both come a long way to get to this place.'

Then he looked around him, from the coconut palms to the beach, and laughed out loud. 'And what a place. You always did have great taste, girl, but this would take some beating. In fact, this village had got me thinking.'

'And I thought the burning smell was from the road. What are those trucks burning? Cooking oil?'

'Funny girl. And yes, they might be burning cooking oil, but actually I was thinking more along the lines of a series of articles about regional development and the culture of Southern India. What do you think? It could be a winner and the paper would cover all of the costs. Providing, of course, I could find someone who was willing to put me up around here. Know any local hotels or guest houses?'

Sam was so close that all she could focus on was the gentle rise and fall of his chest and the caress of the warm breeze on her skin. Time fell still so that she could capture the moment.

'What do you say, Amber?' he asked, his pale blue eyes smiling into hers, and with just a touch of anxiety in his voice. 'Could you put up with me if I came back here to stay for a while? Say yes. Say that you will let me be part of your life. And you know that I am not just talking about a few weeks. I want to be with you for the long haul.'

Say yes to having Sam in her life? Here in India at the school?

'Are you sure?' she asked, her voice hoarse and almost a whisper. 'I thought that your life was going to be in the London office from now on. It's your dream job. Don't you want that editor's chair any more?'

Sam replied by sliding his long, strong, clever fingers between hers and locking them there. Tight. His smile widened as his gaze scanned her face as though he was looking for something, and he must have found it because his grin widened into an expression of such joy and happiness that was so infectious that she had to smile in return.

'A clever woman has shown me that it is possible to go beyond your dream and never stop following your passion until you know what you finally want. I like that idea. I like it a lot. Almost as much as I like those girls of yours.'

He snorted out loud. 'You never thought that you would hear me admit to loving kids. But there is something about this place. And about you, Amber DuBois. In fact, this might not be the comfiest chair I have ever sat on,' Sam said as he patted the log, 'but I do know what I want. And I'm looking at what I want at this very minute.'

And just to make sure that she got the message, Sam bent forward and tapped her on the end of the nose with the soft pad of his forefinger.

'That's you, by the way,' he said in a voice that could have melted an iceberg, 'in case you're not keeping up.' And then he sat back up straight and winked at her.

Amber blinked and tried to take it all in.

The school.

Her dream.

Her Sam.

This was a chance of happiness with this man who she thought she had lost ten years ago. This amazing man who had come back into her life only a few weeks ago, and yet at that moment she felt even more connected to him than she had ever done before.

She felt as though they were two parts of one whole heart and soul. She had known happiness in her music and her teaching but nothing compared to this.

Could she do it? Could she take him back and take a risk on heartbreak?

Sam was holding her dream out to her, and all she had to do was say yes and it would be hers.

And that thought was so overwhelming she faltered.

Amber inhaled a deep breath and tried to keep calm, which was rather difficult when Sam was only inches away from her, the fine blue linen of his shirt pressed against her tunic, begging her to hold him and kiss him and never let him go.

'Why me? We tried to be together once before and it didn't work. And we both know how hard long distance relationships can be.'

Amber let out a long slow breath as his fingertips moved over her forehead and ran down through her hair, sliding off her hair barrette before coming to rest on her shoulder.

'You're right. We would be spending time apart. But it would be worth it.'

His forehead pressed against hers. 'You are the only woman I want in my life. I lost you once, Amber. I can't stand the idea of losing you again.'

'I know. And I want you too. Very much. It's just...'

'Just what—go on. Please, I want to know what is holding you back and what I can do to help you.'

'It has taken me ten years to build up all of these heavy barriers around my heart to protect it from being broken again by being rejected and abandoned. You were the only man that I ever let into my world. The only one. I fell in love with your passion and your fire and I was pulled towards you like a moth to a flame. Rico and Mark had that same spark and I knew that I could get burnt, but I couldn't help but be drawn to them. You had ruined me for ordinary men, and I have only just realised it. I want to give you my heart, Sam. *Truly*. I do. But I'm scared that it would never recover if it was broken again this time. That's why I'm scared of making this leap.'

'All or nothing. It's the same for me. So here is the plan. We both know what hard work is like. So we work at our relationship and make our love part of the joy we find in everything that we do. We might not be in the same room or even the same country but we would still be together. We can make this work. I believe it.'

'*All or nothing*. Oh, Sam.'

Suddenly it was all too much too soon to take in.

She looked across at the new school building and was instantly transported into what life could be like. The school. Her concerts. And then, maybe, the tantalising prospect of playing with the girls in the lovely garden of the orphanage with Sam by her side.

By reaching up and taking hold of Sam's hand in hers, she managed to regain some control of herself before words were possible. His fingers meshed into hers, and he raised one hand to his lips and gently kissed her wrinkly dry-skinned knuckles before replying.

'I know a good opportunity when I see one and, from what I've seen, we would make a great team. You can do this, Amber. You can teach and run this school. I know you can.'

The pressure in her chest was almost too much to bear as she looked into his face and saw that he meant it. He believed in her!

'You would do that? You would fly back to India just to be with me now and then?'

'If it meant I could be with you and the girls? In a heartbeat. You are bound to spend some time in London, especially over the monsoon season. And the rest of the time we have these amazing new-fangled technical inventions which mean that I can see you and talk to you any time I want. In fact I intend to make myself the biggest pest you could imagine.'

His presence was so powerful, so dominating, that she slid her fingers away from below his and pushed herself off the log and onto the hot sand on unsteady legs. Sam was instantly on his feet and his fingers meshed with hers and held them to his own chest as it rose and fell under her palm.

She forced herself to look up into his face, and what she saw there took her breath away. Any doubt that this man cared about her flashed away in an instant.

No pity, no excuses, no apologies. Just a smouldering inner fire. Focused totally on her. She could sense the pressure. Trembling, hesitant, but loving.

He was the flame that had set her world on fire. Nothing would ever be the same again.

Which was why she said the only words she could.

'Yes, Sam. Yes. You are the only man I want in my

life—the only man that I have ever wanted in my life. I want you and I need you and I never want us to be torn apart again. Never again. Do you understand that?'

Sam looked into those perfect violet-blue eyes which were brimming with tears of joy and happiness and fell in love all over again. All of the clever and witty things he had intended to say to make her laugh and look at him drifted away onto the sea breeze, taking doubt and apprehension with them.

This was it. He had finally found a woman he wanted to be with. As a girl, Amber had taught him what the overwhelming power of love could be like. But Amber the woman was a revelation. She was so beautiful his breath caught in his throat just at the sight of her.

And now this woman, this stunning, clever, open and giving woman, had just told him that she wanted to be with him as much as he wanted to be with her.

And, for once, words failed him.

How could he have known that the path to happiness led right back to the first girl that he had ever kissed and meant it? How ironic was that?

Frank Evans and that editor's desk were not important any longer.

All that mattered was this woman, looking at him with tears in her eyes. This was where he wanted to be. Needed to be. With Amber.

He dared not speak and break the magic of that moment, that precious link that bound him to Amber for this tiny second in time. But he could move closer, closer, to that stunning face. Those eyes filled with the love and tenderness he had only imagined was destined for other men. And now she was here. And he loved her. This was no teenage crush but a tsunami of love which was more shocking and startling but destined to last.

He. Loved. Her.

Finally. It had happened. He had known lust and attraction. But the sensation was so deep and overwhelming that the great loner Sam Richards floundered.

He was in love.

The lyrics of every love song he had ever heard suddenly made perfect sense.

Without thinking, his hands moved slowly up from her arm to her throat, to cradle her soft and fragile face, gently, his fingers spreading out wide. As her eyes closed at his touch, he had to blink away his own tears as he moved closer, so that his body was touching hers, his nose pressed against her cheek, his mouth nuzzling her upper lip, as his fingers moved back to clasp the back of her head, drawing her closer to him.

She smelt of every perfume shop he had ever been into, blended with spice and vanilla and something in her hair. Coconut. The overall effect was more than intoxicating; he wanted to capture it for ever, bottle it so that he could relive this moment in time whenever he wanted.

And then her mouth was pressing hotter and hotter into his, his pulse racing to match hers. Her hand was on his chest, then around his neck, caressing his skin at the base of his skull so gently he thought he would go mad with wanting her, needing her to know how much he cared.

Maybe that was why he broke away first, leaning back just far enough so that he could stroke the glint of tears away from her cheeks with the pads of his thumbs.

'Why didn't you tell me that you were still recovering

from meningitis when you came to my dad's garage in London? I could have swept you away to a long holiday in California.'

Amber grinned despite the turmoil inside her heart. 'Each day is a new day for me. A new start. It could have been a lot worse. Instead of which, I am here with you. Who needs a holiday? I am just grateful to be in one more or less working piece.'

She pressed her head into his shoulder as his arms wrapped around her body, revelling in the touch of his hands on her skin, the softness of his shirt on her cheek, and the way his hand moved to caress her hair.

'Me too. I understand that you want your independence. I get that. But when you need help, you have to know that I am right here. I am not going anywhere without you in my life.'

He was kissing her now, pressing his soft lips over and over again against her throat, and tilting his head so he could reach the sensitive skin on her collarbone without crushing her plastered wrist and hand.

His mouth slid slowly against her hot, moist skin and nuzzled away at the shoulder strap of her dress. Her eyes closed and she leant back just a little further, arching her back against his strong arm, which had slid down her back to her hips.

Amber stopped breathing and inwardly screamed in frustration when his lips slid away and she could no longer inhale his spicy aromatic scent.

His hot breath still warmed the skin on one side of her neck, and she knew that he was watching her. And her heart and mind sang.

Amber closed her eyes tight shut and focused on the

sound of her own breathing. Only it was rather difficult when the man she wanted to be with was holding her so lovingly.

Tempting her. Tempting her so badly she could taste it. She wanted him just as much as he wanted her.

His voice was hoarse, low, intense and warm with laughter and affection, and something much more fundamental.

'I have an idea.'

'Umm,' was all she could manage. His fingers were still moving in wide circles on her back.

'Let's hold our own private concert. Just the two of us. Your place is closer. I'm sure the girls would understand. But, one way or another, we need to get off this beach before we get arrested for bad behaviour and setting a bad example for the girls.'

The girls! The concert!

Amber opened her eyes, shook her head once from side to side and chuckled into his shoulder. 'Are you mad? They would never forgive us! I promised them a little Mozart if they had done their piano practice.'

Then she raised her eyebrows coquettishly as Sam groaned in disappointment.

'Maybe—' she took a breath '—you could escort me home afterwards, Mr Richards?'

The air escaped from his lungs in a slow, shuddering hot breath against her forehead, and he lowered both hands to her waist.

'It would be my pleasure. Do you think they would notice if we skipped dessert? My stomach is not used to those syrupy sweets yet.'

'That sounds wonderful. Although I will have to insist on having an early night.'

The brilliant grin grew wider, although she could still sense the thumping of his heart in tune with hers. 'I'm sure we could manage that.'

Then the reality of what he was asking hit her hard. 'Oh, I'm sorry, Sam. I completely forgot. I arranged a meeting with the local governors after the concert. They are keen to organise some legal guardians for the new babies who are still being brought in every week. They are so adorable I'm tempted to offer to put my name down. But that wouldn't be fair on them with my life being so unsettled at the moment. Looks like I shall have to wait to have my own children.'

As soon as the words left her mouth, she regretted them. 'But we have a few hours tomorrow before you fly back, and I'll be in London in a few weeks. The time will fly by.'

The man who had been holding her so lovingly, unwilling to let her move out of his touch, stepped back. Moved away. Not physically, but emotionally.

The precious moment was gone. Trampled to fragments.

His face closed down before her eyes. The warmth was gone, and she cursed herself for being so clumsy. She had lost him.

It took her a few seconds to form the words of the question she had to ask, but was almost too afraid what the answer would be.

'You don't want children, do you?' Her voice quivered just enough to form the syllables, but she held her breath until he answered.

Sam shook his head slowly as his chin dropped so their foreheads were touching. His breath was hot against her skin as the words came stumbling out. 'No, my darling, I have never wanted a family. I want you, and only you. Can you understand that?'

Amber took a slow breath and squeezed her eyes tight shut, blinking away the tears. 'And I want you. So very much. I had given up hope of ever finding someone to love. Only I so want to have children of my own. You would be a wonderful father, Sam, and I know that we could make a family. Besides, you're forgetting one big thing. We aren't our parents. We're us. And we can make our own happiness. I just know it.'

'A family? Oh, Amber.'

'I saw you working with the girls, Sam,' Amber replied with a smile. 'You were wonderful and I know that any child would be lucky to have you as their dad.'

His back straightened and he drew back, physically holding her away from him. Her hands slid down his arms, desperate to hold onto the intensity of their connection, and her words babbled out in confusion and fear.

'Let's not talk about it now. You are going to have a busy few days at the paper. And your dad will be back from holiday. That is something for you to look forward to.'

He turned away from her now, and looked out onto the shore and the distant horizon, one hand still firmly clasped around hers.

'Children need stability and love. I saw what happened when my parents divorced and so did you. The kids always suffer when a relationship breaks down and I would hate that to happen to us.'

The bitterness in his voice was such a contrast to the loving man she had just been holding. The world stilled, and the temperature of the air seemed to cool, as though a cold wind had blown between them.

She stepped back and wrapped her arm around her waist, closing down, moving away from the hot flames that would burn her up if she kissed him again, held him close to her again.

'Oh, Sam. Are you really telling me that you don't believe that we could stay together and make our marriage work?'

'I love you so much and I don't want to lose you. But I can't wipe away twenty years of resentment in a few days. Maybe you're right but it's going to take me a lot longer than that. We have each other. We don't need a piece of paper or children to make us a couple. You are all I need.'

She raised both of her hands in the air so that Sam couldn't grab hold of them.

'You're breaking my heart, Sam. Is it wrong to give a child a loving home with two parents, in this hard and cruel world? Can't you see that is part of my new dream?'

'Amber! I need some time.'

She paused and spoke very slowly, with something in her voice he had never heard before and did not ever want to hear again.

'Oh, don't worry. I'll get through the concert tonight and see you off at the airport tomorrow with a smile on my face. I care about you so much, but I have to protect myself from more heartbreak down the road. So it might be best to stop this now. You have your life thousands of miles away, but this in my new home and I don't want to give it up. If you care about me, then let me go, Sam. Let me go.'

The only thing that stopped Sam from running after her was the heartbreak in her words and the unavoidable truth that he did care about her enough to stand, frozen, and watch her walk away across the sand.

FIFTEEN

Sam waited impatiently in the baggage reclaim area as more bags were unloaded from his flight. He slung his laptop bag over one shoulder and rolled back his shoulders as the time difference and lack of sleep started to kick in.

The huge echoing hall was jam packed with families and people of all shapes and sizes from his flight, all jostling to find their luggage and get back to their normal lives.

He closed his eyes for a moment, then blinked them open again. He was used to air travel—that was part of his job, but that didn't mean to say that he liked it.

Especially not tonight.

It was hard to believe that only sixteen hours earlier

he had been sitting on the beach looking out over the ocean with the morning sun on his face and the colour and life and energy of India whizzing around him. Now he was back in this white, cold, sterile land in a city of stone and glass which he called home.

And he had never felt as lonely in his life.

Amber had kept her word and travelled with him to the airport but her forced smile and tense face only served to make him feel even more uncomfortable and awkward. Their easy friendliness and connection felt strained to the point of snapping completely.

When he wrapped his arms around her to kiss her goodbye, Amber's gentle tears had almost broken his resolve. It would have been so easy to forget all about the flight and the London job and find some way of working as a freelance in India. Other people did it and so could he.

But how would that change the way he felt? Staying would only prolong the agony for both of them. It was up to him to have the strength to walk away.

Over the past ten restless hours in the cramped aircraft seat where sleep was impossible, he had come to the conclusion that Amber was the strong one. She had the courage to change her life for the better and do something remarkable that she was passionate about, and he couldn't be more proud of her. He counted himself lucky to know her. Care about her. Love her.

He had loved working with those girls at the orphanage. Loved being part of Amber's life and sharing her world.

The fact that she actually cared about him in return was something he was still trying to deal with.

So what was the problem?

He was scared of not being worthy of her love.

Scared about not being the man and husband she wanted and needed.

He was scared of letting her down.

He cared enough for her to leave her and walk away from the pain he would cause if he stayed—but he already missed her more than he'd ever thought possible. An Amber-shaped hole had formed in his heart and the only person who could fill it was thousands of miles away, teaching little girls how to make music.

A huge over-stuffed suitcase nudged his foot and Sam turned around to see a gorgeous toddler grinning up at him, followed by a laughing man about his age who swung the giggling child up into his arms and hugged him and hugged him again then apologised profusely but Sam let it go with a smile and jogged forwards to grab his bag off the belt before it went around again.

He had to smile because at that moment his throat was so tight he wouldn't have been able to talk even if he had wanted to.

That was the life that he had turned his back on.

He glanced back over one shoulder. A pretty pregnant blonde girl had her arm looped around her lucky partner's waist. And just for a second she looked like Amber, and his heart contracted at the sight of her.

Amber wanted to be a mother so much. And she would be.

How was he going to feel when another man had made her his wife and given her children, when he knew that Amber had loved him and offered him her life and her soul?

And he had turned down the chance of a family life with the only woman he had ever loved. Why?

The answer screamed back at him so loudly that he was surprised that the other passengers didn't hear it above the sound of the tannoy.

Because he was a coward.

Which made him the biggest fool in the world.

Sam strolled out through the customs area and peered around the cluster of people waiting impatiently in the arrivals hall at Heathrow Airport, looking for the familiar face of his father. And there he was, one hand raised in a friendly wave.

Sam had never been so grateful to see a friendly face after a long exhausting flight.

A quick back slap and a greeting and they were on their way to the car park and a small family hatchback that Sam had never seen before.

'What's this, Dad? Don't tell me that you have finally got around to buying yourself a little runabout to take you to the supermarket? About time.'

'Don't be so cheeky. No, I borrowed it from your Auntie Irene.'

'Auntie Irene? I thought my lovely godmother was living in France these days?'

'She moved back to London about six months ago, so she's renting out her house in the Alps as a holiday let. And it's a great place. I know I enjoyed it. The views are unbelievable.'

'Ah, so that was why you chose the Alps. And here I was thinking it was all about driving around those hairpin bends and mountain roads. You don't get a lot of that around London. Or are you getting too long in the tooth for that kind of driving?'

His dad snorted a reply as he loaded Sam's bag into the boot and closed down the lid. 'Hey. Watch it on the "too old" bit. And, as a matter of fact, we did squeeze in a driving tour around the lakes, then went over to Switzerland for a few days. We had a great time.'

Sam's eyebrows headed north as he fitted his seatbelt in the passenger front seat. 'We? I thought you went on your own.'

His father started to say something, then paused. 'I'll tell you about that when we get home,' he replied and reached forward to turn the key in the ignition.

Sam rested his hand lightly on his father's wrist and looked into his startled face.

'Dad, I have just had a very long flight after an exhausting few days with Amber DuBois. And I have come to one very startling conclusion. If you need to say something, then just say it. Please. So. What is it? What do you have to tell me?'

'Okay, son,' his dad replied with just enough lift in his chin for Sam to inhale slowly so that he was prepared for whatever was coming.

'It's your Aunt Irene. Over these past few months we have been seeing a lot of each other one way or another. She needed someone to help her settle into the town house I had just renovated and it's just two streets away from the garage, so it made sense for me to show her how things have changed around our part of London in the past twenty years.'

He took a breath and licked his lips before going on.

'Do you remember when Irene used to come around

to the house to see your mum and take you out when you were little?'

'Auntie Irene. Yes, of course. She was mum's best friend. I always knew that we weren't related but she liked being called Auntie Irene and I didn't have any other aunties or uncles. I missed her when she went to France. And I still don't see where this is going.'

'Then I'll make it clear. Irene invited me to stay at her home in France to have a bit of a holiday and, well, when we were away, she finally confessed to me that she had been in love with me for years. Before I married your mum we all used to go out in a big group of friends together. But she knew that I only had eyes for your mum, so she didn't tell me how she felt. But in the end it was too hard to watch our marriage fall apart so she moved away.'

He shot Sam a glance. 'She hated leaving you. But she couldn't stay.'

Sam blew out a long whistle. 'Is that why she never married? I always wondered if she had a secret boyfriend in France somewhere.'

'She had a couple of relationships but never met anyone else.'

'So Auntie Irene has been burning a candle for you for thirty years. Did you know? Or even suspect?'

His dad nodded quickly. 'About a year after I divorced your mum, Irene turned up at the garage one day out of the blue. She cooked us both that lovely French meal. Do you remember that? After you had gone to bed, she asked me if I wanted her to stay and take your mother's place. And I said no.'

'You turned her down,' Sam said in a low voice.

'Wrong time. I was still hurting and you needed me to be there for you. So I sent her back to France.'

He banged the heel of his hand against his forehead.

'I was a fool. I lost the woman who loved me and who had always cared about me as a friend. I have spent the last years alone when I could have shared them with Irene and had some happiness. But these past few weeks have shown me that it's not too late. She is a wonderful woman, Sam, and I have decided to take a chance on love for the second time in my life. I hope that is okay with you.'

'Okay? You don't need to ask my permission. I think that it's fantastic. Good luck to you. Good luck to both of you.'

'Thanks, son. Right. Let's get this car started. Because I want to hear exactly what you have done this time to mess up your chance of happiness with Amber. And I won't take no for an answer. Oh, and you had better get used to seeing Irene around—she's moving in. So. Start talking. And there's your first edition of the paper if you want to catch up with the latest. I think I saw something about Amber in it.'

'What?' Sam picked up the paper and turned the pages until he found it. It was the photo he had taken of Amber on the beach.

His blood ran cold and the more he read the more chilled he became.

It might be his photograph but he had not written one word of this article.

Frank had given the fluff piece to someone else to write. And that was so wrong that he didn't even know where to start.

He snatched up the paper and started reading, desperate to find out how bad it was.

He couldn't believe it. Frank had taken the quotes and twisted them around to portray Amber as a shallow, selfish woman who was creating a vanity project for her own glory—just the opposite of what Sam had intended. His idea had been twisted around to focus on Amber and how foolish she was to risk her health and try to teach with a broken wrist.

'Son, are you okay? What's happened?'

'Frank Evans has sold me out,' Sam replied in a low voice, the paper on his lap. 'This is not about Amber, this is about rumours and lies and half-truths for a headline. And it makes me feel sick to my stomach.'

He looked up at his father and took a breath. 'Dad, I need your help. But before that I need to say something and say it now. I was a brat when Mum left. And I am sorry for making your life such a misery. I truly am. Can you forgive me for that?'

His dad shook his head and smiled. 'I've waited a long time for you to grow up. Looks like it's finally happened. Past history. What do you need?'

Sam exhaled long and slow and stared out of the car window. 'A family house with a garden where Amber can play with our kids.'

The silence in the car was so thick that it was hard to breathe, but it was his dad who finally broke it by asking, 'Do you love Amber that much?'

'She is the only woman I have ever loved and ever will love. It has taken me ten years to realise that. I can't lose her again now.'

The instant the words came out of his mouth Sam realised what he had just said and chuckled. It was the truth and he had been a fool to pretend otherwise.

'Then I have just the house for you. Welcome home, son. Welcome home.'

SIXTEEN

From: Amber@AmberDuBois.net
To: Kate@LondonBespokeTailoring.com; Saskia@Elwood-House.co.uk
Subject: On my way back to London
The June monsoon rains came! At last. And how. We are flooded out and the girls have either been sent home for a few weeks or moved to the old school further inland. Any building work has stopped and the lads have taken off.
   I am just waiting for my connecting flight back to London and should be with you for breakfast tomorrow. Cannot wait to catch up. See ya soon. Amber

From: Kate@LondonBespokeTailoring.com
To: Amber@AmberDuBois.net
Subject: On my way back to London
Brilliant—but do not read the newspaper at the airport. Seriously. Don't. We need to talk first. K

Amber strolled into Saskia's kitchen conservatory room, yawning loudly, her good hand stretched tall above her head. There was no sign of Kate or Saskia but, instead, stretched out on a lounger with his feet up and a steaming cup in his hand was Sam Richards.

He looked as casual, cool and collected as if he had just come from a business meeting. Come to think of it, he was wearing a suit and a shirt with a tie.

Amber glanced back towards the hallway. 'How did you get in? Saskia is going to have a fit if she sees you here, drinking her coffee.'

'I climbed over the garden gate,' Sam replied with a quick nod. 'They might want to think about making it a little taller. I can still clamber over, even at my age. Although I probably have dirt on my trousers.'

'Which you are now putting onto her favourite lounger. Sheesh. What cheek.'

Amber peered at his jacket, then physically recoiled. 'Has anyone ever told you that you have the worst taste in suits? Our Kate needs to take you in hand.'

He smiled up and waved his coffee mug in her direction.

His gaze slid up from Amber's unpainted toenails to the tip of her bed-head and gave a low growl of appreciation at the back of his throat to indicate how much he liked what he saw.

Amber instantly tugged the front edges of her thin silk pyjama jacket closer together as her neck flared with embarrassment.

'A lovely sunny good morning to you too. And thank you for a warm welcome. And, as for the lovely Miss Lovat? Kate may have called me to let me know that you have come back to escape the monsoon rain, but Kate is not the woman I want to take me in hand,' he whispered, and then spoilt the moment by wagging his eyebrows up and down. His meaning only too obvious.

Amber's heart soared but her head took over.

He seemed determined to make leaving him even more difficult than it would be already.

'Are you always this much trouble in the mornings?' she asked.

'Want to find out?' he replied in a low husky voice.

Amber dropped her head back and rolled her shoulders.

'What? No. You do not do this to me on my first morning back from India. Especially when I am not awake yet.'

She blinked several times. 'Wait a minute. Did you just say that Kate called you? That is not possible. Because you are officially off our nice man list. You snake. Your magazine did a real hatchet job on me. You have no right to interfere with my head like this. In fact, I shouldn't even be talking to you.'

'Of course you should. I am the new media and fund-raising manager for the Elwood School.'

'Oh, no, you are not. We don't need a media... Wait a minute, okay, maybe the school does need a fund-raising manager but the last person I would choose would be an investigative journalist with a chip on his shoulder the size of a pine tree who delights in stitching me up. Sorry.' She peered at him and sniffed. 'Nice tie. Best of luck with your job interview. Are you going to your newspaper today?'

'Already been. I had a little chat with the editor in chief and we agreed that I should leave the magazine to explore creative opportunities outside of GlobalStar Media.'

Her eyes shot open and she slumped down on the edge of the sofa. 'Oh, no, Sam. You've been sacked.'

'Actually, I resigned. I didn't like the way they changed the meaning of your article without asking me first. Let's just say that we had an honest and open discussion.'

'You stomped out.'

Sam touched two fingers to his forehead. 'I stomped out.'

'Oh...but what are you going to do? Your dad is so proud of your new job—this is what you've been working for.'

'My dad is back home and when I left this morning my godmother was making him breakfast and giving him a cuddle. My dad is in heaven and loving every minute of it—and my lovely Auntie Irene is the wealthiest woman I know. The last thing he needs is an out of work layabout of a son cluttering up his love life.'

'Oh, I am pleased; I like him so much. He deserves some happiness.'

Sam raised both hands and gave a flourish from his lounging position.

'At last we have something we both agree on. And in case you were wondering, he has always liked you too. You should be grateful, you know. There are plenty of other job opportunities for a man of my experience in this town. I could even work with my dad in his new property development business. But no, I came here to offer you my services before anyone else snapped me up.'

She flashed him a freezer stare but it was obvious from his smug smile that Sam had no intention of doing anything other than what he wanted or letting her get a word in sideways.

'Your ploy to drive me away will not work. Not listening. We are officially working on this together. Full-time job. Sorted. You see, I have been thinking about our last discussion—' he nodded, his brows tight together '—and it seems to me to point one way.'

'Ah. Thinking.' Amber smirked and pretended to waft away some horrible smoke from in front of her face.

'Funny girl. But not always a clever one. In fact, after several hours of deep consideration, I have come to a serious conclusion.'

Sam swung his legs off the sofa and pointed to Amber. 'Amber DuBois, I have decided to appoint myself the job and save you the time and effort in advertising and then going through a series of tedious interviews before deciding that I am the one and only candidate.'

He flung one hand towards her, palm upwards. 'I know. It is not a job for the faint of heart, and it would mean giving up my dream of joining the astronaut programme, but I am willing to take on the task. I am the man to do it. Starting today.' He beamed a wide-mouthed grin. 'What do you think of that?'

'What do I think?' Amber replied and started pacing the floor, her eyes wide. 'I think you need to cut down on the dose of whatever you are taking because it is making you quite delusional. I have never heard such arrogance in my life—and I'm used to working with prima donnas in major orchestras.'

'It's okay, you can thank me later.' Sam shrugged.

'Thank you? Oh, I don't think so. Now, listen to me when I explain, Are you listening? Good. First, I do not need help finding a project manager. Full stop. I am quite capable of taking care of myself and when my wrist heals

I shall be back on fighting form. And second, you never had any intention of joining the astronaut programme. You only sent off for the forms from NASA so that you could impress your science teacher with your knowledge of hydrogen and hydrazine.'

'You remembered—' Sam grinned '—how sweet.'

'Of course I remembered. I think you only did it because Heath was thinking of being a pilot for all of two days and the girls in my school thought that was amazing. Astronaut, indeed. As if anyone would be impressed by that.'

'Did it impress you?'

Amber paused just long enough for Sam to sit back smirking. 'I thought so. And you're missing the point. You need someone to take care of the business side of the project because you are going to be busy with Parvita and the other girls in the school.'

'We already have cooks and housekeepers and an office receptionist, thank you. I'm not sure how many, but plenty.'

'Ah, I had better add that to the job description.' He tugged a smartphone out of his pocket and began keying in as he spoke. 'Sort out staffing. Got it.'

'Job description? What job description?' Amber asked, blinking in confusion.

'The one I came up with during my thinking session—you know, the one you should be writing if you were not so very confident that you can do everything yourself.'

'What makes you so sure that I can't do everything myself? I have managed very well so far, thank you.'

'Have you? Have you really, Amber?' He pointed to

her wrist. 'Look at you. Your hand is hurting and you're hardly sleeping. You are worrying like mad about the girls in Kerala, even though you talk to them every day, and now you are intent on going over there and making things worse by barging in with the best intentions when your architect is quite capable of sorting things out himself.'

'What?' Amber called out and raised her hand into the air in a rush, blinking and shaking her head in disbelief. 'He has problems and is asking for answers based on out of focus photographs. I feel so accountable. I need to go there and see for myself and take responsibility for the project. I have to make sure the money isn't wasted on work that has to be repeated and...oh.'

She only wobbled for a fraction of a second before Sam took her hand and half tugged, half helped her across to the dining table.

'Sit. Head between your knees. Deep breaths. Then breakfast. Here. Finish my coffee.'

'Well, this is embarrassing.' She sniffed as she lowered her head and tried to stop feeling dizzy.

'Not for me. It's actually rather satisfying.'

Sam slid onto the fine oak floor and sat cross-legged so that his face was more or less in line with hers.

'Now. About this job interview. I may have just proved my point that you need someone to help talk to the architects and works manager and all of the suppliers and the like while you do what you do best. Teach. Play your piano and fill those girls' heads with the sounds of wonderful music that they will never forget. Because that is what happens when I hear you play. You transport me to a better place. A place where I want to stay and never leave.'

'I do?'

'Every time. You always did. Probably always will. Those girls are going to have a wonderful teacher. The best. And I want to help you to make that happen. If you will let me.'

He turned his head and flashed her a full strength beaming smile. 'Will you let me, Amber? Will you let me work with you and travel with you and be part of your life?'

He nodded towards the sofa. 'I have my laptop in my briefcase and can print out my resumé if you like.'

'You might get bored without your career,' Amber countered. 'It's been your life.'

'No chance. Not around you. And look who's talking.'

Amber sat up slowly in her hard dining chair and stretched out both hands and took hold of Sam, who stayed exactly where he was.

She could tell that his breathing had speeded up to match hers.

This was it. This was where she had to make the decision.

'You know that I want to take over from Parvita some time soon. After what happened...are you ready to move away and be accountable for a whole school-load of children? Because I don't want to bring you into their lives only for you to take off. That wouldn't be fair, Sam. On them or you. On any of us.'

'I know,' he replied in a serious voice that she had never heard him use before. 'And I wouldn't be offering unless I was in it for the long haul. I mean it, Amber. I want to help you run this school. You can do it on your own, I have no doubt about that, but with the two of us... we could achieve some remarkable things.'

'Are we still talking about the project manager's job?' she asked, smiling.

'What do you think?'

'I think that you care about me, but I would need a lot more than that.' Amber took a breath. 'I need to know how you feel before I agree to have you in my life. Working with you is one thing, but more than that is just setting me up for heartbreak, and I don't know if I am up for it.'

'Hate to break the news to you, gorgeous, but I am already in your life. And I am not going anywhere. From the second you walked into my dad's garage that day I have felt an overwhelming sense of recognition and connection. I have absolutely no intention of letting you go again. And, from what I saw, that orphanage needs someone who is handy with a car repair kit and those girls could use someone to teach IT and my version of English. I can probably fit all of that in around my freelance writing work.'

'I'm scared, Sam.'

Sam silenced her by pressing his fingertips to her lips. 'I know. But you haven't heard the rest of the offer. My dad has just finished renovating a sweet little two bedroom terraced house within walking distance of where we are sitting.' His lips turned up into a smile. 'The whole place is about the size of your penthouse living room. But it has a garden. A garden fit for children and pets. And all it needs is a little love to make it a family home. It's ours. All you have to do is say the word.'

He stood up and pressed one hand onto each of her shoulders.

'I should be going. My dad needs me to help him plaster a wall. But you know where to find me when you decide that you are crazy in love with me after all. And Amber, don't wait another ten years. Be seeing ya.'

And, before Amber had a chance to reply or even move from her chair, Sam had started walking back into the kitchen.

He was leaving.

And this time it was through the front door.

Amber shuffled off her chair and opened her mouth to reply, then closed it again. This was it. Decision time. She had to take Sam as he was, faults and all, or risk losing him for ever.

Wait a minute. He had just offered her a home. A real home. *Their home. With a garden fit for children and pets.*

He understood. He understood everything.

She did need him. But she wanted him more.

'Sam. Wait.'

His steps slowed until he was more shuffling forward instead of striding.

'Stay. Please. Stay.'

Sam turned around just in time to catch her in his arms as she flung herself at him, her arms around his neck.

Her feet swung up into a perfect curve as he lifted her high off the ground, his arms wrapped tight around her waist as he pressed his lips to her forehead, eyes, then onto the waiting hot lips with all of the tender passion that Amber had been dreaming about most of that night.

The energy and passion of his kiss sent her reeling so hard that Amber had to step back and steady herself before leaning into his kiss, focusing her love into that single contact as she closed her eyes and revelled in the glorious sensation.

When she eventually pulled away her eyes were pricking with hot tears.

'It's okay, darling,' Sam laughed. 'It's okay. I'm not going anywhere without you ever again. You want to go to India, I'll go to India. Timbuktu, I'll be there. There's no way you are going to get rid of me.'

She replied with a wide-mouthed grin and her heart sang at the look of love and joy on Sam's face.

'Timbuktu wasn't on my list before but it sounds good to me. Anywhere with you. Oh, God, Sam, I love you so much. I don't care what happens any more. I just know that I love you.'

The tears were real now, her voice shaking with emotion as she forced out the words he needed to hear, afraid that they were getting lost in his shirt as she slid to the ground.

One arm unwound and lifted her chin high enough for their eyes to meet, and her heart melted at what she saw in his eyes as he grinned down at her, eyes glistening in the bright sunlight.

'I've loved you since the moment you stepped out of the limo with your mother at your back all of those years ago. It just took a while for it to sink in.'

He took her face in between the palms of his hands

and confessed, 'I never imagined that I could love another human being on this planet as much as the way I feel at this moment. Come here.'

Somewhere close by was the sound of whooping and hooting from Saskia and Kate but Amber didn't care who saw her kissing the man she loved and would go on loving for the rest of her life.

* * * * *

THE WEDDING DRESS DIARIES
Aimee Carson

ONE

'Can I get you a drink?'

The busty brunette behind the bar at the exclusive Manhattan restaurant was addressing the guy at the end of the counter. And, when Amber spied the man, she did a sharp double take that would surely leave her with a crick in her neck.

Parker Robinson.

Blinking, Amber adjusted to the sight as the sounds of Reese's engagement party faded.

When Parker didn't respond, the bartender repeated, 'Can I get you a drink?'

Attention finally caught, Parker drew the sexy smirk like a gun from a holster. No doubt he wasn't even aware. It was more like an automatic response, like most people would say please or thank you or mutter an excuse me when they accidentally stepped on someone's toe.

'Why, yes, you can,' Parker said.

The brunette puffed up her chest, clearly pleased she'd finally earned an attentive smile, and Amber resisted the urge to roll her eyes. Apparently Reese hadn't exaggerated; her half brother's attitude toward women hadn't changed much since adolescence. Amber had witnessed that grin directed at girls often enough, that knowing twinkle in his eye communicating that females liked what they saw, and he knew it.

A cocky confidence that, on Parker Robinson, was more endearing than annoying.

The sun-streaked blond hair of his teens was now a light brown with leftover golden highlights, like keepsakes from his childhood. He still wore it tousled with soft spikes up front, and the little-boy, rough-and-tumble look totally suited him, hair begging to be tugged. Years ago she'd longed to do just that, to pull him in for a kiss. Had fantasized about him teaching her how. And while his hair hadn't changed much, his masculine features were better defined, cheekbones and jaw now sharp enough to cut cold butter. Yet he straddled youth and maturity with an ease to be envied, that cocky teen housed in the bad-boy adult making a killer combination.

His gaze collided with Amber's and held, and a pit yawned wide beneath her stomach. The brilliant green eyes hadn't faded with time. Pulse pounding, she realized, belatedly, that he'd caught her staring, and the shameful memory barreled into her. The day when he'd called her out on exactly that. But she wasn't the besotted little preteen anymore, the one that had followed him around like an adoring puppy.

'You a friend of Reese's?' he asked.

Amber was proud she didn't laugh out loud. Amazing. Ironic that the guy she'd spent every summer in the Hamptons with from the ages of seven to twelve—the guy she'd loved from the ages of eight to fifteen—didn't even remember her.

Though, in his defense, she'd been in the sixth grade the last time he saw her.

In jeans and a leather jacket the color of burnt butter, Parker picked up his glass and came closer, moving with that easy earthy stroll that came with a confidence few could dream of. It had been captivating on Parker the teen.

On Parker the man, it was absolutely breathtaking.

He slid onto the bar stool next to hers and leaned his elbow on the counter, facing Amber. Parker cleared his throat and lowered his head a little to look up at her face—most likely a *stupefied* face—as if worried her lack of response meant she wasn't completely sane.

Parker seated this close was definitely threatening her sanity.

'Are you a friend of Reese and Dylan's?' he repeated.

It had been fifteen years since she'd seen him, had been close enough to *touch*. She gripped her glass and sipped her wine, hoping she looked more sophisticated than she felt.

Amber managed a nod of her head. 'I've known Reese a long time.' *I've known you a long time.* 'Why would I be at their engagement party if I didn't know them?'

'Could be a party crasher, here for the expensive food and free drinks.'

It was surreal to be having this conversation with her childhood crush, protected by her unknown identity. Because she had plenty to be embarrassed about when it came to Parker.

From the time Reese had asked her to handle her wedding, Amber had been dreading the moment she had to measure this man for his tux—an event that needed to occur soon. But she'd thought she could relax tonight because Reese had said Parker would never show. He hadn't attended any of the other parties for his half sister and her fiancé. So why had he come now?

'Is that why you're here?' she said with a smile. 'For the free food?'

Parker let out a bitter scoff. 'If only.'

He didn't want to be here.

The realization hit her with all the force of a sledgehammer on steroids. It fit with what Reese had told her, the man who refused to have anything to do with the Michael family anymore. Not that Amber could blame him. But ever since her engagement, his sister had been trying to pull him back into, well, if not into the fold, at least within touching distance.

He tipped his head with an almost boyish curiosity. 'Do I know you?' he said, and Amber's heart froze. 'I definitely think I know you.'

He pursed his lips contemplatively, and Amber wished her memory of his mouth hadn't been so spot on. He *did* have the most gorgeous lips in the world. Full. Sinful. Utterly kissable. Pretty savvy of a stupid twelve-year-old to notice, if she did say so herself.

Enjoying the rare sense of power in Parker's presence, she sent him another smile. 'Maybe.'

'A name would be helpful,' he said.

Amber let out an overly thoughtful *hmm,* as if she were seriously considering giving him the information. But suddenly, the moment she'd been dreading, her first meeting with Parker, was more about fun than fear.

'That would be too easy,' she said.

Parker's understanding smile at her tone set her pulse fluttering. 'Okay,' he said, settling in as if for a prolonged conversation, the light in his eyes sizzling. 'I'll bite.'

God, she wished he would.

'Do I know you through your work?' he said.

Amber bit back the smile. 'Could be,' she said with laughter in her tone. 'I used to be a seamstress, but now I own my own bridal shop.'

He actually recoiled as if slapped, and the look on his face as he backpedaled made her laugh. Clearly, Parker Robinson was offended at the thought of frequenting an establishment that dealt with weddings.

'Definitely not through your work,' he said gruffly. 'Maybe through mine?'

Amber pretended not to know. 'What do you do?'

He narrowed his eyes at her. 'I work Homicide down at the fifty-seventh precinct. Maybe I interviewed you as a witness before?'

'Maybe I was once a suspect,' she said as coolly as she could.

The roll of his eyes, that sarcastic 'yeah, right' expression made her suddenly sentimental. She remembered that look from her childhood, and a small part of her was glad he hadn't changed too much.

'Do I look too innocent?' she said.

'No,' he said bluntly. 'I just remember all my perps.' His face grew tight, and a harsh laugh escaped his mouth, and he slid his eyes to somewhere beyond her shoulders. 'And yeah, you look too sweet. But, trust me,' he said with a light tone that he didn't quite pull off. He took a sip of his drink and carefully set the glass down, his tone distant. 'No one is as innocent as they look.'

There was a hard set about his eyes, the crinkles at the edges more about experience than age. A bitter fatigue that had started in his teens and now was fully realized.

That bold green gaze was back on her, intrigued. *Interested*. 'Maybe we attended the same school?'

She shook her head.

'Did we meet at a party once?' he asked.

Enjoying his frustrated curiosity, she sipped her wine. 'Try again.'

His eyes narrowed in thought. 'Well, I know we haven't slept together,' Parker went on, sending her stomach plummeting to her toes.

God, only in her teenage dreams.

'Because, although you're certainly attractive,' he said, 'you're definitely not my type.'

Amber ignored the sudden surge in her pulse and maintained an even tone. 'Is that the *only* reason we couldn't have slept together?' she said. 'Because I'm not your type?'

The reflexive sexy smirk lit up his face.

And as the words finally sank in, she drew back a touch in surprise. 'Wait,' she said. 'What type do you think I am?'

His gaze traveled down her body, leaving her hot in places that normally...weren't. Her A-line dress was simple, with a classic cut. Nothing seductive. No overt 'I'm yours for the taking' in the way it clung to her body.

He hiked a brow dryly. 'You own a bridal shop, which means you believe in the institution of marriage.'

'And you don't?' she said softly, only pretending the statement was a question.

Sure enough, a bitter sound escaped those beautiful lips. Not that Amber could blame him.

'Hell, no,' he said.

Heart bleeding a little for him then, she remembered the day she'd found him by the dock, devastated by his mother's words.

You were a mistake.

Amber had grown up knowing she was wanted. Secure in the knowledge her parents had been devoted to each other, were devoted to *her*. Her dad had died when she was a child, and her mother had loved him so much she'd never remarried. And Amber's bridal store revolved around proving that love existed every day, with every client.

But Parker...

Well, Parker's experiences were opposite in every respect.

And the boy who'd given Amber her first taste of romantic love—*unrequited,* but love nonetheless—had grown into a man who mocked its very existence.

'You've made weddings your business,' he said. 'So, obviously you believe.'

'And that's how you've concluded I'm not your type?' she said. 'Because of the dress I'm wearing and what I do for a living?'

He sat back a bit to study her, no teasing, seductive tone now, but a kind of gaze that could see through your soul. 'No,' he said, shaking his head softly. The thoughtful look on his face was deep and, for the first time, he actually looked at her. *Really* looked at her. 'It's the light in your eyes,' he said with a simple shrug. 'You still believe.'

Her lungs slowly collapsed, forcing the air from her body. Believed in what? In love?

In *life*?

The thought instantly drained from her mind when he shifted closer, and the scent of his leather jacket drifted in the air.

'I can't remember who you are.' Simmering gaze on hers, he said, 'How about throwing a poor guy a hint?'

'Okay,' Amber said. After the years of crushing on Parker the teen, now that he was looking at her as a desirable woman, she wanted to work the moment for all she was worth. 'You once pressed your lips against mine.'

Parker's eyes widened, and he dropped his gaze to her mouth, pulling all the oxygen from the atmosphere. Amber's breathing increased in an attempt to suck in enough air.

'Awesome.' His voice slid lower, like heated silk. 'I approve of my choices.'

He leaned close, his eyes glowing, sparking embers she'd thought long dead—those secret pieces of a young girl in the throes of her first sexual attraction. Not really understanding the full extent of what she felt.

His teasing grin was hot enough to light the Christmas tree at Rockefeller Center. 'Did I get to second base?'

Skin vibrating at the thought, her smile was strained.

'Sorry, only first,' she said.

And technically, it was probably only *half* base, but she was having too much fun to clarify the exact nature of how their lips had touched.

'Did I slip you the tongue?' he said.

'No.'

'My loss,' he said, and his mouth parted a bit, as if imagining righting that previous wrong.

The tiny peek at his tongue sent a shot of adrenaline through her body, surely leaving her glowing. Fine hairs standing on end.

'And as first kisses went,' she pressed on, 'it could have been better.'

Mostly by being *real*.

The offended expression on Parker's face was comical. 'Could have been— Wait...*first* kiss?' He shot her a skeptical look. 'Either this was a really long time ago or you've confused me with someone else.'

'I definitely don't have you confused with someone else.' When he looked at her as though he was beginning to suspect she truly *wasn't* sane, Amber sent him a smile and gave up the pretense. 'I practically grew up at your mother's house because my mom worked as her personal assistant,' she said. 'Which was the fancy title for glorified gofer girl.'

There was a three-heartbeat pause that felt like thirty as Parker's expression remained blank.

'I'm Amber Davis.'

'Amber Davis,' he said slowly, as if pulling the name from a memory long buried. Recognition finally shot through his face, and his shoulders snapped back. 'Well, hell,' he breathed out. 'You're the one who tried to drown.'

TWO

———

Fifteen years earlier
The Hamptons, Long Island, New York

Swimswimswim

Eyes fixed on the dock, the chant rang on and on in Amber's head. She'd lost sight of her paddleboard ages ago, swept away by the Sag Harbor current. Crap, she was *so* getting in trouble for this.

Mom's gonna kill me if I drown.

A fresh slice of panic surged. How was she going to marry Parker now if she died? At the stupid age of twelve. Jeez, she'd never even been kissed before! Frowning, she paddled harder. She should have played Spin the Bottle at Nancy Kruger's last month. Okay, so Amber probably would have been stuck kissing Jimmy Stevens, better known as lizard tongue, but at least she wouldn't be drowning with virgin lips. An epically lame end to the suckage that was her life.

All except for Parker.

Parker.

So what if he was in the eleventh grade and she was only in sixth. She'd loved him since she was eight years old. He'd briefly been replaced with Justin Timberlake from 'N Sync, but even she knew that was pretty unlikely to happen. And Parker was cuter. She wanted to marry him so bad that she'd picked out her wedding dress ages ago. Course, it had taken her four months to whittle it down to her top five favorites. Her obsession with tulle and satin and lace was growing pretty strong. This summer, in a fit of boredom, she'd planned the whole ceremony. Reese would have been her maid of honor cuz she was Parker's half sister and Amber's sort-of friend.

Stupidstupidstupid

Sneaking off and forgetting the life vest. But she'd really *really* wanted to get better on the paddleboard. Mostly cuz she wanted to impress Parker. Last summer he'd taught her how to stand and maneuver a turn, but this summer he was more interested in kissing Susie Frances. Amber scowled. And he never helped her bait a hook or capture crabs anymore.

The current was scarily strong, and the dumb dock was slipping farther away. The chill from the water seeped deeper with every passing minute, despite how hard Amber swam. Teeth chattering, her arms and legs grew heavy. So much so it was a struggle to control them now.

A sob ripped from her throat, and she fought back the fear, closing her eyes.

Giveupgiveupgiveup

Her muscles screamed for a break, her lips quivering, the taste of salt a mix of seawater and frustrated tears. The furious pounding of her heart was now just as much about terror as tiredness, and she was sure her chest was gonna explode.

Her thoughts began to drift and grow foggy. She knew there was something she was supposed to be doing. Swimming? Finding Reese?

'Amber!'

The call shook her out of her daze. God, she really *was* drowning. Was she already in heaven? Now she was hearing Parker calling out her name.

The voice grew closer, the tone urgent. *'Amber.'*

Exhausted, she turned and spied Parker sprawled on his board, sleeves pushed to his elbows as he paddled toward her like a madman. She sucked in a breath, getting a mouthful of salt water that burned her throat, and she coughed and gagged, slipping beneath the surface. The cold closed over her head and she stopped fighting for a moment. It was peaceful. Quiet. And she was so, so tired; it was nice not to fight so hard to keep her head above water.

She drifted, floating, until an arm circled around her chest and heaved her up. She had a vague sensation of being hauled onto something hard, but she couldn't move. It took too much effort to breathe.

And then there were lips on hers and warm breath filling her lungs and she had an overwhelming urge to cough again. She rolled, gagged and then threw up a bunch of salt water that stung as much coming up as going down. Shattered, she collapsed again, drifting in and out, only half-aware as Parker paddled the board for shore and dragged her up on the beach.

That was when the shivering started for real. Water dripped down his nose as Parker gathered her close, fear making deep lines in his forehead. She gazed up at him, dazed, her heart pounding from the feel of his arms cradled around her. The feel of his breath, *Parker's breath,* on her cheek was awesome. But the close-up of his face was just...was just... And as she blinked, her mind clearing, it hit her.

Parker had kissed her!

Her heart fluttered like a hummingbird stuck in a cage. Okay, true, it was more like he'd given her mouth to mouth, but still... She closed her eyes, remembering the hard press of those soft lips she'd been obsessing about for years. Pressed against *hers.*

OMG...it was almost worth drowning for.

His dark blond hair looked brown when wet. A smattering of freckles bridged his nose, and thick lashes framed the prettiest pair of green eyes in the history of *ever.* Eyes that always did funny things to her stomach when they locked on hers. Used to be they'd look at her with patience and, when she was *really* lucky, a hint of fondness. Now that Parker had gotten older there was a lot of irritation. But it wasn't *her* fault his mother made him watch out for her and Reese when Amber's mom wasn't around.

She clutched his arm. 'You can't tell my mom,' she croaked out.

'Aw, come on, Amber.' Parker's face scrunched up tight. 'You nearly freakin' died.'

'I did not.'

He rolled his eyes in that ever-sarcastic 'yeah, right' way of his. 'What if you get sick or something?' he said. 'She needs to know.'

And be grounded? Amber had been looking forward to

summer vacation for *months*. As the daughter of Ms. Michael's personal assistant, Amber had practically grown up in the Michaels' home. Parker never visited his mother in the city anymore, so summer at the Hamptons was the only time she got to see him.

She pulled harder, panicking now. 'If you tell, I'll— I'll—'

Her mind sputtered as she scrambled to come up with a good threat. And then a memory filled her mind. A vision of Parker, lids rimmed red, sniffing as she stumbled on him down by the dock. He'd yelled at her, of course, scrubbing at his face as he'd told her to scram. As always, her heart hurt when Parker got that look in his eyes. And the only person in the world that could make Parker that upset was his mother. It had been a long time since she'd seen him sad about his mom. Lately, his reactions more often resembled anger.

She straightened up. 'I'll tell Susie Frances that I caught you crying like a baby.'

His gaze flashed to hers. 'I was not crying,' he said. 'I got salt water in my eyes, is all.'

They both knew it was a lie, and she fought the temptation to look away. This was too important.

'Fine,' he said. And then he jabbed a finger in front of her face. 'But you have to stop the creepy stalker stuff.'

Heat flaring up her face, she was horrified by the words. Had she been that obvious?

Suddenly, she wished she'd been swallowed up by the waters of Sag Harbor. 'Fine,' she said, mimicking him. But then her bravery ran out, her voice growing small. 'I don't suppose we can find the paddleboard?'

Parker stood, and right away she missed the heat of

his skin. He swiped a hand through his hair, leaving it spikier than usual. 'The board's long gone.'

Jeez, it all seemed so *unfair*. Blinking back the tears, she looked across the water. Petrified Parker would see her cry, she dragged her hand across her eyes and sniffed. Another shiver racked her body, and the rustle of clothing brought her attention back to Parker.

He'd taken off his hoodie. 'Don't worry about it, Ace,' he said gruffly, pulling his sweatshirt down over her head.

Her heart soared, both from the touch and the words and the protective tone in his voice. And she'd always adored his nickname for her. She jabbed her arms into the damp sleeves, savoring the heat from his body, the smell of *Parker*.

'I'll take the blame for the board.' Those too-beautiful lips flattened grimly. A dark look crossed his face. 'My mom already hates me, anyway.'

A needle pricked her heart, the sharp pain familiar. Ms. Michael was all *Reese Reese Reese*, spoiling her daughter rotten. But Parker? He barely even existed in the Michael household. No wonder he chose to live with his dad.

'Thanks,' she said, hoping she wasn't tearing up like a baby again.

His lopsided smile appeared, leaving her weak in the knees as he said, 'Let's get you home.'

Parker gripped his whiskey glass.

Amber Davis.

Discovering the redhead's identity had been like a cattle-prod shock to Parker's nervous system, his mind reeling with the memories of his youth. He struggled to ignore the beautiful woman who'd trailed after him as a kid, hanging on his every word. His every move. The one who'd witnessed his most humiliating moment.

You were a mistake.

Tossing back the rest of his drink, he tried to focus on his goals for tonight. Avoid his mother at all costs, speak to Reese and tell her no and then get the heck out of here.

Attention firmly on him, Amber asked, 'Do you remember—?'

'Yeah,' he said gruffly, fixing his eyes on his empty glass. No way was he letting her finish that question. 'I remember.'

He could feel Amber's gaze, but he needed a minute to adjust. Several of them, actually. Because he sure as hell wasn't ready to face the lady who, years ago, had found him sniffling like a wussy little girl.

Thank God for his cell phone.

Parker glanced at the incoming number flashing in time with the vibration, answering with his pat 'What's up, Robby boy?'

'Why aren't you at Rosie's Bar?'

Parker let out a discontented grunt, longing for the bar that was the watering hole for most of the fifty-seventh precinct. His gaze swept across the elegantly attired guests at the restaurant, the fancy venue most likely chosen for its bird's-eye view of Manhattan. The only bright spot had been the pretty redhead that he'd known was too sweet and *all* kinds of wrong for him. Resisting a little harmless flirting had been impossible.

But, man, was that ever a freakin' mistake.

'I'm busy,' Parker said to his partner as he shot a look at Amber.

Creamy skin, wide mouth and eyes the color of maple syrup. Her auburn hair was pulled back in some sleek knot that looked more professional than dressy. If he'd known she was gonna turn into a stunning redhead, he might have actually paid more attention. But she had been all knobby kneed, gap-toothed, with gangly arms and legs. A quiet kid.

A lamb among wolves at the Michael household.

He'd always felt a little sorry for her, a bit protective. Some of that had been drilled into him, to watch over Reese and Amber when Amber's mother couldn't. And more than anyone, he knew how it felt to be an outsider in the Michael household.

Now Amber was gorgeous, but there was still a lingering sense of the innocent openness that she'd had as a child. He could see it in her clear, honest eyes, the face that left everything on display. Parker couldn't remember ever being innocent.

Had stopped *believing* in innocence long ago.

Gaze locked with the redhead's, Parker spoke to Rob, who was waiting patiently on the other end of the phone. 'Trust me,' he said. 'I'd rather be spilling a beer with my partner at Rosie's Bar than at this fancy restaurant.'

'Get your butt down here,' Rob said.

'Sorry, Robby boy.' *Christamighty* was Parker sorry he was here instead of there. 'Got something I've got to do first.'

There was a long pause on the end of the phone. 'This isn't about the Miller case, is it?' Rob asked.

Parker's insides felt as if they'd been hooked to two tractor trailers racing in opposite directions. Shoulders tense, he rolled them back. 'No,' he said, careful to keep his voice casual. 'I've done this job long enough that noth-ing shocks me anymore.'

He knew his partner thought the turn of events had affected him. Was worried, somehow, that Parker was burning out on all they dealt with day to day. But he was more disturbed by the fact that he *wasn't* affected. The latest case had taken a twisted turn that most people could never fathom and, yet, Parker hadn't felt a speck of shock. Zip, zilch, nada.

The hollow darkness surrounding his heart expanded, and Parker refused to admit how much it scared the hell out of him.

Rob cleared his throat on the other end of the phone. 'I hate that our number one suspect is a teen, especially given his parents are total dirtbags,' he said.

Parker huffed in agreement. 'Yeah, sometimes fam-ily sucks.'

Eyebrows tenting at his words, Amber frowned.

And as he said goodbye to Rob, Parker let out a sigh and addressed the redhead. 'You got something you want to say?'

'Just wondering if you've spoken with your sister yet,' Amber said.

'Haven't had the time.'

'Haven't *made* the time.'

As if on cue, a feminine voice called his name, and he turned to face Reese. She was crossing the hardwood floor in a cocktail dress, her blond hair in a delicate twist.

'Be nice,' Amber whispered.

Parker frowned. 'I'm always nice.'

As Reese drew closer, he slipped his phone in his jacket, bracing for the upcoming conversation. Confronting his sister and telling her no appeared to be the only way to get her off his case. Emails hadn't worked. The phone calls had been a failure. Seemed the only way to get her to accept his no was a face-to-face conversation.

You can do polite.

But when Reese went to hug him, for a moment he panicked. Freakin' *panicked*. A master at deflection, he shifted on his feet, subtly placing his shoulder forward, blocking her attempt. Fortunately she interpreted his body language accurately and abandoned her attempt.

He didn't do public displays of affection.

He'd learned long ago not to do affection *period*.

'I'm glad you came,' Reese said with a small smile. 'I hope this means you've changed your mind about the wedding.'

Parker bit back the urge to say *hell, no*.

Now that she was getting married to her supposed dream guy, Reese was suddenly all 'peace on earth, good will toward men.' More persistent in her insistence they pretend they were a real family. They lived in the same town and hadn't seen each other in two years.

Mostly his fault, sure, but *still*...

'I came to talk to you in person,' he said.

'And to catch up with old friends?' Reese said.

His sister shot the redhead at his side a curious look before addressing Parker.

'So...' Reese said. 'Are you and Amber setting an appointment time for you to get measured for your tux?'

Parker's lips quirked in surprise as he slid his gaze back to Amber. She was watching him as if assessing his every move, the beautiful woman's attention sending a thrilling shimmy down his spine. *Amber* was supposed to measure him for his tux?

Interesting notion, but not enough to get him to change his mind.

'Come on, Reese,' he said, trying to be the diplomat he wasn't. 'Can you really picture me in a monkey suit?'

How many more times did he have to say no?

He wasn't a part of the Michael family, had never been welcomed. And at the age of thirty-two he wasn't going to start pretending now.

'Of course we want you there,' Reese said. 'You're my brother —'

'Half brother,' he said bluntly, knowing he sounded callous and trying to care. 'With emphasis on the half.'

Amber briefly touched the back of his hand and flashed him a disapproving look, and he chose to ignore the warning and the stimulating warmth of her touch, the fleeting feel of soft fingers. Reese eyed him warily. As if, after knowing him forever, she was still trying to figure him out.

Yeah, well...good luck with that one. He was still working on that himself.

'Listen,' he said. 'I'm happy that *you're* happy that you and that fiancé of yours are finally tying the knot.' He did his best not to scoff out loud. 'Not that I believe in the whole marital thing. But you know, to each his—or her—own delusion.'

'Parker,' Reese said gently, and he hated the worried look in her eyes. 'Love isn't a delusion.'

'Oh, yeah?' Parker screwed up his face, hoping he looked more doubtful than like the caustic bastard that Jessica had called him before breaking it off. After four months, a real record for him, it was almost a relief to have her gone. 'If I remember right—' he studied his sister '—you've pledged 'till death do you part' before.'

Amber's fingers returned to his wrist, gripping him hard. The contact briefly short-circuited his brain, bringing to mind better reasons she could be holding on to him so tight.

Not your type, Robinson. Not your type.

He discreetly pulled his wrist from Amber's clasp. 'Mason was your ex's name, wasn't it?' Parker said, lifting a brow at his sister.

Pink staining her cheeks at the mention of her first husband, Reese ignored his comment. 'Being in the wedding doesn't mean you're endorsing the institution.'

He plowed a hand through his hair, not caring if it stuck out in all directions. 'Reese—'

'Please,' she said, her face the picture of sincerity. 'You're family.'

Every muscle in his gut tensed with the hit. As far as he was concerned, his family died the day his father had passed away.

And the void that had started with his mother's *you were a mistake* had grown through the years, only to expand to unbelievable depths the day his dad had died. Since then he'd felt numb, as if nothing touched him. Detached. A black hole that threatened to consume everything.

Amber shifted slightly on her feet, and his eyes went of their own volition to land, *again,* on the pretty tagalong from his youth. She pressed closer until their shoulders brushed, a distracting touch. But she was giving him an emphatic stare that screamed *Don't you dare break her heart*.

Because Reese didn't deserve it, not really.

It had taken him years as an adult to realize that his sister wasn't responsible for the way their mother had treated him. That Reese's precious-princess status in the Michael household was her parents' doing, and not his sister's. She'd been a clueless, pampered kid adored by her mom and dad. And wasn't that the way life was supposed to work?

But Parker Robinson wasn't a fake.

He puffed out a breath. At this point, he was just gonna have to let her be disappointed when he didn't show up for the Big Day.

'I told you,' Parker told his sister. 'Dylan needs to pick someone else for his fifth groomsman.'

Parker headed for the elevators, and Amber spied the crestfallen look on Reese's face.

'He's never going to say yes,' Reese said.

Amber hated seeing her so down. Helping her childhood friend plan her dream day—complete with a reunion with her three college roommates as bridesmaids—was vital. Because she'd watched Reese work hard at her marriage to Mason, had *seen* how devastated she was when it failed. It had been painful to watch her friend suffer. Reese deserved her happily ever after with Dylan.

'Parker will say yes,' Amber said. 'Because deep down he knows you care about him.'

'You care about him, too,' Reese said with a knowing look in her eye.

Her stomach lurched. 'That was a long time ago.'

'And you're both grown-ups now,' her friend said, tone riddled with subtext.

Shooting Reese a look, Amber said, 'Anyone who chooses to get involved with Parker is a glutton for punishment.' She cast an eye at the man as he waited for the elevator. 'And I don't chase men.'

'No,' Reese said with a sigh. 'You just sit back and let life pass you by.'

'Hey,' Amber protested. 'Romance will happen when it's good and ready.'

Her mom had always said loving her father had been easy. Reese and Dylan's relationship always looked effortless, too. They were the perfect couple. Amber's other friends chased love as if it were something to be hunted down and captured, torturing themselves in the process. Amber knew when she met the right man, love would happen naturally.

Until then, she'd help others plan their perfect day.

Reese let out a *hunh*. 'Maybe you should be more proactive in getting what you want.'

'Listen,' Amber said, changing the subject. 'I'll talk to Parker about the wedding.' Amber gave her friend a hug. 'You go find Dylan and enjoy the rest of the party, okay?'

Heart pounding, Amber followed in Parker's path. But who was she, really, to try to convince Parker Robinson of *anything*?

The elevator doors were beginning to shut, and Amber picked up her pace and slid inside just before they closed.

Tension bounced off the walls, making the space feel especially small.

Parker sent her an overly tolerant look. 'Did Reese send you to try to change my mind?'

'No,' Amber said truthfully. She knew she needed to ease her way into this conversation. Years of resentment weren't going to be undone with a one-minute elevator ride. 'I was hoping you could give me a lift home.'

He straightened up and stared at her.

'Are you coming on to me?' he said. There was no seductive tone. He actually sounded amused by the thought.

Amber sent him a disgusted look she didn't feel. And why did he find the idea *funny*? 'No,' she said. 'Will you give me a ride, anyway?'

'I'll give you a ride because you're *not* coming on to me,' he said. Before she had time to process the unsatisfying words, Parker pushed the button and went on.

'Where do you live?' he asked.

'In a loft above my shop,' she said. 'Down under the Manhattan Bridge overpass.'

An emotion she couldn't quite place swept up his face. 'I would have thought Reese wouldn't be caught dead in a shop anywhere other than on Fifth Avenue itself.'

Affection flared across her heart. Reese's wedding to Dylan Brookes was one of *the* social events of the year. The Michaels and the Brookeses were two of the most prominent families in the city. Handling the account was going to put her shop on the map, and she would forever be grateful for her friend's business and her trust.

'Reese has changed,' Amber said as they exited the elevator. She knew that better than anybody. 'I know she was a little oblivious as a teen...'

Parker chuckled at the understatement, though there was no malice in the sound.

They entered the lobby and Parker held the door open for her, and Amber passed through onto the busy, night-time sidewalk. Traffic whooshed by, the smell of rain heavy in the air.

'Honestly, I don't care how much she's changed.' And as he gave his ticket to the valet, he shot Amber a sharp look. 'I'm not convinced this thing with her and Dylan is even real.'

'You're just cynical about relationships in general,' Amber said with a small scoff. 'Everyone knows they're perfect for each other.'

'Regardless,' Parker said. 'I'm not going to be in her wedding.'

Heart shifting lower in her chest, Amber curled her fingers in her hand, determined to change his mind by the end of the ride home.

No matter what it took.

THREE

———

'What is this?' Amber asked when the valet pulled up with Parker's car.

'This,' Parker said, unable to hold back his grin of affection, 'is a 1967 Ford Mustang Fastback with a 390 cubic-inch, V-8 engine.'

Face blank, she stared at him.

'She's fast and she's furious and she's as badass as me,' he said, knowing the response it would produce. And so what if he enjoyed the roll of Amber's eyes. He blamed the small slice of pleasure for the words that slid from his mouth next. 'It belonged to my father.'

A look of tenderness leaped into her eyes and his chest clenched hard, the black hole cinching tight around his heart.

Stretching out her arm, as if to take his hand, she said, 'I'm sorry—'

'Don't.'

He stepped back before he knew what he was doing. He wasn't sure where the harsh word had come from. But

Parker also knew he couldn't bear to hear whatever she was going to say next.

And no way could he stand to have her touch him in comfort.

They settled into his car, and he was grateful for the distraction of merging with traffic. The misting rain turned into a steady drizzle and the *swish swish swish* of the windshield wipers filled the vehicle. Riding in silence, the awkward commute felt longer than it should have, and Parker was almost relieved when they drew closer to her turnoff and he had to ask her for directions.

Once he parked on her street and turned off the car, the rain began to come down a little harder. He slid off his jacket and turned to toss it onto the backseat, noticing her eyes on his chest. And the sharp stab of lust to his groin was unexpected.

'I'll walk you to the door,' he said, gearing up for a goodbye.

'No need,' she said. 'There's no sense in two of us getting wet.' She twisted in her seat to look at him. 'Parker, about the wedding—'

Stomach knotted with tension, he bolted out of the car and rounded to the passenger side, opening Amber's door. 'We're a block away,' he said. 'We should get moving.'

He closed the car door behind her with a forceful *thunk,* because the former stalker had lied to him. She was going to try to convince him to change his mind. And the last thing he needed were *two* females hounding him about an impossible task.

Amber frowned. 'It won't take long to get there, so we can—'

'We better hurry before the rain gets worse,' he said, taking her arm.

Leading her up the sidewalk, he glanced at the red-head from the corner of his eye. She had a nice figure. Slim, but curvy enough in the right spots to capture a man's attention.

'Parker,' Amber said, sounding impatient. 'We need to—'

The skies opened up and began to release a load of rain as if it had grown too heavy to hold. Their mad dash to the awning wasn't fast enough, and, when they arrived, water dripped down their faces.

Parker turned to Amber, trying hard not to appreciate how good she looked wet.

'The last time I saw you that soaked you were trying to drown,' Parker said.

Sending him an overly tolerant look, she opened her mouth to speak again. But Parker had other ideas.

'There's something I gotta ask.' He narrowed his eyes at Amber with a curiosity that was genuine. 'Were you just pretending to be dead so I would do mouth to mouth?'

The shocked and offended expression on her face was instantaneous, and her mouth dropped open wider. 'I—'

She blinked and tried again. 'You—'

'Hey,' he said by way of protest. So far his choice of conversation had left her practically mute, which was exactly what he'd planned. 'You *followed* me around. I mean, come on, I couldn't seem to get rid of you.' A smile split his lips at the memory. 'I even caught you watching me make out with Susie Frances.'

Pink coloring bled up her cheeks. Parker would never

forget the gaping look on Amber's face when he spied her peeking at them from behind the lifeguard house. He knew his gruff 'You got some kind of voyeur kink going on there, Ace?' had been totally out of line. But the expression on her face had been priceless. Poor kid didn't have a clue what he'd been talking about, but he remembered the look in her eyes.

From an awkward twelve-year-old it had been embarrassingly uncomfortable.

From a beautiful twenty-seven-year-old it made him embarrassingly uncomfortable in his jeans. Case in point, the way her eyes had skimmed over his chest in the car.

'I did not mean to spy on you while you were with Susie,' she said.

'Feel free to keep lying to yourself,' Parker went on. 'So...did you?'

She blinked. 'Did I what?'

'Pretend to be dead.'

'Yes,' she said with a huff of sarcasm that told him it wasn't true. 'And vomiting up seawater was part of my evil seduction plan, too.'

'Come on, you know you wanted to kiss me back then. It was hellaciously embarrassing, let me tell you,' Parker said.

The color climbed higher up her cheeks. 'Trust me, I didn't plan out almost drowning just so I could get your lips on mine,' she said. 'Which is a good thing, too, because it would have been a terrible disappointment.'

'You keep saying that.'

'Because it's true.'

'Awesome,' he said with a dry twist of his lips. 'My skills are being judged on a one-time incident of giving you mouth to mouth—' he paused, as if for emphasis '—while you were trying to, you know, *die*.'

'Sorry,' she said with a delicate lift of her shoulder. 'It's my only basis for comparison.'

In a fit of madness he wanted to wipe that look off her face. 'Well,' he said as he stepped closer, hating how rough the word came out. 'There's an easy fix for that.'

Hands on her arms, he was vaguely aware goose bumps prickled her skin, and he wondered if it was from the chilling rain...or his touch.

No matter. He intended to be quick in his efforts, to dazzle her with his finesse. Get in; get out. Hopefully blow her mind. Or at least replace a stupid ten-second mouth-to-mouth moment with a kiss that was worthy of being judged. His pride was at stake here.

But when his lips touched hers, she let out a whimper that slayed him and canted her head up, opening her mouth beneath his as if she'd been waiting all night to do exactly that. And if he took advantage of the offer to sweep his tongue against hers, and instantly followed through on the crushing need to repeat the act, well... he was as weak as the next guy when faced with a beautiful woman in his arms.

He might have arched against her.

His breath might have caught in his throat at the glorious feel of her soft body.

Before he knew what he was doing he was shifting closer, his hands in the silk of her hair, and angling her head to increase the contact. To maintain the seductive slide of tongue against tongue. She tasted like maple and smelled like the syrup that matched the color her eyes.

For a heart-stopping moment he pushed aside the fact

that she was too sweet. That she was the sort of woman that would expect more than he could give.

That she was the one person who knew the truth about how weak he'd once been.

The mood-killing thought hit like a jolt of lightning, and he tried to pull away. But her soft hand on his neck didn't allow him to escape too far, now only an inch of space separating them. Her breath was sweet, warm and moist on his lips.

Heart thumping harder than it should have from a simple kiss, he stared into the golden-brown eyes.

And then she feathered her mouth across his in a way that was so soft, so barely there, that Parker didn't know what to do with the moment. As lips ghosted across his, he frowned, frozen, adjusting to the foreign feel of something *not* focused on the act of sexual gratification. The barely-there touch of skin on skin that managed to gut him so thoroughly. Affect him more than any other more carnal action could have.

And an odd, soft feeling was seeping into his chest. A feeling he didn't quite know what to do with.

But he did not do sweet. Not in his relationships, not in his work, not in his *life*. Yet, for some unknown reason, he couldn't pull away. He didn't respond, but he couldn't move, either. Like a stupid deer in the freight-train-lights moment.

When she finally leaned back, her throat was flushed the same shade as her face, her fingers stroking against the hair at the base of his neck. Sending goose bumps, freakin' *goose bumps*, down his back.

What the hell?

Rain pounded the pavement around them, gushing

off the awning and cocooning them in a rushing wall of water.

'So,' Parker finally said. He cleared his throat. 'I'd say that puts the kiss issue to rest.'

But, man, did it ever create a whole new set of problems.

Because he was staring at her face, still wet from the rain. A drop dripped from her hair and slid down her cheek, slipping past the corner of her mouth, and Parker was struck by the gut-wrenching urge to lick the trail. The slender body in the dress that now clung to curves he hadn't *truly* appreciated without the addition of water. And, as if the *want* wasn't bad enough, the strand of hair that clung to her temple added an air of vulnerability that was far worse than the feeling of lust.

From this proximity he could reach out and brush the lock from her forehead. Not that he planned on following through, or that he longed to. At all.

Damn it.

'You seem awfully confident,' she said softly.

'I am.'

'Shouldn't I have a say?'

Lifting a brow, he waited.

'It definitely puts the issue to rest,' she said.

And the smile on her face left him wanting to kiss her again, and he fisted his hand.

He worked in a world of bitterness and darkness and death and she dealt with joy and lightness and happily ever after. He couldn't bear the thought of being the one to snuff out those good feelings. And he would, too. Every woman he'd left behind him had been just a little more jaded, a little less innocent. Had believed a little less.

He didn't want to...

No, he *wouldn't* do that to Amber.

'Take care, Ace,' he said as he set her back.

And then he headed out into the night and the rain, before she could say something they'd both regret.

Focusfocus*focus*

Amber clutched her purse as she trotted up the steps leading to Rosie's Bar, hoping Parker was here. Three days after she'd set out to get him to change his mind and gotten so deliciously sidetracked, she'd finally recovered enough from his devastating kiss to face him again. It had been all she'd imagined and more.

And after years of fantasies, that was a supersize order beyond belief.

The beautiful lips had been softer than she remembered, the slide of his tongue electrifying. The smell of the leather jacket clung to his T-shirt in its absence. Hands hard on her head, he'd held her still as the kiss had quickly shifted from a teasing joke to something more, until he was nearly mauling her mouth with an intensity that had sapped the air from her lungs.

She pushed aside the swirl of heat in her stomach. No more getting distracted by her memories or the way he made her feel. She'd followed Parker into the elevator that night with every intention of convincing him to agree to be in Reese's wedding. But once she'd climbed into the car and been enclosed in the small space, his enticing smell, those captivating eyes and that finely honed body had derailed her plans.

And of course, then there'd been the leftover strain in the air from the mention of his father....

No, that wasn't right. The tension had come when she'd tried to show him how sorry she was for his loss. All she'd wanted was to offer a bit of sympathy. She might have been small when her father had died, but she still felt the loss acutely. And she'd been overwhelmed with the need for a simple squeeze of her fingers to communicate that she knew how he felt.

But Parker...Parker wouldn't allow even that small comfort.

The vision of him averting Reese's hug swam before her eyes, and Amber's lips twisted in disappointment and concern. He hadn't always been so distant. In fact, as a kid he'd been open and easy and fairly demonstrative. But that had changed as he'd grown into an adolescent. Amber had witnessed the slow transformation under his mother's treatment, and it was disheartening to realize that it remained a permanent fixture of his personality.

Bracing herself for another Parker encounter, she opened the door and entered the chaos of the noisy sports bar. She weaved her way through the throng of people, scanning the crowd.

And then her gaze caught on the back of ruffled brown hair with streaks of gold, spying Parker at a small table. He wore well-worn jeans, a long-sleeved T-shirt and the brown leather jacket. A black-haired man in slacks, a navy peacoat and no tie shared the table.

As she approached, Parker's green eyes collided with hers. 'What are you doing here?'

The words were delivered with more surprise than annoyance, but the pause that followed was uncomfortable, filled with Parker's heated gaze, chatter and the sound of clinking glasses.

The man sitting beside him sent Parker a curious look before sticking out his hand. 'Rob Winston,' he said with a smile and an accent that sounded southern. Texan, maybe. 'Ignore my partner here.' She returned his shake as he tipped his head in Parker's direction. 'His momma didn't hug him enough as a child.'

The words sent a shock through Amber's system. There wasn't a flicker of emotion in Parker's expression, the muscles in his face rigid. By the nonchalant way Rob had delivered the words, Amber knew that Parker's partner had no idea how close to the marrow his words had drilled. It was written in the way Parker was studiously avoiding her gaze.

Because she remembered...

'Don't get your ovaries in a wad, Robin,' Parker huffed, though there was no real annoyance there, either.

'Don't be such a dirtbag, Parker,' Rob said good-naturedly.

Amber had the distinct impression that these words were uttered on a daily basis.

'So—' eyes on Amber, Rob indicated for her to take a seat, but she hesitated '—how do you know my dumbass of a partner here?'

'We grew up together,' she said.

This seemed to prick Rob's interest. He sat up higher in his seat and folded his arms on the table, leaning in with a light in his gaze that was unmistakable.

'I bet you have some good stories about my friend here,' Rob said. 'Please—' he waved at the chair beside him again in invitation '—join us and share.'

Ignoring Parker's gaze, Amber bit back the smile as she sat down. It was hard not to respond to the open friendliness in Rob's face, the amusing curiosity in his eyes. Which made it easier to bear Parker's disconcerting attention.

'You're right, Rob.' Her eyes slid to meet Parker's, who was staring at her with a heat that burned her to the core, making her words just a little too husky. 'I do have some doozies to tell.'

The responding flash in Parker's gaze sent a thrill tripping through her limbs.

'Was he always an obstinate SOB?' Rob said.

Amber smiled at the memories. 'Definitely.'

'He's relentless,' Rob said with an acknowledging nod of his head. 'He once chased a suspect ten blocks before tackling him in the alleyway of a pawnshop. And that was *after* the guy had dumped a pail of rose-colored paint over Parker's head.'

Amber laughed at the image of Parker in pink sprinting up the street.

'He spent one whole summer teaching me how to hold a crab,' she said. Remembering her yells and Parker's patient laughs, she twisted her lips wryly. 'I kept shrieking and drawing my hands away. But he kept insisting I try again, no matter how loud I screamed.'

He'd paddled like a madman to rescue her from drowning.

He hadn't given up then, either.

Tilting his head, Rob went on. 'You should see him in the interrogation room,' he said. 'Of course, my hell-on-wheels partner here is the reason we have the highest closure rate in the department.'

That Parker was the best at his job didn't come as a surprise.

Chuckling, Rob glanced around. 'We should have the waitress bring you a drink,' he said to Amber. 'So we can swap war stories. Was he a shameless flirt back then, too?'

'The summer he was seventeen he dated three girls—' eyes fixed on Rob, she leaned in conspiratorially, ignoring Parker's frown '—at the *same time*.'

'I don't remember that,' Parker said.

Gazing at Rob as if Parker hadn't spoken, Amber went on. 'Leslie Campbell, Sharon Howell and Susie Frances.' She hoped no one would comment on why she remembered the girls' names when Parker didn't. 'Once I even caught him—'

'Hey.' Clearly unhappy with the turn in the conversation, Parker waved a hand in the air between his tablemates' gazes. 'I'm sitting right here, people.' He tossed a loaded look at his partner. 'Why don't you make yourself useful and go find the waitress.'

Rob chuckled again. 'But I'm—' his curious gaze slid to his partner, where he must have seen something interesting, because Rob cleared his throat and stood '—just going to find the waitress.' He sent Amber a quick nod. 'Nice to meet you.'

After an answering smile, Amber watched the man walk away to join a boisterous bunch at the end of the bar. Her gaze lingered more from a nervousness about looking at Parker again then from any real interest in his good-looking partner.

'Why are you here, Amber?' Parker asked, his voice wary.

Feeling the need for a sense of power, she shifted higher in her seat. And from his laid-back position, legs stretched in front of him, they were almost eye to eye. Her foot brushed his, and a flash of awareness lit his gaze, an awareness that reminded her that she had been well and thoroughly kissed by Parker.

'You know why I'm here,' she said.

'We're not finishing what we started.'

Was he talking about their make-out session or the conversation where she insisted he be in the wedding?

And why was the former more disappointing than the latter?

Amber lost track of the thought when he shrugged out of his jacket to loop it behind his chair, the muscles in his chest flexing from the move. The long-sleeved T-shirt stretched across his gorgeous form nicely, the pectorals and biceps filling it in a way that made coherent thought briefly impossible.

'You need to come get measured for your tux,' Amber said.

Parker let out a grunt. 'I'm not going to be in the wedding.'

'You have to.'

His gaze pierced her. 'I don't have to do anything.'

'Please, Parker,' Amber said, all teasing long gone. 'I know it means nothing to you. But it's really important to Reese.'

At the mention of his sister, Parker's gaze slid off into the distance and Amber could see the conflict on his face. He wanted to, but he didn't. And suddenly, it seemed imperative that Parker accept this little bit of his family's affections. Or, more accurately, his *sister's* affections. Somehow Amber just knew that if he didn't follow through with this he would remain distant, not only to his family, but to, well…*life*.

'I'm busy, Amber,' he said. 'I'm here with my friends.'

'And as soon as you agree to the simple deed that will make your sister happy,' she said easily, leaning back to get comfortable, 'I'll get out of your hair.'

The twist of his lips betrayed his displeasure. But this was too important. And much bigger than just one wedding.

When he didn't relent, Amber crossed her arms and pulled the same stunt she'd pulled after he'd saved her from drowning. 'If you don't agree to be in Reese's wedding,' she went on with an expression so innocent she knew Parker could see through it, 'I'll agree to that drink with Rob.'

Parker's gaze barreled back into hers. 'You wouldn't.'

'I would.' She sent him a small smile. They both knew she had enough stories to embarrass him from now until forever. 'I bet Rob would *love* to know you listened to 'N Sync.'

'When I was twelve,' he barked, eyebrows scrunched in horrified protest.

'You were seventeen when you let Susie Frances paint your toenails.'

'That was *joke*.' He glanced around nervously, as if suddenly realizing the potential risk to his reputation. 'And besides—' the sexy smirk edged up his face '—she made the humiliation totally worth my while.'

And Amber *really* didn't want to hear how.

'Okay,' she said. Time to go big or go home. She leaned closer, and this time her smile was brilliant. 'I'll tell Rob about the time I walked in on you in the bathroom and caught you—'

'Stop.' His hand landed on the table with a *thump,* and he eyed her as if half tempted to muzzle her mouth. His voice gruff, he muttered, 'Holy mother of—'

The curse—a creative one, no doubt—died as he plowed a hand through his gold-tipped hair, leaving it more tousled than usual.

'I'll do it, okay?' he said.

The boyishly ruffled hair, his obvious embarrassment and his agreement sent a twist of affection to her heart, and she leaned in close enough to smell the leather of his jacket.

'Thank you,' she said sincerely as she reached out, overwhelmed with the need to touch his hand in simple appreciation.

He must have misread her intentions, because his gaze grew dark as he drew back out of reach. 'You've had your kiss,' he said dryly. 'And that's all you get. As a matter of fact,' he went on, lifting his brow as if in challenge. 'Hands to yourself from here on out.'

Amber was surprised the surge of heat didn't leave her in a puddle in her chair. Her nerves pulled into a knot, partly from the mention of their kiss and partly in annoyance at the reminder she wasn't his 'type.' Which apparently included everyone *but* her. She inhaled a soothing breath. Parker Robinson seemed to avoid anything he didn't want to talk about—emotions, thoughts, feelings, his *past*—by burying it in sexual innuendo.

She remember Parker arching against her body, the catch of his breath against her mouth...and the pulse of pure, unadulterated pleasure knowing that she had caused both.

Clearly, he'd enjoyed kissing her. No one could fake that kind of response. And he was still attracted, she could sense it in his gaze, in his very posture. Except he kept insisting he'd never touch her again. Any other guy and she wouldn't care.

For some reason, Parker's attitude was starting to tick her off.

'I'm measuring you for your tuxedo,' she said, amazed she managed to sound so calm. 'Touching kind of goes along with the activity.'

She forced her eyes to remain steady on his as an impressive whirlwind of emotion swept across his face. Annoyance. Resentment. And a whole lot of lust.

Lust.

Chest slowly squeezing the air from her lungs, she desperately reminded herself that she didn't do casual hookups, no matter how attracted she was. More important, she'd never, ever, seduce a guy. And she wouldn't *dream* of chasing a fellow who was throwing up caution signs all over the place. Especially like the man seated across from her, a man who was less like a stop sign and more like a road-totally-closed-ahead kind of guy.

But...but she'd wanted Parker her whole life and the desire was so strong she was seriously considering making him an exception.

'Fine,' he said gruffly. 'But I work long hours, so it will be late before I can stop by your shop.'

Visions of him in her store swam before her eyes. At night. The two of them alone. All she could hear in her head was Reese's 'You should be more proactive.'

And if anyone was worth taking the initiative to seduce, it was Parker Robinson.

Decision made, anticipation coursed through her veins, and Amber swallowed so hard it hurt.

She cleared her throat. 'I make special, after-hours appointments fairly regularly,' she said. 'Just tell me when you can be there.'

Parker heaved out a breath and grabbed his beer bottle. 'Nine-thirty tomorrow night,' he said, taking a sip as he shot her a loaded look. 'Just a quick couple of measurements and then I'm gone.'

The set of those beautiful lips and the tone of his voice made it abundantly clear he was done. But Amber...

Well, as far as she was concerned, she was just getting started.

FOUR

———

    At nine-thirty the next night Parker pulled the door open to Amber's Bridals. The bell tinkled way too merrily for a frustrating day that had started with a dead end on the Miller case, expanding the black, vast void in his chest. Which meant he'd spent the rest of today numbly going through the motions. Or maybe the numbness had been a problem for months.

Perhaps *years*.

Rolling his shoulders uneasily, he glanced around. He had to hand it to the kid, she had one helluva store. Classy to the core, the shop contained sleek hardwood floors and an abundance of white dresses lining the walls, veils, fake bouquets and pictures of models in wedding getup. And bowls of...what were those? Rose petals?

Parker couldn't help himself. He let out a shudder.

'Don't worry.' Amber's voice came from behind. 'No one has to know you were here.'

He let out a barking laugh. 'I'm losing every masculine mark I ever earned just by passing through these doors—'

Turning, he was hit with a vision of Amber that

knocked him on his virtual ass. How had the geeky pre-teen grown into such a vision? Red hair flowed past her shoulders. She was dressed in dressy jeans and a sheer top that clung to her breasts, the long-sleeve blouse flaring at the waist and sleeves. She managed to look young and sweet and incredibly sexy.

And with the current case he was working on, he felt old and hardened and done with humanity.

Amber crossed to lock the door and then turned to face him, remaining silent. The staring contest grew uncomfortable as Parker realized he was alone in a shop with a beautiful woman who had, at the age of twelve, looked at him as if he hung the moon, the stars and the bloody sun to boot. Unfortunately, the appreciation in her face now held the weight of experience. Not to mention the lady was a walking, talking advertisement for Happily Ever After and Parker was quite convinced that Content for Now was beyond his capabilities. Toss in the fact that they were surrounded by swarms of puffy white dresses—and, holy mother, were those fake *tiaras*?—and the situation was less amusing than downright *concerning*.

She hiked a brow that didn't ease the tension. 'You ready?'

What was that supposed to mean?

'Of course,' he said.

He wasn't an amateur. He refused to be intimated by the little slip of a thing that he'd taught how to capture crabs on the beach.

As he followed her down the hall, he made a point of ignoring the gentle, seductive sway of her slight hips and the fluid walk. Fortunately, the view was easier to ignore when she stepped into a large room containing two couches, an armchair and a coffee table mimicking an elegant living room, the furniture facing a small space surrounded on three sides by floor-length mirrors. And while he was sure broad daylight and the addition of people encouraged the appropriate air for viewing a dress, somehow the whole setup hinted at something...almost erotic. Especially with just the two of them. Alone.

Damn, what had he agreed to?

'Take off your jacket and shoes,' Amber said, waving in the direction of the furniture.

Parker shrugged out of his leather jacket and tossed it on a couch, toeing off his shoes.

'Uh—' her eyes dropped to his shoulder holster containing his weapon and handcuffs '—the gun, too.'

For some reason he hesitated.

'What?' she said, hand on her hip. 'You don't mind taking off the jacket and shoes, but you draw a line at the weapon?'

'Maybe it brings me a sense of security,' he said with a small grin. When she waited for him to go on, the oft-repeated joke tripped off of his tongue. 'Most people respect the badge,' he said. 'But everyone respects Smith & Wesson.'

'Is that why you do what you do?' she said, gesturing for him to step forward to the space in front of the mirror. 'For respect?'

Black void expanding exponentially in his chest, he frowned. Shoot. He'd been teasing and she'd jumped straight to the serious talk.

'How long is this going to take?' he said as he crossed to the designated spot.

She pulled out a small, flexible tape measure and

moved closer, pulling his gut a touch tighter. 'I need to measure you for a shirt, jacket and pants,' she said.

Which was really no answer at all.

And suddenly she was right in front of him, bringing her scent and the clear skin of her beautiful face close to his. He leaned back and looked down at her dubiously, his frown drawing his brows down until they tried to merge with his eyes.

'Relax,' she said. But something in her tone made the suggestion impossible. 'This isn't going to hurt.'

He elected to ignore the twitch of her luscious lips and hoped to hell she was talking about being measured for the tux. Innocent expression clashing with the knowing light in her eyes, she looped the tape measure—and consequently, *her arms*—around his neck, setting his heart tapping harder in his chest.

The slight smile on her face made him nervous. 'There's something I've been meaning to discuss with you,' she said as she took the measurement, her fingers whispering against him just beneath his Adam's apple.

The simple brush of skin on skin sent a line of goose bumps streaking up his back. And how was that possible when she was only touching his stupid neck?

'Are you going to your mother's dinner party in two weeks?' she went on.

Fortunately it was a question he could answer without thought, because thinking was difficult with her so close. 'No.'

The word came out a little harsher than he'd intended, but the feel of her fingers was sending an uncomfortable thrum through his body. And how long did it take to get an accurate measurement? She wasn't launching a nuclear warhead here. An approximation would do just fine, thank you.

'Why not?' she said as she dropped her hands and stepped over to the laptop on the coffee table.

Free of her disturbing touch, Parker let out a breath of relief.

'Because I don't have anything to say to my mother,' he said. 'And if I show up I'll have to talk to her.'

A small frown tugged on her lips as she entered the measurement into her laptop. 'When was the last time you two had a conversation?'

The gaping pit around his heart seemed to expand twofold, and Parker worked hard at *not* frowning at the memory.

'She called my cell the day my father died,' he said, remembering the feeling of desolation, the sense of aloneness. 'I didn't answer.'

She turned and stepped closer again, studying him silently for a moment. The assessing gaze, the topic of conversation and her skin that looked as if it tasted of cream made the situation wholly uncomfortable.

Without a word, she came to his side, and he stared at her profile in the mirror.

'You should talk to her,' she said.

'I've got nothing to say.'

The pause was slight, but he sensed she had more to share. The words that followed were not what he'd been expecting.

'I'm going to measure your sleeve length,' she said.

With more care than he thought necessary, she measured from the spine at his neck, to his shoulder, and then drew the tape down his arm to his wrist. His T-shirt offered no protection from the slow slide of her fingers against his bare arm, and he ignored the shimmer of awareness that came with the move.

The simple brush of skin on skin on his arm shouldn't be so arousing, either.

'You did that on purpose,' he said.

Despite the unfortunate husky tone of his voice, she said, 'I have no idea what you're talking about.' She sent him a sedate look. 'Now raise your arms.'

He shifted on his feet, uneasy. 'Why?'

She rolled her eyes. 'No need to be so suspicious,' she said. 'I just need to measure your chest.'

Something in the set of her posture and the light in her eyes told him he needed to proceed with caution. To be on guard—and not because of the conversation about his family. The mood was electric. Heck, the air was so heavily charged he was surprised they both didn't glow. And he could see in her eyes that she knew it, too.

'Arms,' she said as she stepped in front of him again.

Sending a sharp look down at her too-close-for-comfort face, Parker complied, raising his hands as if surrendering. Which he wasn't, blast it all.

Amber looped her arms around his back, and, for a moment, the world came to a grinding halt....

He couldn't think.

Couldn't breathe.

If he leaned just a fraction of an inch closer, he would be able to feel the soft press of her breasts against the harder planes of his chest. She was looking up at him with those wide, beautiful eyes, and her face almost glowed. As though she was lit from within. A light that just might be able to absorb the blackness that churned inside.

Where had that thought come from?

Looking dazed, Amber stared up at him with her arms around his torso, and the words that came from her mouth were a surprise. 'You took off your jacket.'

Her tone of voice suggested there was more to that less-than-brilliant bit of observation.

Parker's brows pulled together, the rest of him frozen. 'You told me to.'

She looked as stunned as he felt.

'No. Not that...' she said, her voice stumbling a bit. 'I mean—you still smell like leather.'

A succession of emotions filed across her face, moving on from the shock and eventually ending with something that looked like anticipation. And...damn, there was no ignoring the vibe any longer because—

'But maybe that's just your signature scent,' she mused.

—it was written all over her face.

'Are you trying to seduce me, Amber?' he asked softly.

Sometimes it was best just to punch the elephant in the room in the face.

She blinked, as if clearing her vision, and then brought her hands back around to finish measuring his chest. 'Yes.'

Apparently she had no qualms about laying her cards on the table.

Tipping his head, he paused, feeling stronger now that they'd addressed the issue. He could handle this. He'd handled her starstruck adoration as a kid and he could handle her desire now. Feeling better, he watched her cross to enter the latest numbers and then return to stand in front of him again.

Everything would be fine, if he just didn't look at her face, or her mouth, or her chest....

Bracing himself, he held his breath as she measured around his waist, her fingers skimming just below the level of his belly button, too close to more...*sensitive* parts of his body. And his abdominal muscles clenched as if punched, despite the T-shirt between them.

'You should at least come to your mother's party to see Reese,' she said as she bit the corner of her mouth in concentration.

Leaving Parker with the intense need to lick the damp spot from her lip. His head was spinning, and his shaft was thickening, and coherent thought took him a moment.

'Why?' he croaked.

See, he could form words. Sort of.

'Because she's family,' she said. 'And we all need family.'

Despite his discomfort, he let out a small huff of laughter. She thought she was going to seduce him *and* get him to talk to his family? Man, she really was a believer.

And then she knelt before him, and... *Oh, God*.

In the mirror, the vision of her on her knees in front of him sent his pulse bounding out a rhythm that threatened to burst from his body. She was joy and hope and light and the intense need to bury himself inside her, to take a little of that faith for himself, to sink into her *belief* was almost his undoing.

His mouth worked, struggling to function. 'Nothing about this scenario is going to work on me, Ace,' he said hoarsely, proud he could still form words.

'I'm just taking your measurements.'

A sarcastic scoff escaped his throat.

And then she measured from his waist to his heel, and Parker blew out a breath, relieved the act was fairly tolerable. Even being so stupid as to congratulate himself on his self-control as she entered the measurement into her computer.

'Next, your inseam.' She returned to kneel in front of him, and he braced himself. 'Spread your legs a bit.'

Sweat broke out along his lip at the erotic image her words produced. Parker was busy battling the flash of heat when Amber, with one end of the measuring tape, reached up between his thighs. His chest seized around his heart, preventing it from doing its job. And when her fingers brushed just to the left of his groin, pleasure pooled in his stomach.

Paralyzed, he used his gaze in a vain attempt to burn reason into her, his voice almost a growl. 'Does measuring my inseam include touching my junk?'

Eyes wide, she looked up at him. But beneath it all, he was sure he detected a note of false innocence. And a hint of nerves.

'Sorry,' she said as she drew the other end of the tape down to his heel.

With a wary scowl, he said, 'You don't look sorry.'

She swallowed and cleared her throat. 'Assume your normal posture, please.'

'I am.'

'You look like you're slumped over,' she said with a doubtful look.

That was because he was so hard now his body was protectively hunching around the sensitive area.

'And now I need to get the last measurement,' she said.

He should have known he was in trouble by the fine tremor in her voice. By the way she nervously licked her lips. But he was too mesmerized by the slide of pink tongue across her mouth to register what she was doing.

One hand holding the tape at his waist in back, she reached between his legs and pulled the measuring tape down his backside.

'You're measuring my ass?' he rasped.

'I need your crotch length,' she said.

Crotch length?

There was a joke in there somewhere, but, for the life of him, he couldn't formulate the wisecrack. Especially when her hand slowly pulled the tape up between his thighs.

And Parker knew he was well and truly screwed.

Breathing a distant memory, a tiny speck in his rearview mirror, he couldn't move as her fingers flirted with touching his erection. She skirted too close for comfort as she continued up his crotch toward the front of his waist. Wringing his insides. Dragging his nerves through razor wire. And, just when it was almost over, she lightly brushed the tip of his shaft.

Desire burst like a supernova, jump-starting his flagging brain.

'Jesus, Amber,' he ground out, grabbing her wrist. Body throbbing, he narrowed his gaze. 'Is this measurement even necessary?'

She gazed up at him, looking stunned. 'You can never have too much information,' she murmured.

'Hell yeah, you can.' His grip grew firmer around her wrist.

Case in point: her skin was warm, her pulse bounded

beneath his fingers and her expression was nothing but honest—pure, unadulterated want innocently on display. Along with something else. He should have pushed her wrist as far from him as possible, but he was transfixed by the light in her eyes. As if he deserved much more than just sex.

And the crushing need to capture a little of that hope for himself, to briefly fill the black hole that had been surrounding his heart for years, was too much.

'You win,' he muttered, and he hauled her up by her wrist, gaze intent on her mouth.

Amber didn't utter a word of protest as Parker pulled her body flush with his. Her wrist still clutched in his fingers, he tucked their arms behind his back until she was giving him a partial hug. But it wasn't a real embrace, because his other hand hung loosely at his side.

Green eyes holding hers, his voice gruff, he said, 'You know this is all you get, right?'

They were pressed together from chest to groin, and she was momentarily rendered speechless by his too-blunt words and the feel of his erection. The longing to be wrapped in his arms for real was intense. But he maintained his current posture, patiently waiting for a response, and he wasn't going to continue until he was sure he'd made his point.

She'd never chased a man before, had never actively pursued what she wanted. And she *wanted* this.

With an intensity that was too great to be denied.

'I understand,' she said.

The tension radiating from him since she'd taken his

measurement suddenly dissipated, and he lifted his free hand to her face, lowering his mouth to hers.

God, it wasn't fair.

He was strong and sure and oozed a confident sensuality as his lips slid over hers, as if trying to absorb something more than a simple kiss. Meanwhile she was quaking, literally *quaking* at the knees. She was a grown woman with plenty of experience under her belt. She'd been around several blocks along the way but, for some reason, this time the trip felt different.

Amber supposed it was only natural, as she'd waited for this moment since she was a preteen. Before she really even knew what, exactly, her body longed for....

She remembered the heat from innocent brushes of skin on skin as she'd accepted the crab he'd gently placed in her hand. She remembered her heart pounding from dreams too vague to recall, only that they'd contained *Parker*.

And she remembered the mesmerizing mouth that had always triggered an anxious flutter in her stomach. Parker's lips were now slicking across hers, wet and warm and working her mouth so deliciously she had to clutch his T-shirt, dizzy.

With a small movement, his tongue tested her bottom lip, and a needy catch escaped her throat as she opened her mouth wide. He finally relented and gave her what she wanted, his tongue against hers. The taste, the soft strokes that went on and on, sent her senses soaring. Twisting his T-shirt tighter, she fought to have her other arm freed from his grip.

'Slow down, Ace,' he murmured against her mouth.

Pleasure flared higher. As a kid, the nickname had always made her feel special in Parker's eyes. She hadn't been, she knew. But it was the way he said it, as if she were the only one on the planet that was important. And right now he was licking, kissing and nipping his way down her neck, leaving her feeling the same way.

Against the bounding pulse at her neck, he said, 'There's no hurry.'

Oh, but holy heaven, *there was*.

Summers of innocent longing. *Years* of fantasies.

The mother lode of mental foreplay.

'Please,' she said, pulling against the fingers wrapped around her wrist.

He released her.

Instantly her fingers gripped the edge of his T-shirt and shoved, unceremoniously, up his torso. When he didn't lift his arms fast enough, she abandoned her plan to take it off and dropped her mouth to his naked chest. He tasted of salt and smelled of leather, as if the essence of his jacket had fused with his skin. She pressed open-mouthed kisses across his muscles, with the ridiculous thought that she could inhale this moment and keep it forever. Parker mumbled something she couldn't understand, something about taking their time, but Amber ignored him. She nosed a nipple and then licked the nub until it was raised enough to scrape her teeth across.

He sucked in a breath. 'Okay, okay.'

All thought came to a halt when his hands dropped to the T-shirt bunched just beneath his arms. Stunned, she watched the shifting of pectorals and bone and sinew as he shrugged out of the garment and tossed it aside. The strength in his shoulders, the easy play of muscle a beautiful, breathtaking sight.

Without hesitation, she spread her hands across the gorgeous display and pushed him back against the mirrored wall.

'Jesus, Amber,' he hissed.

Ignoring him, she stared at the light dusting of hair on his flat abdomen as she fumbled with his belt and the fastening of his jeans, finally pushing everything to the floor. The vision of lean hips, well-muscled thighs and a full erection left her breathless. Unable to continue.

And Parker finally seemed to grasp the urgency of their situation.

Hands and lips and teeth seemingly everywhere at once, he divested her of her clothing efficiently. When gone, she pressed her body to his, refusing to blush at the groan that ripped from her chest at the glorious feeling of, *finally*, skin on skin.

Parker swept a hand up her back and buried his fingers in her hair, his kiss raw. Mouth realigning this way and that as if to consume her from every angle. She lost track of time until the fingers in his other hand found their way between her thighs.

The visceral hit to her system left her pulling back from the kiss, gasping for air.

Lips parted, he breathed through his mouth—open hunger on his face as the fingers between her legs turned bolder. Until the desire grew so great tears pricked the backs of her lids.

Closing her eyes, she whispered, 'Parker.'

Which came out more like a strangled sound of pleasure than an actual word.

As if inspired, Parker's lips crashed back to hers. He pressed his hard shaft against the skin of her belly, as if seeking friction. The overpowering sensations were full of need. And want. And *need*. Amber could barely coordinate herself to return his kiss properly. Parker didn't seem to care, rocking his hips and nipping and pulling at her mouth for all it was worth. When he withdrew his hands, her body clenched in disappointment. Until he bent to pull a condom from the wallet in his jeans, sheathing himself.

Amber's mouth lost all moisture as she watched, transfixed, half terrified this was a dream and she'd wake up too soon.

Bracing his back against the mirror, Parker reached for Amber and lifted her up. Surprised, limbs clumsy, she didn't follow the logic until he spoke.

'Wrap your legs around my waist,' he said.

Oh, *God,* yes.

Praying her muscles would cooperate, she complied, yet all she could manage was to hold on as he buried himself inside. Eyes wide, she froze, adjusting to the pleasurable pressure that threatened to send her flying apart. A threat that escalated when he gripped her hips and began to move in earnest, each time taking her a little deeper.

Heat swamped her senses, until she was no longer frozen. She wrapped her arms more firmly around his neck. Tightened her legs around his hips.

And threw herself into a carnal kiss, scraping her teeth lightly across his tongue.

The swearword that shot from Parker's mouth into hers was explicit. He clutched her close, buried himself to the base of his shaft and then paused.

It felt *incredible.*

Chests pressed together, heart thundering against his,

Amber whimpered greedily and rolled her hips, seeking more friction.

'Amber,' he groaned as he slowly slid down the mirror until she was seated in his lap, his back against the wall.

Hands on her shoulders, blunt fingernails clutching her skin, he began to rock up into her. Friction, wonderful, glorious friction again. His movements slow and sure and hard.

'I need…' he mumbled, eyes closed.

His head drifted to hers.

Each hot press of his mouth was interspersed with a flick of his tongue against her lips, all in rhythm with his hips. As if he needed every part of her, everything, all at once. The pace didn't increase, but the intensity did. Until starved, naked, needy noises began to spill from his mouth.

Nothing had ever been this ridiculously, spine-tingling delicious. The feeling of wholehearted—and, heaven help her—*reciprocated* want.

Digging her nails into his sweat-damp shoulders earned her a garbled reply.

'I can't—' he slurred.

Greedy, Amber arched her back, fitting their hips closer together, taking more.

Wringing an incoherent response from Parker. 'Ah, 'mgonna.'

With the garbled word of warning his movements grew too needy for finesse, hips bucking as if seeking fusion with every thrust. Too far gone for a coordinated kiss, their mouths pressed close, damp and hot as they breathed each other in. The feel of him slicking between her thighs, beneath her, *in* her, tightened the cord of pleasure, pulling harder. Until she was so taut she feared being stranded on the edge of this precipice forever.

Afraid she'd never take that beautiful fall.

But then he gripped her shoulders, arched and thrust hard, groaning as he shattered.

And the sound of her name on his lips as he came pushed her off the ledge. A fiery electric pleasure shot through her veins, and her orgasm burst, painting colorful fireworks behind closed lids.

With a mumbled 'Parker,' she collapsed against him, and let herself be swept away by the aftershocks.

The smell of leather and sex filled Amber's nose as her breathing finally slowed enough for her to think straight. Bit by bit she became aware of the hard chest under her cheek, Parker's pounding heart gradually recovering beneath. They'd managed to shuffle their way to the thick rug in front of the wrought-iron coffee table. Now, sweat-slick bodies cooling in the aftermath, she was draped across Parker, her palms resting on his shoulders.

His hands, however, were resting by his sides.

Parker gripped her arms, gently shifting her off, and her chest cinched tight at the movement. 'I should find my clothes,' he said, his voice rough from exertion.

She briefly pressed her lids tight, knowing he was doing more than pulling away physically. He was pulling away mentally, too, and the memory of his words punched the breath from her throat.

You know this is all you get, right?

Pushing up on her elbows, she stared at Parker. The sex had been fantastic, and now his soft hair was spiked in all directions, delectably mussed by her fingers. His cheeks were flushed from the energy he'd expended. And he'd exerted a good deal of energy.

After they'd finished the first round, while Amber was still limp and essentially incapable of thought or movement, he had rolled them over onto the rug, pinning Amber beneath him. And started in on her again.

No one had ever made her feel so sensual.

No one had ever pulled so much pleasure from her body.

But he didn't want more.

She watched him rub a hand down his face with a faint frown on his mouth, and a memory rose, unbidden, in her mind.

That last fateful summer she'd caught Susie and Parker making out, and while it was clear he knew exactly what he was doing, there was no emotion behind the act. As if he could have replaced Susie with either of the other two girls he was dating and been just as happy. And while, yes, horny teens were pretty much a given, from what Reese had said Parker hadn't changed his ways much.

Random women, random relationships and nothing that lasted longer than a few months.

Amber's gaze landed on his holster draped across the arm of the couch, an idea forming in her head. He wouldn't like it. Heck, he might even wind up *hating* her for it. But getting the stubborn man to let someone in, even if it was his sister and not Amber, suddenly overwhelmed everything else—even her intense need to flee the presence of the man she'd so shamelessly seduced.

The one who seemed incapable of wanting more.

Chest tight, nerves taut, she reached for his holster, and when he reached for his pants...

She snapped the handcuffs around his wrist.

FIVE

———

The click of the cuff around his wrist snagged Parker's immediate attention.

Rolling onto his back again, he stared up at Amber. Her hair was mussed, her lips bruisingly red from his kisses, and guilt pierced his chest. So, yeah, things had gotten a little rough there toward the end. But he was only so strong, and Amber's frantic words and feverish hands had hacked away at his control until he really shouldn't be held responsible for what came after.

The guilt stabbed harder, anyway.

'Okay,' he said, his voice like gravel as he dangled the handcuffs in the air, his body twitching with interest. 'I'm assuming you want another round.'

The edgy smile, the blush that crept up her face and the way she shifted her eyes to the left had him chuckling.

'For the record, Ace—' he stretched out his leg, resting on his elbows '—any woman who goes for the handcuffs has no business being nervous.'

She stared at him a moment more and it was as if she

was looking everywhere but at his groin. Which wasn't the *only* part of his body that wholeheartedly approved of the addition of restraints, but it was the only part that could communicate its consent.

And then Amber reached for his boxers.

Frowning, Parker simply watched as she hooked the underwear on his feet, sliding them up his calves.

He lifted a brow. 'FYI,' he said, 'the addition of handcuffs usually means you're taking the clothes off, not putting them back on.'

Ignoring him, she slid the boxers higher.

Now he was *really* curious.

'Okay, I'll bite,' he rumbled. She met his gaze as he lifted his hips to allow her to pull his underwear into place, and he sent her a smile. 'You got a clothes-on fetish, right?' The thought sent a thrill working its way down his back, wrapping around his growing erection. 'I can work with that.'

Now that he was covered, she scooted until she was resting against the coffee table.

'No fetish that I know of,' she said. 'I just can't concentrate when you're so naked.'

She reached for the loose end of the handcuffs, looping it through the ornate leg of the wrought-iron coffee table before clipping it around his other wrist.

Totally intrigued now, he grinned at his helpless position—which was really kinda *hot*.

'That's one of the advantages of being naked,' he said. 'The inability to focus on anything else.'

Gaze admiring all the creamy skin before him, he took in the curve of her breasts and hips.

He shouldn't encourage her. He shouldn't be so weak.

He shouldn't crave absorbing that mesmerizing light radiating from her expression. From her eyes. Seemingly from her very skin.

But he needed just a little bit more.

Desire licked at his limbs and his voice reflected his thoughts.

'You just need additional practice,' he said. 'And I'm—'

She reached for her blouse and slid it back over her head, and Parker stared, stunned. And while she had been rendered mute by the sight of him naked, he had a similar problem with the vision of her putting her clothes *on*.

When she picked up her underwear and pulled them into place, he finally found his words.

'What the hell are you doing?' he asked.

She studied him for a moment, and Parker was briefly grateful that the long expanse of her legs was available for admiring.

Amber said, 'You clearly aren't a man who likes to cuddle.'

The statement slammed into him. 'Cuddle?'

So what if the word spit from his mouth with a vengeance. He didn't like the turn in the conversation.

'And if there is anything that Parker Robinson needs,' she went on, eyeing him steadily, 'it's a good cuddle.'

Heart thumping in agitation, he was sure he made a ridiculous sight, what with being handcuffed to a table leg and his mouth opening and closing like a fish.

When he finally found his voice again, it was rough. 'Amber—'

'We're going to talk, Parker.'

The swearword that echoed through his mind wasn't fit to be uttered out loud.

Scooting over to sit by his side, Amber's eyes settled on his. 'Why didn't you answer the phone when your mother called the day your father died?'

The one-two punch to his chest had his jaw falling open wider, and then he slapped his lips shut, his mouth growing grim.

'Damn it, Amber,' he said, struggling to prop up on one elbow, despite the restraints. 'We're not high school sweethearts.' Frustrated he couldn't even plow a hand through his hair, he went on. 'Let me up.' Anxiety pressed in on his chest, leaving it difficult to draw in a breath. 'I don't want—'

She gently cupped his cheek, her thumb landing at the corner of his mouth, and he froze, unable to do anything but blink like an idiot.

Looking up at her, he wanted to curse and rant and rail against the understanding in her eyes and the bloody confinement of the cuffs. He finally managed to pull off a sparse rattling of the chain between his wrists.

Which, unfortunately, earned him a gentle swipe of her fingertip along his lower lip. It was just a simple stroke, barely noticeable, but the tenderness curled like a knot in his belly.

'Why?' she asked again.

He lobbed a hard look in her direction and didn't spare the truth. Sweet little Amber wanted to know, so sweet little Amber was going to hear.

'You were following me that day,' he said. 'You heard what she said.'

Amber didn't pretend she had no idea what he was talking about.

Her gaze warm on his, she said, 'I heard some of what your mother said, yes.'

Unsure of which parts she'd missed, he gave her the full version. 'Marrying my father was a mistake.' His next words came out louder than he'd intended. '*I* was a mistake.'

Letting the words echo in the room, he forgot to breathe for a moment.

'I was just a symbol of everything my mother had done wrong,' he said. 'Of everything she regretted.'

None of it mattered.

The mantra had served him well in the past. He'd learned as a kid it was best to exist on the surface and ignore or bury or compartmentalize the rest. Because it was the rest that bit you in the ass.

Be polite to your mother, but don't try to get her to show you she cared. Hugs weren't necessary, but an occasional expression of some sort of affection would have been nice. He'd given up looking around the age of ten.

None of it mattered.

Or at least, that's what he'd told himself.

Until the summer he was seventeen and he'd tried again. But the years of being the rowdy boy who only got noticed when he got into trouble had taken a toll. Maybe by then his mother couldn't have cared, even if she'd wanted to.

'She hated my father's job,' he said. 'Looked down on what he did for a living.'

And Parker had *despised* her for being such a snob.

'Which was exactly why you followed in his footsteps,' Amber said as, still cradling his cheek, she stroked his lip again.

His mouth twisted beneath her finger. Man, she always was such an observant little thing. Even as a too-sweet, freaky stalker of a kid.

'Maybe in the beginning,' he said, though he knew she was absolutely right. Growing weary of his awkward posture, he laid down on his side. 'But now...'

Well, not *right* now. Cuz right now everything was dull and flat and he got little enjoyment out of much of anything. But there was a time when helping victims' families find justice had been incredibly satisfying.

'You've always been good at taking care of people,' she said.

Barking out a laugh of disbelief, he tilted his head as he stared up at her, amazed she was still cradling his face. Strangely, he was starting to like the comforting feel of her palm.

'Who did I take care of?' he said.

'Reese,' she said. 'When we were kids, anyway.'

She gazed down at him, like she had as a kid. That same light in her eyes. He just didn't get it. What did she see in him then? What did she see in him now?

And then she went on. 'And you took care of me....'

He couldn't talk about how he'd felt that summer he left his mother's home and never went back. As a seventeen-year-old he'd been too cool to admit he'd missed Reese's and Amber's company. As an adult it seemed too late to confess the truth.

With a huff of humor, he said, 'You're just saying that because I saved you from drowning.'

Finally dropping her hand from his face, she sent him a small smile. And he didn't miss her touch. Not at all. Damn it.

'Your father loved you,' she said, and he swallowed back the groan.

Apparently, nothing in his history was sacred.

His dad hadn't been the type to hug or tell you he cared with his words. But he'd shown him in other ways.

'But then he died,' Parker said, and he hated the way the words came out so harsh. So bitter. He tried to ease the mood with a small smile, failing by a mile. 'Cuz life is mostly just a nasty little bitch who's looking to collect.'

Amber's expression shifted into one of sadness and he hated that he put that look on her face. The urge to take it back, to put a smile on her mouth, was overwhelming. And then suddenly she was crawling over him and sliding onto her side to lie next to him. Shocked, he didn't move as she wiggled her way up between his cuffed arms, settling against him as she embraced his chest.

Staggered by the comforting contact, the press of bodies from torso to toes, he took a moment to respond.

'You know,' he said dryly, 'I don't do the morning-after thing.'

'I'm not asking you to.'

'And hugs don't count if they're not freely given.'

'I know,' she said as she gave him a gentle squeeze. 'That's why I'm freely giving this one to you.'

Paralyzed, he didn't know what to do with himself. Silence stretched between them as they lazed on the floor, wrapped in each other's arms. His by force. Hers by choice

And it was really intimate in a way that sex usually wasn't, and wasn't that just the kicker?

Something in Parker shifted. Just a little, but enough to voice the thought he'd been having for weeks. 'Plenty of people have it worse than me,' he said quietly.

He didn't know why he needed to say the words. Other than the fact that they were the brutal truth. And if there was anything he was comfortable with, it was the brutal truth. Maybe it was the comfort of her arms that seduced the words from his mouth.

'Who?' she asked. 'Who has it worse?'

He didn't want to look into her eyes, so he stared up at the chandelier on the ceiling. 'I'm working on this case,' he said. The dark cloud encasing his heart grew thicker, denser. Something he hadn't thought possible since the day his dad had died.

An acid rain just waiting to break.

'Our current suspect is just a stupid seventeen-year-old,' he said. 'And his parents...'

He didn't want to repeat the words they'd said about their son.

'You know,' he said instead, his voice hoarse. 'Family should stick by you, no matter what.'

Man, now the woman had both hands on his cheeks.

Turning his head to face hers, her gaze clear, she said, 'Yes, they should.'

Staring into her amber eyes, he clenched his jaw.

The case had been eating at him for a while, draining what little color remained in his already-mucked-up life. He refused to lean into the warmth of Amber's palms, but the urge was there. He remembered the stricken look on her face when she'd overheard his mom that day, and the comforting hand Amber lay on his shoulder later.

Not that he'd wanted her sympathy. No, he'd hated the caring in her touch, the gesture of concern from a twelve-year-old when he couldn't even get that kind of emotion from his own mother.

Something in him had died that day, something vital that he'd lost. And damned if he knew how to get it back. He was pretty sure he didn't even *want* it back.

Blocking Amber's beautiful gaze, Parker closed his eyes and concentrated on keeping his breathing even. She held his face, and her sweet scent surrounded him, the silky legs entwined with his. But it was the warmth of her body that captivated him the most. Surprisingly, he wasn't really thinking of her skin in a sexual sense, but more of the gentle give-and-take of shared heat. It was refreshingly simple. And kind of nice.

Like a handful of summer sun on a dark winter's day.

But the unfamiliar feeling of comfort, of contentment—of...*happiness*?—scared the bejesus out of him.

Parker didn't know how much time passed as he grappled with the dueling urges to push her away or pull her closer. Maybe he should do something more productive, like bang his head against the nearest wall.

'You're right, family should stick by you,' she said, and he lifted his lids. 'No matter what.' Amber raised her chin to look up into his face, her eyes warming him in ways he'd never imagined. 'Which is why you should come to your mother's dinner party,' she went on, and Parker didn't bother suppressing the groan.

Christamighty, not this again.

'To support Reese,' she went on.

Without warning, she slid down from between his arms, and he instantly missed the feeling of warmth.

That tiny bit of...security, for lack of a better word.

'You should go to the party, Parker,' she said again.

After sitting up, she slipped on her jeans. Her shoes came next, and he absolutely did not panic that she was dressing to leave. Because that would be a stupid thing to do.

'Why?' he asked.

'Because your sister loves you,' Amber said as she stood to look down on him.

Something inside him rejected the notion, and not just because Reese had never said so in as many words.

'And if you can't do it for Reese,' she went on. Her voice dropped an octave, creating an ominous pressure in his lungs. 'Then do it for me.'

This time the word came out harsher. 'Why?'

Reese stared down at Parker, her heart pumping wildly in her chest.

'Do it for the kid who saw you as worthy of adoration all those years ago,' she said.

The rest was on the tip of her tongue as she hesitated. But her insecurities suddenly seemed so insignificant compared to all that Parker had been through. He deserved the truth. He needed to *hear* the truth.

So she went on. 'And do it for the woman who's falling for you now.'

Denial, exasperation and a massive dose of confusion flared in his eyes just before he slammed his lids shut, muttering, 'Damn.'

She hadn't started out intending to share so much. But suddenly her choice to tell Parker the words that were so simple and complex, the words she was pretty sure he'd never heard in his life, was important—not just for Parker, but for herself. An extension of her decision to finally *fight* for what she wanted. And she wanted this man in her life.

Not the boy she'd obsessed about in the past, but the *man* of today.

Ironic, given it might be too late for Parker to ever truly let himself love anybody.

When he finally opened his eyes, a blank look on his face, she simply picked up the holster containing his keys and gently dropped it by his foot. Going on, she looked at him and spoke the words she knew he needed to hear.

'I'm falling in love with you,' she said. 'And you deserve to be loved, Parker Robinson.'

SIX

Whywhy*why?*

Two weeks later Amber was dealing with her last customers of the day and preparing to leave for the Michaels' dinner party, still unsure she'd made the right decision to abandon Parker with his keys to free himself. Which he had, of course. She'd checked, just to be certain. Part of her thought she'd been making a statement by walking out, taking the first step in seizing control of her romantic life by seducing the man she'd dreamed of for ages, sharing the truth of how she felt about him and then exiting with her head high. The other part knew the truth.

Coward*coward*.

Because she didn't have the strength to stick around and *really* deal with the repercussions of her confession.

Fabulous, Amber.

Staring at the couple deciding on the style of the tuxedo for their wedding, she smiled, a tiny bit envious. When the groom-to-be leaned over and kissed the top of his fiancée's head, Amber's lips twisted. Such a simple gesture, shared and accepted so freely. As if the act was a given.

For some people displays of affection came easily.

Amber's cell phone rang and, grateful for the distraction, she turned her back on the couple and answered.

'Amber,' Reese said. 'You'll be there tonight, right?'

'Of course.' Without thinking, she went on. 'Have you heard from Parker?'

My. God.

Would she always sound like that twelve-year-old little girl who loved Parker Robinson?

'No,' her friend said with a sigh. 'But at least he agreed to be in the wedding, so thanks for that.'

Amber murmured a 'No problem.' And how did she tell Parker's sister that the only reason he'd agreed to be in the wedding was because her friend threatened to tell embarrassing stories to his partner? Maybe Parker really was that shallow. Deep in her heart she knew he wasn't.

But if *Parker* believed it, then the truth didn't really matter.

Clutching her phone, Amber forced herself to focus. 'Your dress is due to arrive next week,' she said to Reese. 'I'll set up a time for the first fitting.'

Reese's enthusiastic 'Good' was heartwarming. She knew Parker had his doubts about his sister's marriage, but Amber envied Reese and Dylan because their relationship always looked so comfortable and easy. Just as Amber always thought love should be. Of course, Parker's very DNA made acknowledging the possibility of forever near impossible.

Behind her, the tinkle of the bell over the door signaled another customer. Signing off the phone, she slipped it in her pocket as she turned...and spied Parker just inside the entranceway.

Her head spun, her gut tensed and her heart hurt too much to function. Unfortunately the overly dramatic angst of her teen years didn't compare to the real, grown-up pain of a woman. Falling for him again was turning out to be easy. Doing something about it would be hard.

Now that she'd adjusted to his presence, her eyes roved lovingly over him. He wore jeans and his leather jacket, as usual. The only difference was the button-down shirt that he wore.

No matter, Amber was sure it smelled of leather. She'd spent enough time in his arms, kissing every inch of his skin to know his scent inside and out.

When the couple called out their goodbyes, Amber waved, working hard not to feel a sliver of jealousy as they held hands on the way out. Uneasy, she glanced at Parker, who was watching them leave. The slow barrel roll her belly was attempting wasn't helping her nerves, and she swiped a damp palm down her dress pants.

'Tuxedo rental,' she managed to say lamely, nodding at the retreating couple.

His brow furrowed in humor. 'Did you measure his crotch, too?'

'It wasn't necessary.' Despite everything, she had to bite back the smile. 'Only for you.'

His mouth quirked. 'I figured as much.'

Five heartbeats pounded in her chest before the awkward silence was broken.

'So...' Parker leaned a shoulder against the wall, crossing his arms with that earthy easiness that was so seductive. And how could such a simple movement be so sexy?

'What kind of woman leads a guy on by handcuffing him to a table and then up and leaves?'

'I put the holster with the key in reach of your foot,' she said. 'I knew with a little bit of time and effort you'd eventually escape.'

Parker let out a cocky *hunh*. 'I was free and out the door in two minutes.'

Clearly he was proud of his skills.

Hiking an eyebrow at the expression on his face, she said, 'Ten.' She tipped her head. 'It was *ten* minutes.' And when he shot her a sharp look, she gave a small shrug. 'I was watching your car from the window.'

The pleased look on his face was comical. 'You worried I wasn't going to get free, Ace?'

And here he was, choosing the shallow route again. As if the amount of time it took him to retrieve his key from the holster and unlock the cuffs around his wrists—not an easy task, she was sure—was the most important thing they needed to discuss.

'I think we already established that I *do* care,' she said.

Parker closed his eyes, and the easy look on his face died, his voice low. 'Damn, Amber.' He rubbed his neck and met her gaze again. 'I got good news today, so I'm in a first-rate mood. And you were the one who convinced me to go to my mom's tonight.'

Her heart soared at the words, and she realized that also explained his button-down shirt.

Frowning, Parker went on. 'But I don't think I'm ready for...'

He dropped his arm to his side and looked at her. Shifting against the wall, his movements were now stiff. He looked as if he was braced for battle.

A million questions crashed through her mind like a ten-car pileup, but she decided to start out simple.

'What's the good news?' she asked.

'That teen I was telling you about? The suspect in my latest case?' he said. 'Turns out he's innocent. He's been cleared.' The small shrug was simple yet meaningful. 'I don't know if that will help him with his parents or not, but at least he's got a second chance.' The relief on his face was obvious.

And *this* was why she was falling for Parker all over again. He liked to pretend he was above those pesky things called emotions. To pretend he felt no fondness or affection or hope. To pretend he didn't care. But it wasn't that he had no heart. The problem was his heart was so big, had been through so much, the need to protect himself was automatic.

Today was an encouraging step, but there was a real risk this instinct might never be undone completely.

'I'm glad you're going,' she said. 'I know Reese will appreciate it.'

Thick dark lashes slowly blinked across a mesmerizing green gaze as he stared at her for several moments. 'I'm not going just for Reese.'

Her breathing stalled, and she barely managed to murmur, 'No?'

Two pounding heartbeats passed as she longed for him to clarify.

'No,' he said. 'I'm also going for me.'

And while she breathed out a sigh of relief that he'd finally decided that he wanted family in his life, a small part of her was crushed he wasn't going for *her*. She'd known all along the most she could hope for was to help him reconnect with Reese, and this was as good a start as any. In truth, it was a miracle he was going tonight. And while Amber was glad Reese's wish would come true, the truth was, having him here—having him near *her*—was hard.

Because a part of her would always long to be loved by Parker.

'Well,' she said, shifting closer to the exit. Distance. She needed *distance*. Time to regroup. 'Your sister will be happy to see you.'

'Yeah, but I can't say I'm thrilled with the idea of making polite conversation with my mom and stepdad,' he said, his feet firmly planted in place. 'Cuz I know things won't have changed.' His expression grim, he went on. 'William Michael of the Park Avenue Michaels hates any reminder that he wasn't my mother's first husband. My mother is weak, petrified he'll leave her. And, way back when, Reese was too young to notice,' he said with a tiny shrug. 'I've accepted all that.'

By the look on his face she knew it was true. He cleared his throat, suddenly looking uncomfortable.

'I was hoping we could go together,' he said. 'Having you around might make things a little...smoother.'

A confusing mix of tenderness and disappointment flushed through her chest, and she picked up her purse, heading for the exit. 'Then let's go.'

Amber could feel him following.

'But the other reason I came was because I wanted to see you first,' he said.

Her feet stuck to the floor.

'About—about what you said,' he said from behind.

Clutching her purse harder, she turned to face him.

'You know...' He shrugged awkwardly. 'Before.'

I'm falling in love with you.

The lag time from one heartbeat to the next seemed to lengthen to uncomfortable levels. So much so Amber was amazed she didn't pass out.

'As a kid—' he puffed out a breath grimly '—it sucked not getting what I needed from my mom. And it's...' With a small scowl he plowed a hand through his hair before gesturing at Amber. 'You're...' He dropped his hand, frustration etched in his every word. 'You know everything I don't want *anyone* to know.'

The raw, naked look on his face lasted several seconds before he let out a scoff.

'Which makes you the last person on earth I should want to see,' he said.

My God, this wasn't getting any easier.

'After that night,' he went on. 'I spent the first few days thinking you had some sort of...*misguided* sense of hero worship because of the whole drowning incident.'

She could hear the hesitation in his voice.

'And then I spent the rest of the time hoping it was more than that,' he finished in a low voice.

Her voice resolute, she said, 'It is.'

Now the lag time between heartbeats was ridiculously short as she watched the emotions parade across his face. Relief. Followed by something that looked like contentment before landing on that cocky smile she loved so much.

Parker stepped forward, all awkwardness gone. The easy stroll was back, carrying him right up into her personal space, and her stomach swooped at the sight. The gorgeous green eyes. The ruffled hair. And that mouth, that beautiful, beautiful mouth that had first captured her attention oh so long ago. Little had she known then how good it would feel pressed against hers in a *real* kiss.

'But the rescue was an incredibly awesome move on my part,' he said with a grin.

She rolled her eyes, delighting at his responding bark of amusement. When he reached out to brush the hair from her cheek, her stomach swerved.

He paused, his voice uncharacteristically riddled with self-doubt. 'Even the thought of trying for something that lasts past a few months scares the crap out of me.'

Inhaling slowly, Amber steadily held his gaze. She'd spent years pining after something that could never be hers. Parker, specifically. And as lame as the idea was, especially given she'd been just a ridiculous *preteen,* it was time to admit the years of unrequited feelings had had a profound influence on her choices in life. And the thought of putting herself in a vulnerable position again was almost incapacitating. But Parker had spent years hoping his mother would change, and was willing to venture back into her circle again with little likelihood that the relationship would improve.

'That's the thing about letting someone in,' she said softly. And if he was willing to put his heart on the line for his sister, for *himself*...well, then maybe she should take a risk, too. 'It's both a beautiful and a dangerous thing.'

His eyes searched hers. 'So why me?'

Drawing in a deep breath, she tried to put her thoughts into words.

'I think over time,' she said slowly, 'the closer you get to a person, and the closer you let them *get to you,* the more the light and the shadows inside become more vivid. Clearer. More sharply defined.'

Love wasn't easy. And sometimes, especially with a man like Parker Robinson, it would be especially difficult. But she loved the parts of him that were dark just as much, if not more, than she loved the lighter bits. Because they defined him the best.

And for a moment, she almost felt sorry for Reese and Dylan. A comfortable relationship would definitely take less work, but Amber wouldn't trade the conflict or passion she shared with Parker for all the ease in the world.

She reached up to cup his face, and nothing, *nothing* would ever be as wonderful as the slight tip of his head into her palm. The contact wasn't much. But enough.

Encouraging her to go on. 'And knowing all those bits about a person makes it both more difficult, and—just as important, I think—more imperative that you take that chance.'

The tiny, nervous lick of his lips was almost heartbreaking.

'So...' he said. 'You want to give this thing a whirl?'

'Do you think it will work?'

'Almost definitely maybe.' His mouth curled at the edges. 'We have several things in our favor.'

'Such as?'

'First, I'm adorable and you worship the ground I walk on.' She lifted her eyes heavenward with a 'whatever' look, and he let out a chuckle. Amber wasn't sure if his shallow reply was a coping mechanism or if he just liked to see her reaction. She suspected it was a bit of both. 'Second,' he went on. 'I *want* it to work. And third...'

Amber didn't miss how quickly he'd rushed through

the second, almost as if embarrassed. She'd let it slide. For now.

'And third?' she asked.

The quirk in his lips was adorable. 'I'm just stubborn enough not to give up.'

Eyes stinging, she swallowed back the mushy words and sent him a smile.

'I'm not going to have to handcuff you for every hug I want, am I?' she said.

He reached out and took her hand. The gesture was hesitant, the fingers that squeezed hers gentle. But the light in his eyes?

Sizzling.

'Oh, you'll need the handcuffs, all right,' he said, his voice husky.

And then Parker Robinson drew the sexy smirk like a gun from a holster. 'Just not for a hug.'

* * * * *

REQUEST YOUR FREE BOOKS!
2 FREE NOVELS PLUS 2 FREE GIFTS!

YES! Please send me 2 FREE Harlequin® Kiss novels and my 2 FREE gifts (gifts worth about $10). After receiving them, if I don't wish to receive any more books, I can return the shipping statement marked "cancel." If I don't cancel, I will receive 4 brand-new novels every month and be billed just $4.30 per book in the U.S. or $4.99 per book in Canada. That's a savings of at least 13% off the cover price! It's quite a bargain! Shipping and handling is just 50¢ per book in the U.S. and 75¢ per book in Canada.* I understand that accepting the 2 free books and gifts places me under no obligation to buy anything. I can always return a shipment and cancel at any time. Even if I never buy another book, the two free books and gifts are mine to keep forever.

145/345 HDN FVXQ

Name	(PLEASE PRINT)	
Address		Apt. #
City	State/Prov.	Zip/Postal Code

Signature (if under 18, a parent or guardian must sign)

Mail to the Harlequin® Reader Service:
IN U.S.A.: P.O. Box 1867, Buffalo, NY 14240-1867
IN CANADA: P.O. Box 609, Fort Erie, Ontario L2A 5X3

Want to try two free books from another line?
Call 1-800-873-8635 or visit www.ReaderService.com.

* Terms and prices subject to change without notice. Prices do not include applicable taxes. Sales tax applicable in N.Y. Canadian residents will be charged applicable taxes. Offer not valid in Quebec. This offer is limited to one order per household. Not valid for current subscribers to Harlequin Kiss books. All orders subject to credit approval. Credit or debit balances in a customer's account(s) may be offset by any other outstanding balance owed by or to the customer. Please allow 4 to 6 weeks for delivery. Offer available while quantities last.

HKI3

She hadn't seen him in ten years and he chose
her wedding day to show up...

THE UNEXPECTED
WEDDING GUEST

"Surprised to see me, Park Avenue?" The familiar, sexy rumble
and the nickname added to the surreal nature of being transported back ten years in time when she had laughingly told
Mason her college roommates' nickname for her, Park Avenue
Princess. And then he'd made the name his own, dropping
the *princess* part. Which for some strange reason had pleased
her no end.

But she was not pleased to see Mason.

Days away from her *wedding*.

Reese gritted her teeth, struggling to retain her cool as the
anger finally built high enough to surpass every other emotion—
shock, doubt and dread, just to name a few. Why was he coming
to see her again? After ten years, why *now*? Right when all of
her dreams were finally about to come true.

She forced her voice to remain smooth. "And the last time
I saw you, you were dodging the dog tags I hurled at you."

"Your aim was good."

"I should have used your baseball bat."

"It still made a nice punctuation mark for your demand for
a divorce." The corners of his eyes crinkled. "Claimed irrecon-
cilable differences, if I remember right."

She tipped her chin higher. "Temporary insanity was more like it."

"A *lust*-induced state of insanity." Heat flushed through her like a flash fire, though he steadily held her gaze. His expression more reflective than affected, he murmured, "A drug, that."

Her chest pinched, making breathing more difficult. Bad enough he had to still look good, now the unwanted memories invaded. Memories of Mason making love to her. The incredibly intense state of happiness they'd achieved, right before it had all been blown to hell. Correction, right before *Mason* had blown it all to hell.

Remember, Reese. Never again.

Never *again.*

"The sex wasn't a drug," she said, though at the time, she'd thought the same thing. But God knows she'd learned her lesson the hard way. She was no longer susceptible to the whims of her hormones. "It was quicksand."

And just as deadly to her peace of mind. Her sanity.

He hiked a brow and studied her a moment more. "Maybe," he said softly, his lips curling at the edges. "But what a way to go."

**Pick up THE UNEXPECTED WEDDING GUEST
by Aimee Carson, on sale June 18,
wherever Harlequin books are sold.**

Four friends. Three weddings.
Two explosive secrets.
One unforgettable
summer!

THE WEDDING SEASON

Reese, Cassie, Gina and Marnie were best friends.
Until *that* night.

They haven't seen each other in years, but now Reese is
getting married and she wants everyone there.

It will be a reunion to remember—and the wedding of
the year! But what these feisty women hadn't planned
on are the sizzling, scandalous and *very* surprising
consequences....

**Look for this fabulous quartet from these talented
Harlequin KISS authors—Aimee Carson,
Amy Andrews, Heidi Rice and Kimberly Lang.**

Starting June 18 with
THE UNEXPECTED WEDDING GUEST
by Aimee Carson

www.Harlequin.com

HKCONT0613